the
WARSEC
Interstellar Series

the
WARSEC
Interstellar Series

3

EXHIBITION

2 0 9 7 - 2 1 0 0

ASH GAWAIN

ASHGAWAIN.COM

Published by Ash Gawain

ISBN: 978-91-639-7451-9

Cover design, illustration & interior formatting:
Mark Thomas / Coverness.com

TABLE OF CONTENTS

Map of Earth: 2097

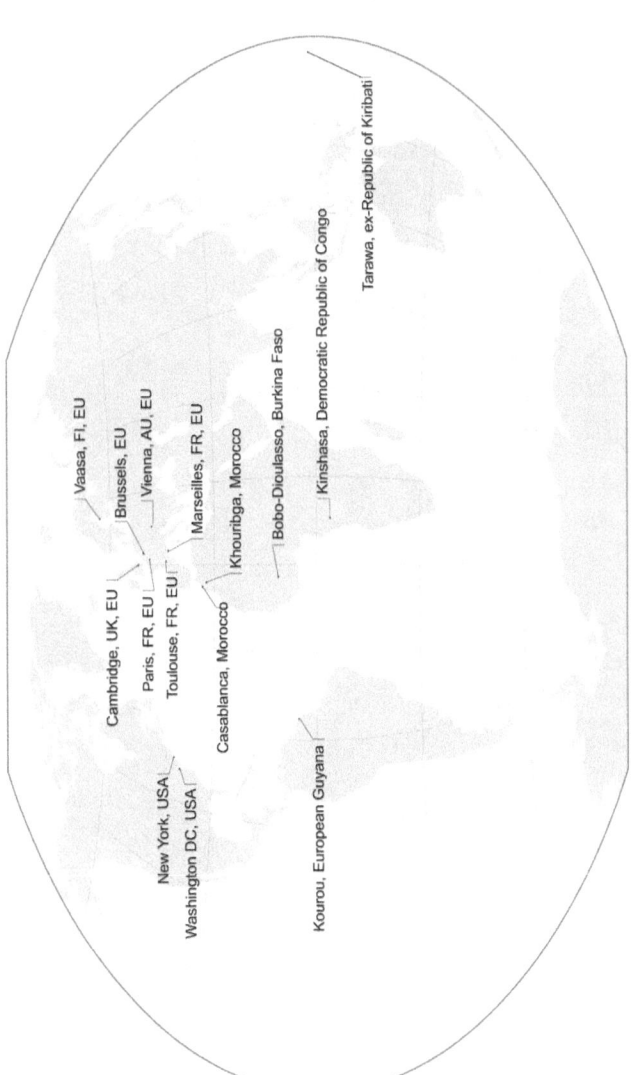

Vaasa, FI, EU

Brussels, EU

Vienna, AU, EU

Marseilles, FR, EU

Cambridge. UK, EU

Paris, FR, EU

Toulouse, FR, EU

Khouribga, Morocco

Bobo-Dioulasso, Burkina Faso

Casablanca, Morocco

Kinshasa, Democratic Republic of Congo

Tarawa, ex-Republic of Kiribati

New York, USA

Washington DC, USA

Kourou, European Guyana

EU = European Union.

INTRODUCTION

During the second half of summer 2097, the geopolitical situation on earth had deteriorated at an unprecedented rate since the middle of the 21st century. Two opinion pieces, published at seven week's intervals illustrated the rapid shift in the state of minds of the contemporaries.

Published on Friday 26 July 2097 in the New York Times, the first Op-Ed had been written by Dr. Anatoli Govorov, the co-recipient of the 2095 Nobel Prize in Physics for the unified gravity theory, and also a member of the first crew testing faster-than-light travel on board the *Alcubierre*, back in 2094. His Op-Ed was entitled '*Interstellar Exploration to Commence before 2100*':

"Why has mankind still not gone interstellar?" Such is the question I hear over and over again, and I will now try to answer it.

Of course, there are those among the older scientists who

claim that the Voyager probes leaving our solar system and going into deep space back in the 2010s are the first human interstellar spacecraft. I shall disagree with them. These two Voyager probes have indeed gone 'exostellar', but they have not gone interstellar. They won't until they reach another star system, probably not before a few million years. I will therefore side with the people harassing me. Mankind has still not gone interstellar and thus the question remains: "Why has mankind still not gone interstellar?"

In 2091, Dr. Tintin Mutombo and myself succeeded in merging quantum gravity and the general relativity theory into one single 'unified gravity theory'. The physical implications were tremendous. Negative energy fields created within the framework of quantum mechanics were now usable to warp spacetime, thus enabling faster-than-light travel. This led to the funding and assembling of the Alcubierre.

In 2094, I was part of the crew of the Alcubierre, under the command of Dr. Alice Fù, recipient of the 2095 Nobel Prize in Chemistry and inventor of the green matter, the negative-energy attributes of which make the warping of spacetime possible. The Alcubierre performed the first faster-than-light journey between the Earth and Mars.

Since faster-than-light travel was successful within the solar system, why have we still not engaged into interstellar exploration? We have a warp-ship, the Alcubierre. Why is it anchored, idle, at the orbital station?

First of all, I would like to say that the Alcubierre has not been totally inactive. In October 2094, the spaceship was used to rescue the last survivor of the Martian colony and has since then conducted exploratory missions within the asteroid belt.

But why have we not sent the ship to Alpha Centauri, for instance, the closest star to our Sun? After all, the Alcubierre would need only five and a half months to get there.

There are two reasons for this. Firstly, because of her size, the Alcubierre has no cargo bay. What's the point of traveling 161 days if you cannot even deploy scientific equipment at the reached destination? Secondly, there are currently no other spaceships with warp capability. This means that no other spaceship could support an interstellar mission in sudden need of assistance.

This is why mankind has not gone interstellar. Yet.

The next question is: When will mankind go interstellar?

As an employee at WARSEC (World's Agency for the Regulation of Space Exploration and Colonization), I can confidently answer that the first interstellar exploration journey will occur before 2100, at the insistence of the UN member states.

Indeed, much has happened over the last three years, making the first interstellar mission more feasible. The orbital station has been vastly expanded and will open to space tourism in May 2098. WARSEC Ventures is now operating an aerospace shipyard on the Moon, where not only are cheap aerospace shuttles manufactured, but also the assembly of new a class of interstellar ship will start before Christmas. By January 2099, WARSEC will be ready to send a first interstellar exploratory mission to Alpha Centauri.

There may not be anything remarkable to observe in this near star system. But at least, we will be able to say: 'Look, mankind has gone interstellar.'

While Dr. Govorov's column was illustrative of an optimistic state of mind that could offer one the luxury of thinking about interstellar exploration, another Op-Ed, published seven weeks later, on Friday 13 September, was suggestive of the recent geopolitical degradation and the growing pessimism among young Europeans. This second Op-Ed had been published in *The Cambridge Student*, a British student paper from the eponymous university town. It had been written by Sanne Van der Maas, a master's student in economics, who also happened to be the only survivor of the Martian colony. Her column was entitled '*An era of Exhibition*':

More than ever, we seem to live in an era of exhibition. I was born on Mars on 6 July 2076. My parents, like sixteen other couples, had been sent to Mars by the private corporation The Martian Show *to try and establish a colony. The stated goal was to grow a colony while looking for traces of fossilized life. The subsequent cancellation of the colonization, followed by the bankruptcy of the corporation, and eventually, our abandonment on the red planet, made me think that the whole colonization project was nothing but the unfinished idea of an eccentric billionaire wanting to exhibit himself, and us, to the world.*

In a more recent context, pressure has grown on WARSEC to launch an interstellar expedition to Alpha Centauri at the earliest possible date. Like the Martian colonization project before, it does not seem to be seriously questioned. Yet Dr. Anatoli Govorov admits it himself: the purpose of such a mission would primarily be to say 'We mankind have gone interstellar'. Once again, a project driven by a desire for exhibition.

Where does this need for exhibition come from? What is the impulsion driving this desire to display superiority?

At the beginning of July, in an Italian mountain hut, I met three fighter pilots from the EU Air Force. They exhibited a certain sense of dominance due to the potential destruction and death their flying machines could bring, and radiated superiority. Back then, I did not ponder about it.

These three air force pilots said they had practiced hypothetical attacks on Morocco intensely. So much that war seemed certain to them. Back then, I did not ponder about it.

After all, we all know that Morocco has a monopoly on phosphate extraction, phosphate much needed for fertilizer. Diplomacy between the European Union and Morocco has been chaotic over the last two years without leading to any remote risk of conflict. So why take these pilots seriously? Back then, I did not ponder about it.

Until now.

Yesterday, a Moroccan diplomat was arrested in Paris with two tons of cannabis. He had landed in the private jet of the crown prince of Morocco. The European President blames cannabis trafficking on the state of Morocco and has issued an ultimatum with terms difficult to meet.

What is the purpose of it? Is this a way for our good President Bonavita to exhibit an iron will and be re-elected? Is it a way for her to force a conflict and exhibit the deadly might of the European Armed Forces? I honestly don't know.

01: DOWN-TO-EARTH MATTERS (SEPT 2097)

Ralf Åhman did not know why he had remained at the orbital station. Perhaps he did not want face the earthly reality. Perhaps he just wanted to keep his head in the stars for how long he could. Though, actually, his office had no windows, and neither shining stars nor glowing Earth could be seen from there.

It was not because of his rank. As the director of the UN-affiliated World's Agency for the Regulation of Space Exploration and Colonization (WARSEC), he was presently the most senior official in the station. The reason his office had no windows was that the orbital station barely had any windows at all.

In September 2097, the orbital station was not quite completed, but consisted nonetheless of four gravity rings around a 240 m (787 ft) long cylindrical core. Each gravity ring was 40 m (131 ft) wide with a diameter of 150 m (49 ft) and contained fifteen so-called 'gravity decks'. These circular inner decks glided on internal magnetic rails around the core axis and the resulting centrifugal force created a gravity force equivalent to that on Earth.

The two gravity rings at the rear of the station were still under way and were meant to open to the public in May 2098. Soon, tourists from Earth would be able to enjoy a stay in the orbital station, in its Radisson or Sheraton hotel, try some spacewalks and even enjoy a visit in the space attraction park being developed by Vahlroos Travel.

The second gravity ring was leased to all the main aerospace corporations, from Boeing to Airbus, and to all the respective National Space Agencies, from NASA to Roscosmos.

Ralf's office, however, was located in the first ring, the ring reserved for WARSEC, the UN agency that had once been created to regulate space activities. It was somewhere on the fifteenth deck, the one the furthest away from the core axis. As a result, his office was rotating at 4.2 turns per minute along with the whole deck. This was the rotation speed required to reproduce a gravity equivalent to that on Earth.

In that context, it was no wonder that none of the rooms located in the gravity rings had any windows, lest its occupants be prone to spin sickness. And even then, one still required an acclimatization period not to feel sick in the gravity rooms, with their concave floors and convex ceilings.

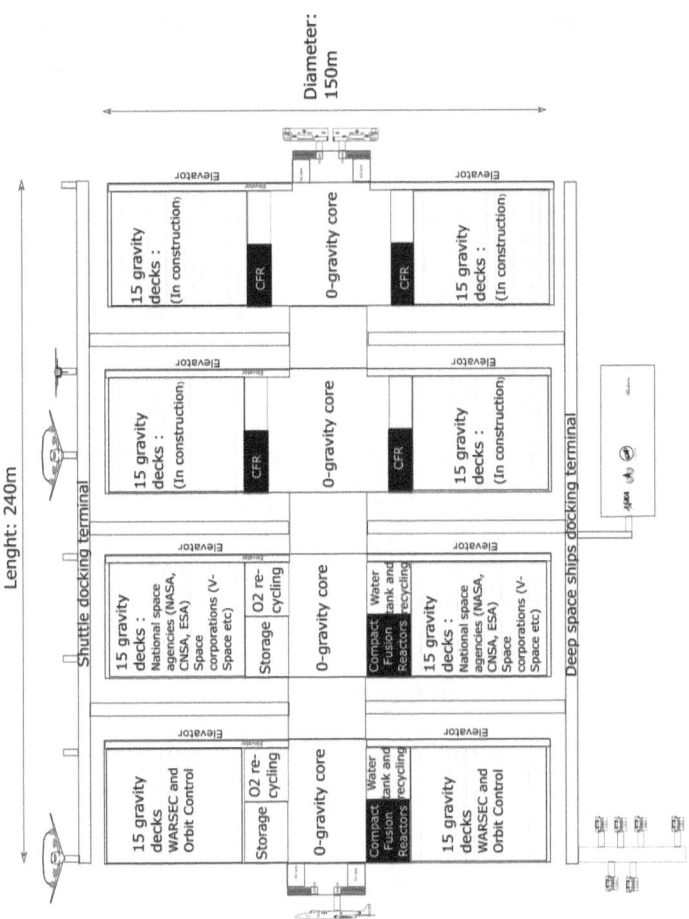

Figure 1: The orbital station in 2097.

On that Tuesday 17 September 2097, the forty-one-year-old director was sitting, or rather crouching, in the sofa corner of his windowless office. A very slightly pot-bellied man of intermediate height, Ralf Åhman had dark brown Afro-hair and pale brown skin. His right eye always seemed half shut. He had worn the same clothes for the last five days. A comfortable purple overall with the WARSEC logo on it. He was pondering over the situation.

17 September. Ralf Åhman did not like that day. A European citizen, he had been born in Finland of a Scottish mother and a Finnish father of African descent. However, he had spent most of his upbringing and student years in Sweden, and saw himself partly as a Swedish UN diplomat.

Swedish UN diplomats did not particularly like the date of 17 September. On that very day back in 1948, the Swedish mediator to Palestine, Folke Bernadotte, had been killed by Israeli terrorists. On that very day back in 1961, UN secretary-general Dag Hammarskjöld's airplane had been shot down by a mercenary fighter jet over Northern Rhodesia.

Yet, three years earlier, 17 September had been a good day for Ralf. On 17 September 2094, the Chinese, Japanese and Russian space agencies had tested the first warp-flight of the Alcubierre. Named after the Mexican theoretical physicist who, a hundred years before, had proposed a plausible, though in practice impossible, approach to faster-than-light travel, the cylindrical spaceship had reached the Martian orbit in twenty-five seconds. Ten times faster than the speed of light.

On that same day, the previous UN secretary-general, an incompetent Pole, had been arrested by the FBI and charged with child abuse. This unfortunate event had at the same time fostered a diplomatic Big Bang, under the leadership of a new UN secretary-general, appointed in emergency. An experienced Nepalese diplomat suffering from innate blindness, Mrs. Hira Dorjee-Sherpa had championed the Vienna Conference. Ralf Åhman, at the time the director for the small UN Office for Outer Space Affairs, had been her direct report.

The subsequent diplomatic marathon had led to the signature of the Vienna Treaties of 8 December 2094 and the creation of the World's Agency for the Regulation of Space Exploration and Colonization (WARSEC). Ralf had been appointed its director.

WARSEC had been tasked with regulating space business and even granted the right to levy a tax on commercial space activities. It had also been tasked with spearheading interstellar exploration. The problem was that the contributions of its member states would not in any way suffice to build an interstellar ship. Without solid financial resources, WARSEC was toothless. Ralf had, however, found a creative and elegant solution to the problem.

WARSEC had been given sovereignty on all extraterrestrial resources and the right to license their exploitation. In the 2090s, robot labor was taxed on Earth, but not in space.

As a result, Ralf had invited all private aerospace corporations, from Airbus and Comac to Boeing and Lockheed, to partner with them in what was to become WARSEC Ventures. The plan was to mass-manufacture cheap aerospace shuttles on the

Moon, using lunar mineral resources and untaxed robot labor. Airline companies would acquire them to open commercial routes to the soon-to-opened orbital station, or to replace their older aircraft with brand new shuttles endowed with suborbital capability and able to travel to anywhere on Earth in less than two hours.

The goal of this joint enterprise was two-fold. One, it would generate much needed cash for the WARSEC treasury, and thus finance the construction of the first interstellar ship, the *Forward*. Second, it would boost commercial space activities by making travel to the orbital station affordable to a greater number of tourists.

The first prototypes of the two models of aerospace shuttles had been completed. The Ventures partners Airbus and Boeing were currently testing the Space Bear and the Space Hound respectively. Both types would be certified by their respective air regulation agencies, including the American Federal Aviation Administration (FAA), by May 2098, a few weeks after the orbital station had opened to space tourism.

Financially speaking, things were going according to plan. Morally speaking, it was another story.

Ralf Åhman had just got back from the Lunar base, where the prototypes had been assembled and done their first flights. Two potential customers had accompanied him. The Ryanair vice-president of procurement had expressed interest in the large Space Bear shuttle, which had originally been an Airbus-cancelled project, now resuscitated by WARSEC Ventures.

And there was nothing wrong with that. With its delta wings on the roof and its two massive CUBIC-R engines the Space Bear could bring up to 700 passengers into orbit and carry a useful payload of 50 tons.

It was the second potential customer who had disturbed Ralf Åhman. A general from the EU Air Force. The European Union was planning to buy up to 200 Space Bears for its air force, as it considered it to be the best means of quickly projecting soldiers to anywhere in the world. After all, the Space Bear could carry a full infantry battalion to any earthly location in less than two hours.

Under other circumstances, it would probably not have bothered Ralf so much. Of course, it was indeed very ironical, as Michael Vahlroos, the CEO of V-Space and Vahlroos Travel, had pointed out to him, that a UN-backed consortium should make their first sales to the armies of this world. On the other hand, armies needed transportation means, and there was not necessarily anything wrong with selling them those means.

However, the geopolitical situation on earth had shifted dramatically over the last few weeks. There had been unrest in Morocco. It had started with some anti-Chinese riots against expats staying in the kingdom. It was unclear what had started these riots.

What was clear, though, was that Morocco had a monopoly on the production of phosphate, and people had been talking about the phosphate peak for over a year now. Phosphate was needed for fertilizer, and fertilizers were needed to grow the food required to feed a planet now inhabited by 10.5 billion human souls.

Since she had been elected EU president three years earlier, Mme Eugénie Bonavita had constantly threatened to take a tough stance on the monopolistic phosphate situation. There had been some diplomatic tensions between Morocco and the European Union on several occasions, though anything worse had always been averted.

It now seemed to have reached a new climax. A few days earlier, a Moroccan diplomat had been arrested in France after landing onboard the private jet belonging to the crown prince of Morocco. Several tons of cannabis had been seized.

It could have remained a non-incident, if the EU president had not sent an ultimatum to the sherifian kingdom, demanding unacceptable terms, among which the extradition of the crown prince to the European Union.

It now seemed that war between the European Union and Morocco was unavoidable, despite all the efforts UN secretary-general Hira Dorjee-Sherpa was now deploying to ease the tension.

As he was trying to follow the news in his office in the orbital station, Ralf had a doubly bad conscience. Not only was he about to fund his UN agency by selling aerospace shuttles to one of the potential belligerents. But while he had been keeping his head in trivial, space-related matters, his boss, the UN secretary-general, had embarked on an impossible diplomatic sprint. And she had not even asked for his help.

02: AN UNEXPECTED BRIEFING (SEPT 2097)

On Sunday 8 September 2097, Aisha Barjaoui was coming from a climbing weekend with her boyfriend Éric, when she got to know the terrible news. When she was back at the garrison, in Saint-Christol, Southern France, she had been told to meet her captain in his office. At first, the short but muscular black-haired legionnaire had been perplexed. Yes, she was part of the European Foreign Legion, an elite outfit of the EU Armed Forces, but what could Captain Antoine Léger possibly want of her on a Sunday evening?

From her standpoint, it could only mean bad news. She was wondering what could have happened as she knocked at the door of Captain Léger, a short, slim 28-year- old white man, with military-cut brown hair and tired brown eyes.

"I have received a message from your father," the captain told Aisha. "He would like you to call him back."

That was not good. Her father had never tried to contact her since she had joined the Legion.

"What happened?"

"There have been anti-Chinese riots all over Morocco. I understood your mother worked as a housemaid for a Chinese businessman. She was in his villa when the mob came and accused her of collaborating with the Chinese. They killed her. I'm sorry to tell you that."

Aisha felt she was about to cry. She tried to restrain herself.

"What about the Chinese businessman?"

"He was killed too. Did you know him?"

Aisha left the captain's office and went to the closest bathrooms and locked herself in. She took some deep breaths but, after a short moment, she was silently crying.

Of course she knew him. He had been the reason she was in the Legion in the first place. Her mother had been working for him. He had a swimming pool in his villa. She had used his pool to learn how to swim. Deng Hoang had caught her. Instead of punishing her and her mother, he had offered to teach Aisha how to swim. It had ended in an affair. Aisha had been sixteen at the time. A few months later, there had been a condom accident, and she had become pregnant. Deng Hoang had helped her to go the European Union to have an abortion.

Somehow, the Moroccan authorities had got wind of it and wanted to put her in jail. Moroccan nationals were not permitted to have abortions, either in Morocco or abroad, and would face at least four years of imprisonment. She had stayed in the EU. As an undocumented young Moroccan girl, she had had no future.

However, in Cambridge, she had meet Samir and Sanne, who, back in 2095, had been doing their civil service in the British university town. Samir had suggested she apply for the European Foreign Legion, the best way for a physically strong, but uneducated and mostly undocumented Moroccan teenager to become a European citizen. She had got in. She had even become a sergeant after only one and a half years of service. This had been mostly due to her actions in Kirghizstan the previous year, something she tried not to think too much about.

The 2nd Regiment of Foreign Engineers (2nd REG – *Régiment Étranger du Génie*) had returned from their peacekeeping mission in Kirghizstan at the end of January 2097. Like all soldiers back from overseas operations, Aisha Barjaoui had been sent to a shrink. Was she thinking a lot about the corpses in the street of Bishkek, or about the mass graves in the south of the country? Barely. She just remembered she was tired and hungry, back then. Was she affected by the fact she had killed ten people with her knife? No. They had been rapists and assholes. She had no problem killing assholes. Overall, was she feeling upset? Not at all, she was so happy to be back in France. The food was so much better. After this short evaluation, the military doctor had assessed her fit for duty.

In February, she had followed an NCO course, and had been

promoted to sergeant. At nine-teen, she was already a sergeant in the mountain engineers! Logically, the following month, she had been sent on another course, in winter mountaineering. There, she had met again Sergeant Éric Legrand, from the Alpine Rangers. That same nerdy sergeant who knew about stars and had been in her glider during the airborne assault on Bishkek. That same sergeant who had lead-climbed the frozen waterfall to help her squad outflank the militiamen, in that hamlet in the Osh province. He had asked her out. She had said yes.

It had not only been a lot of awesome sex, but also a lot of mythic skiing, mountaineering, and climbing. She did not want to offend the legionnaire mountain engineers of her own regiment, the 2nd REG, but Alpine rangers were better at all of it.

In the summer, during an alpine excursion in Italy, she had seen again her old acquaintances Samir and Sanne. Sanne van der Maas, who by the way, also happened to be the only survivor of the Martian colony. This time, they had exchanged phone numbers and upgraded themselves from acquaintances to friends.

In the first eight months of 2097, Aisha had come a long way to become a regular European individual with normal friends, but since she had learnt about the death of her mother, the whole world was collapsing. Was God punishing her for having too much of a good time? She had had a liberal religious education but could not help wondering.

The following week, she decided to focus on her work, to forget her grief. She had asked for leave to go to the funeral in Morocco. The colonel had answered that European soldiers were currently not allowed to travel to Morocco, for reasons unknown to him. Her request had been denied.

As a sergeant, however, Aisha had much more interest in the progress of her squad. She had a competitive instinct and wanted 1st squad of 3rd platoon to be the best of the 2nd company. In her B-team, her support team, she had kept Jean-Claude Rheinfeldt, the tall and bold Luxembourger, as the machine gunner, and Torbjørn Eriksen, the young Norwegian, as the 51-mm mortarman. She had made Corporal Abhisheek Singh, who had recovered from his wounds in Bishkek, the leader of the B-team. Now that she was a sergeant, he no longer bitched with her because she did not clean the dorm enough.

She had assigned Gabriel Tran as the leader of the A-team, the assault team. The short Cambodian had been promoted to corporal after the assault on the hamlet in November the previous year. She had kept Private Gonzales in the A-team, which she had completed with a new recruit, John Nguyen, from Vietnam. Their driver was still Damian Kowalski, the Catholic Pole.

She was looking forward to the exercise planned at the end of September. They would practice urban warfare on a larger scale. After what her squad had gone through in Bishkek and later in the hamlet, she secretly hoped they would be the best.

However, it seemed that the dates of the exercise were elusive. There were rumors it had been postponed to October.

On Thursday 12 September evening, she went out of her room, as she heard some noise in the corridor. It was coming from the dormitory room of 1st and 2nd squad.

"*Bande de connards*," Jean-Claude Rheinfeldt ranted, drunk as usual ('Band of assholes!'). "They have locked the base. I cannot even go out and buy some more Ricard."

"Perhaps it will be your first sober weekend in a year!" Torbjørn joked.

"What's happening?" Aisha asked.

"They have locked the camp," Corporal Tran said. "All the leaves are cancelled."

"Why?" Aisha wondered.

"I can tell you why."

It was Sergeant Paul Uwilingiyimana, the tall Rwandan, also nicknamed Sgt. Uwil. After Bishkek, Lieutenant Hoffman had picked him as his new platoon sergeant.

"Or at least, what I suspect is the reason," the Rwandan sergeant went on.

"Go ahead, sarge," Jean-Claude said.

"A Moroccan diplomat has been caught with two tons of cannabis in Orly airport," Sgt. Uwil said. "He was in a private jet belonging to Morocco's crown prince."

"I don't see the point," Jean-Claude objected.

"Of course you don't, Private Rheinfeldt. Good night."

Sgt. Uwil went back to his room.

On Friday 13 September, the regiment's colonel gathered all the companies in the assembly yard. He was standing on a stage, talking into a microphone.

"Legionnaires," he said. "There is trouble in Morocco. Two tons of cannabis have been seized in Paris onboard a private jet belonging to the Moroccan royal family. This has shed new light on the drug trafficking organized by the ruling family of a neighbor nation. Our President, Madame Bonavita, cannot accept this kind of provocation. An ultimatum has been sent to the Moroccan king. The crown prince of Morocco will be handed over to the European police before 19 September 05:00, otherwise the EU will do whatever it takes to capture the prince on Moroccan soil, including invading the country. You are all asked to hand over your smartphones and private computers to logistics. They are confiscated until further notice. We are from now on not permitted to communicate with anyone outside the base."

What the hell was going on? Was the EU about to invade Morocco because of some drug trafficking? That did not make sense. Aisha was upset her mobile phone had been confiscated. She could not even call her father. She could not call her boyfriend Éric either. She wondered if the Alpine rangers had been mobilized too.

In the mess, most of the TV channels had been deactivated. There were only a few channels left, all belonging to the Bolloré media group. They were congratulating President Bonavita, who was becoming a true 'Iron Lady'. Aisha wondered if any European citizens were demonstrating against Bonavita's stance. There was no information on it on TV, as she could see. Instead, the TV channels showed demonstrations against the high phosphate price by angry European farmers who demanded immediate action against Morocco. They were also showing videocasts of the carrier Jean-Monet and of AF5 Dachshunds practicing close air support missions. The Moroccans had better give up, they did not stand a chance against the EU armed forces!

"Bollox news!" Torbjørn commented, referring to the Bolloré media channels. "Impossible to know what is really happening."

The only thing that was certain was that the UN secretary-general, Mrs. Hira Dorjee-Sherpa had flown from New York to Brussels for talks with the EU president. She was also to fly to Morocco, first to Rabat and then to Casablanca to talk with Moroccan officials.

Aisha had met her in Kirghizstan when she had been awarded the Dag Hammarskjöld medal, meant for wounded peace-keeping soldiers. Aisha had not even been really wounded, only badly beaten up, for a short time, before eventually taking the upper hand. When meeting the secretary-general back then in the Osh province, Aisha had been too exhausted and sore to be really impressed by this blind diplomat from Nepal and the South Asian Union. Now she hoped that she would calm everybody down. She was not thrilled at the prospect of a war with her own home country. That did not make sense!

The next Monday morning, a company from the 2nd Foreign Parachute Regiment (2nd REP – *Régiment Étranger de Parachutiste*) as well as an extra platoon from that same regiment arrived in Saint-Christol.

"Why are they bringing in paratroopers?" Torbjørn asked as the legionnaire paratroopers moved into the assembly yard. "Do they want us to be *Arnhemized* or to be *Dien-Bien-Phued*?"

Aisha smiled, remembering their Finnish drill sergeant in Castelnaudary, where she and Torbjørn had gone to Legionnaire School together. Back then, most of the legionnaire recruits wanted to become paratroopers, rather than infantry men or engineers. The Finnish sergeant, however, had a low opinion of paratroopers. According to her, being a paratrooper was the best way of being slaughtered. 'Arnhem' referred to a 1944 Allied disaster in Holland, where a British airborne division had been annihilated. 'Dien-Bien-Phu' hinted to a similar fate occurring to French paratroopers in Vietnam, ten years later.

Later that day, officers and sergeants of the 2nd Company of Combat Engineers were called to a briefing in the large operation room. Aisha sat down close to Sgt. Uwil and Lt. Guido Hoffman, her platoon leader, a tall, strong blond German. The senior staff of the six platoons of paratroopers sat in the room as well. She also recognized a few glider pilots from the glider squadron based in Orange, the nearby air force base. On the stage were two generals, most likely sent from Brussels.

The two-star general started:

"In short, the Moroccans have still not responded favorably to our demands. According to our intelligence service, they will refuse to hand over the crown prince to us, and moreover, they have mined half of the phosphate mines and plan to sabotage the other half if we proceed with military action against them. This could cause a shortage of fertilizer, and with it a worldwide famine next year. The president of the European Union cannot allow that."

The one-star general took over:

"That's why we have a contingency plan. We want to at least secure the phosphate mine in Khouribga. It lies over there on the map. About 33 degrees north and 7 degrees west."

As all in the room sat silent, the two-star general explained:

"To put it simply: We will have 300 men silently infiltrate the site. That way, we will be ready to intervene if needed."

"What will happen, exactly?" the paratrooper major asked.

"170 paratroopers and 130 mountain engineers will

silently land in Chough gliders directly on the mine south of Khouribga," the one-star general replied.

"And when?" Aisha's captain asked.

Aisha looked at him. Capt. Antoine Léger seemed in a particularly gloomy mood.

"Tomorrow evening," the two-star general replied. "To be more precise, in the following night, at two in the morning."

"But that will be on the 18th of September," Capt. Léger remarked, "Still 25 hours before the ultimatum's deadline."

"Of course," the general said. "The sooner, the better. That way, you will have the time to deploy and camouflage on the spot calmly. Then, if needed, you are ready to secure the phosphate mine in the night before the 19th of September."

"But we cannot invade the country before the ultimatum is ended!" Capt. Léger objected.

The two-star general smiled:

"Who said so? As long as we don't get caught, it's fine."

Lt. Hoffman raised his hand and said: "What if the Moroccan government yields to our demands and the invasion is called off? What do we do?"

"It's unlikely to happen. Not according to our intelligence," the two-star general assured.

"But what if it happened nonetheless?" The paratrooper major asked.

"If it should happen," the one-star general said, "You will have to march discreetly, by night, 250 km southeast to the

Atlas mountain range. There, we will send some gliders to extract you."

"What about us, the gliders," the squadron leader asked. "How do we get there, and how do we get the hell out of there?"

"Good question," the one-star general complimented. "The 300 men will be spread out in fifteen Chough gliders. You will be towed by fifteen AF5 Dachshunds at Mach 3 from Orange over the Mediterranean Sea and Algeria. With that speed and the stealth of both your gliders and Dachshunds, you will reach the Moroccan-Algerian border east of Khouribga undetected. There you will release the cables and glide your way to this position, over there, in the old mine. Your gliders are stealthy and silent. You will not be detected."

"How do we come back?" The squadron leader asked.

"You use your electric engines, take off and fly to the Algerian border and land in the desert. When the sun rises, you let the solar cells recharge your batteries, and you later resume your flight to France."

"But that's 1,800 kilometers [1120 miles]! At 140 km an hour [87 mph, 76 knots], it will take thirteen hours for us to come back."

"The Chough glider can make it," the one-star general answered.

"Yes, but the crew won't," the squadron leader of the glider regiment objected. "There are no toilets onboard the gliders."

"Use some diapers," the two-star general replied. "Astronauts have diapers, and they are the *crème de la crème*".

Some of the officers and NCOs laughed.

"*Mon general,*" Aisha's captain said. "Flying over Algeria and then landing in the desert in Algeria. Is Algeria backing us up in this enterprise?"

"Son," the two-star general replied. "All I can tell you is that Algeria will not shoot down our planes and gliders. You needn't know more. Now let's go through the details of the operation. You will see, it's a very good plan. It may well be a jolly little war, as the president framed it."

After the briefing, Captain Léger looked depressed. Lieutenant Hoffman took Aisha and Sgt. Uwilingiyimana and followed the captain to his room. He had a bottle in his briefcase.

"*Liqueur de génépi, mon capitaine,*" the lieutenant said showing a liquor bottle.

"Come on in, Guido," the captain said. "And you too, Uwil and Barjaoui."

Antoine grabbed four glasses and put them on his little side table, before sitting on his bed and inviting his guests to use the two chairs and the stool. Guido poured liquor into each of the glasses before sitting down on the remaining chair. As he raised his glass, the lieutenant said:

"Génépi. Who would think that these ugly little alpine plants would taste so good in liquid form? À la vôtre!"('Cheers!')

"À la vôtre!" the others replied.

They took a few sips. Aisha liked the taste, and the warmth filling her stomach and brain. She felt a bit happier.

"What do you think of this operation, *mon capitaine*?" Lt. Hoffman finally asked.

Antoine Léger took a few more sips of génépi liquor before admitting:

"I never joined the Army, or even the Legion, to do this kind of black ops. Truly, I'm scared. We are involved in something morally wrong."

The German lieutenant smiled and said: "You are an idealist, sir. According to sociologists, the Army is made of 30% nationalists, 65% opportunists, and 5% idealists. You are a minority. You are like my good platoon sergeant here. Aren't you also, Paul?"

"And what are you, lieutenant?" Sgt. Uwil asked.

"I'm an opportunist, like most of the legionnaires, I would say." Guido Hoffman replied. "Like Aisha here, I just want to be paid to do mountaineering and ski touring. Though that does not make me willing to invade Morocco. That's Aisha's home country. By the way, what do you think, Aisha?"

Aisha was not expecting to be asked her opinion. She thought a while and smiled wearily:

"At Legionnaire School, we had to learn the Legion's history. It was created in 1831 to serve the French Empire and oppress Africa and Indochina through colonization."

"'*The Legion was created to oppress Africa through*

colonization," Lt. Hoffman smiled: "Is it how you learnt it at Legionnaire School?"

"Of course, not", Aisha replied. "The wording they used might have been slightly different."

"The colonization era ended in 1962," Lt. Hoffman said. "It's true it was bad. During the Algerian war, a lot of Germans deserted from the Legion."

"A hundred and three years ago, the Legion was still not exemplary." Capt. Léger said, looking gravely at Sgt. Uwilingiyimana.

"Careful, captain", the tall Rwandan sergeant warned. "You are about to use the R-word. It's forbidden in the legion."

"The R-word?" The captain wondered.

"R for Rwanda." Lt. Hoffman said. "Senior French officers could fire you for that. You're lucky I'm junior and German."

The lieutenant was laughing. The captain was not.

"A hundred and four years ago," Captain Léger said, "France trained and armed genocidaires in Rwanda. During the genocide, France kept delivering weapons to them. After the genocide, they exfiltrated the genocidaires. The Legion was part of it."

There was a chilling silence in the captain's room.

"I would never have wanted to serve France, ever," the captain went on. "On 9 May 2054, the EU became a federation. With it came the dissolution of the French army and the creation of the European Armed Forces. Over the last forty-three years, Europe has never been at war and has only taken part in peace-keeping operations. That's why I joined the army in the first place."

The other legionnaires remained silent. The captain went on:

"I first served in a French-speaking tank regiment, with mostly French officers. A few of them still wanted France to have a king. A King! Yesterday, the Brits elected their first president, and in two days, the last king of England is gonna hand over his power to the new South British president. But those French nationalistic officers still want a king! That's why I joined the Foreign Legion. To be in an integrationist environment, with interesting people. We did a fine job in Kirghizstan. Now, I am leading those men and women into a very disputable operation."

"What do you want us to do, captain?" the lieutenant asked. "Shall we desert?"

"Would it help?" Aisha said. "The invasion is gonna happen anyway. It will be over in less than a week. I'd rather keep my job and have some skiing next winter."

She stood up.

"That's the spirit," Lt. Hoffman said, and also stood up. "*Mon capitaine*, you think too much. It's gonna get you killed."

The legionnaires left their captain in his room with the bottle of génépi.

03: STEALTH GLIDE (SEPT 2097)

Aisha did not sleep well that night. Before the glider assault on Bishkek, eleven months earlier, she had gone to pray. She did not this time. Though she had been raised as a feminist Muslim, she had become less and less religious. She knew Paul Uwilingiyimana and Damian Kowalski were both devout Catholics. However, they looked equally tired, the following morning. Aisha concluded that strong faith did not necessarily improve one's sleep.

At breakfast, her machine gunner, the tall, bald Jean-Claude Rheinfeldt, shortly commented: "Seems everybody has slept poorly! Look on the bright side: exhaustion and weariness are powerful medicines against doubt and bad conscience."

The Norwegian mortarman, Torbjørn Eriksen, asked him to shut up.

After breakfast, Aisha and her squad reported to Lt. Harry Guaino of the 2nd Regiment of Foreign Paratroopers, the 2nd

REP, who was now staying in the same base as the Mountain legionnaires. Her squad of combat engineers had been put at the disposal of his platoon of paratroopers. They had lunch together, in the mess hall.

While some of the legionnaires would secure the Khouribga phosphate mine, the main part of the force would seize the military airport nearby. Guaino's platoon of paratroopers was to lead the assault. Aisha's squad of engineers had been assigned to them to clear the mine fields into the airport.

"Remember," the lieutenant said. "I want to see speed, and clear actions. We must take the hangars by surprise in the night. We are spearheading the assault on the airport. We need to clear it before the rest of the parachute regiment jumps on it."

"*Pas de problèmes, les mecs.*" ('No problem, dudes'.) Jean-Claude Rheinfeldt commented, eating his cheese and bread with his mouth open.

The lieutenant looked at the bald Luxembourger with wide-open eyes.

"Excuse me, legionnaire?"

The tall machine gunner saluted with nonchalance:

"Private First Class Rheinfeldt. I served in Greenland and Kirghizstan. Where have you served? Or sorry, it was a rhetoric question. Paratroopers have not been deployed overseas in twenty years."

"*Mon Lieutenant*, you will say." Lt. Guaino said. "Sergeant Barjaoui, your man shows a total lack of respect."

Aisha was tired. The best was to agree with the Lieutenant. She sighed and said:

"*Oui, mon lieutenant. Personne ne veut de ce con de Luxembourgeois.*" ('Yes sir, no-one wants this Luxembourger idiot.'). That's why my squad is stuck with him. Another two years before his contract expires. He distinguished himself in Bishkek, though."

The paratroopers laughed.

The lieutenant drank from his glass of water and said: "I see. You have some hot shots here. Please remember we paratroopers are also an elite force."

Aisha acquiesced politely: "*Oui, mon lieutenant.* After Legionnaire School, I applied to the Parachute Regiment, but I was never accepted. I was not good enough."

The Lieutenant pointed his knife at Aisha with a gesture implying she had exactly got the point. When he had finally swallowed his bit of comté cheese, Lt. Guaino said:

"You engineers have perhaps served in peacekeeping missions. We paratroopers are kept in reserve for very serious missions."

This made Torbjørn Eriksen sneer. Aisha's Norwegian mortarman said, mockingly:

"*Ooh la la, mon lieutenant! On va se faire Arnhemiser la gueule, ou bien Dien-Bien-Phuter la face?*" (Ooh la la, Sir. Are we gonna get *Arnhemized* or *Dien-Bien-Phued*?")

Aisha's combat engineers laughed heartedly, and the

28

paratrooper lieutenant looked at them in distaste.

The afternoon was mostly about packing and checking the equipment. They would have desert camouflage instead of khaki, and everything had to be planned accordingly.

Now and then Aisha cast a glance at the European flag flying over the assembly yard. She felt some distrust for the flag. She once had been told the EU flag had been different, twelve yellow stars arranged in a circle on a deep blue background. It was supposed to represent harmony. The current flag was also made of twelve yellow stars on a deep blue background, but they were arranged in the atomic structure of diamond. Diamonds were unbreakable and this layout of stars was supposed to represent strength and unity rather than harmony. It was well suited for what they were planning to do.

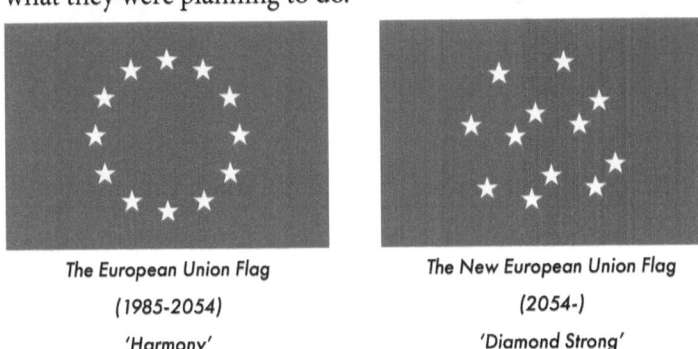

The European Union Flag
(1985-2054)
'Harmony'

The New European Union Flag
(2054-)
'Diamond Strong'

Figure 2: the old European Flag, and the new EU flag, with the dark -blue background and the 12 yellow stars arranged in the atomic structure of a diamond, supposed to symbolize strength, rather than harmony.

They had an early dinner, before leaving for Orange's air force base.

Night had already fallen when they arrived at the military airport, around half past eight. The lights of the runway had been turned off, but Aisha could sense some activity on it. As the legionnaires waited on the tarmac, Aisha's eyes progressively got used to the obscurity. Eventually, she could make out fifteen Chough gliders and fifteen AF5 Dachshunds to tow them.

Aisha had her squad check their equipment one more time. She had forgotten how heavy it could be in some cases. The squad's driver Kowalski had the main radio but, as a squad leader, she had to carry an extra radio. She was also carrying a gas mask, and some explosive. Luckily, they were skipping winter clothes, but they had to bring more water. Regarding her climbing equipment, she had cut it to the minimum, taking only a few slings, nuts, and quickdraw. She had swapped her military harness for her own private one, which was lighter and took less space.

It was damn heavy. Two years earlier, she had been promised a special rucksack designed for women, but she was still waiting. In the meantime, her back hurt.

When they were ready, she met up with her chalk. Aisha's squad was to board the same Chough glider as Lt. Guaino's leader group and his first squad.

They followed the lieutenant into their assigned glider. After the twenty troopers had sat down on their seats in the cabin, Jean-Claude Rheinfeldt, stood up again and went to the rear door on the left. He unzipped his trousers and took a piss.

"They are no toilets on-board, remember?" he said.

Then all the men stood up and queued at the four doors of the glider to pee. As the only woman onboard, Aisha jumped out of the glider, ran to the towing AF5 Dachshund, crouched under its fuselage and relieved herself on the runway.

Once back in the plane, the lieutenant commented it was indeed better to be a man than a woman when one was a soldier.

"As long as you say so, *mon lieutenant*, you are certainly right," she said to be left in peace.

Chough Glider
(Airbus Military)

AF5 Dachshund
(Airbus Military)

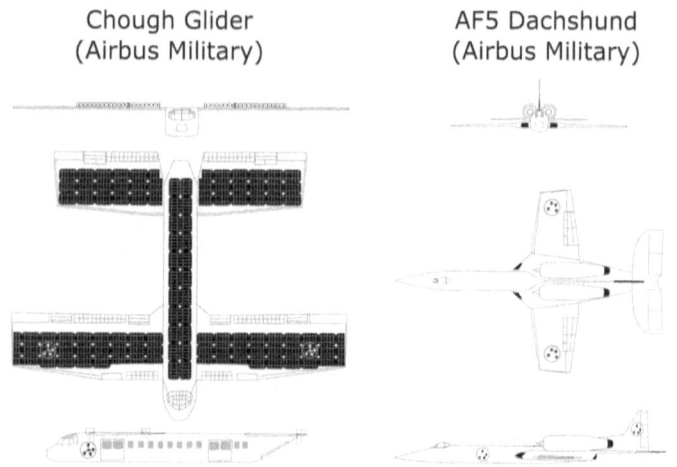

Figure 3: the Chough glider is stealth and can be towed at supersonic speed. Equipped with ducted fans, it can do a vertical take-off and landing and fly at 140 km/h, powered by solar energy. The AF5 Dachsund is equipped with two CUBIC-R engines and a scramjet can fly up to Mach 6 using its ramjets, Mach 17 using its scramjet. Both bear the insignia of the EU Air Force

At 22:10, the engines of the AF5 Dachshund were started.

Five minutes later, the glider was rolling along the runway.

There were a few bumps and suddenly they were airborne and climbing. Through the window, Aisha saw all the lights of the nearby towns disappear as they climbed above the clouds.

Once the AF5 Dachshund reached its cruise altitude, it accelerated to Mach 3, and the legionnaires were pulled sideways in the glider.

Aisha had never been towed in a glider at that speed, and felt like being sick. She managed to hold it back, though.

The towing took one hour.

Then there was a click, and they were gliding.

Shortly after, the glider pilot switched off all the lights in the cabin and announced in the intercom: "Troopers, check your watch. It's 22:25 Moroccan time. It will be a two-hour glide."

Gliding in the dark and in silence had a relaxing effect.

The sky over Morocco was cloudless. To the southwest, she could see a red star shining close to the Moon. Her boyfriend had been a good teacher, and she knew it was Mars. She briefly wondered why she was not living over there instead. After all, her friend Sanne had been born there. The planet was currently not inhabited, though. The Martian Colony project had been the largest recent failure in space history.

Aisha pondered over her own situation. Why was she sitting in a glider on her way to invade her home country? Because of a poor quality Chinese condom and a Moroccan government forbidding abortion. Well, if the Moroccan government got the shit beaten out of them, she would certainly not cry.

This was a weird sensation, this total absence of feeling. She was invading her own country and did not really care. She felt detached from herself. Perhaps, Rheinfeldt was right. Exhaustion and weariness were the best medicines against bad conscience and doubts. Right now, she needed that.

"Landing in five minutes," the pilot notified them.

Aisha saw that the electric ducted fans of the glider's wings had been turned on. It would certainly land vertically, she thought. She was right.

Five minutes later the gliders had landed, and the soldiers exited the aircraft silently. It was 0:23 a.m. Moroccan time.

The fourteen other gliders had landed nearby, and Aisha saw their troopers spreading out in the area like shadows. A moment later, the gliders started taking off vertically one by one and silently flew east toward the Algerian border. Three hundred shadows were left wandering in the dark on the Moroccan soil.

Lt. Guaino took his platoon and Aisha's squad to a position located five kilometers (3.1 miles) north of their landing zone. The forty-one soldiers moved low and quietly.

Aisha's squad was closing the march and found it difficult to keep up with the paratroopers. Engineers were not as well trained when it came to night march. Luckily, it took only one hour for them to reach their camp position. Other platoons were to camp some half a kilometer away.

There, they started digging. They were to build some three-meter-deep trenches, where they would hide until the following day. It was hot, they were sweaty, and the digging was exhausting, but by four in the morning, they were ready, and they could disappear into their trenches, which they covered with camouflage nets.

It was Wednesday 18 September, morning. The ultimatum would end in exactly twenty-four hours, at 4:00 Moroccan time, the next night. They would then seize the airport, located only 6 km (3.7 miles) away.

04: Lightning In The Sky (18 Sept 2097)

In the orbital station, Ralf Åhman had been sleeping on the couch in his office. Or at least trying to sleep. He had not changed clothes in six days, had not showered, and had started to smell 'manly', as his ex-girlfriend would have said.

He had spent all the previous day following the news on Earth to try to guess what was about to happen. A friend of his, Esko Punainen, currently the EU ambassador to Kirghizstan, had told him a few days earlier that President Bonavita was most likely not bluffing. That she would indeed invade Morocco.

In the news, the hawkish rhetoric had been prevailing. Both Fox news and the Bolloré Group TV channels seemed to have the same position: The EU president was a great leader and an Iron Lady. She was the *'first EU President to show some real balls in a while'*. Morocco deserved it anyway since they had jacked-up the phosphate prices and so on. In case of invasion of Morocco, the EU armed forces stood ready. They were great.

They were so great. They were the best-armed forces in the world. Or so was the message on *Bollox news*, as the Bolloré Group had been nicknamed.

The only reliable piece of information Ralf had obtained had been that the UN secretary-general had now left Brussels and was heading for Rabat, and then Casablanca to discuss the crisis with Moroccan officials.

At four in the morning on Wednesday 18 September, an alert on Ralf's smartphone woke him up, if he had been sleeping at all. He was not sure.

He checked his smartphone immediately and smiled: She had done it! Hira Dorjee-Sherpa was simply the best UN secretary-general Ralf had ever seen. She had worked out a face-saving outcome for both parties and a compromise had been reached.

The Moroccan crown prince would fly to Geneva, in Switzerland, where he would answer questions asked by the Swiss police, in the presence of EU police officers. Both the EU and Morocco had agreed to that part of the deal.

Ralf felt relieved and decided to go to his bedroom to spend the rest of the night. He fell asleep immediately. The following morning, it was a rested, showered, and clean-shaved Ralf who was back in his office at the orbital station.

After starting his computer, he realized he had several missed calls from Glover Johnson, his global safety director. He decided to call him back using the video-conference system.

Because of the transmission delay, it was slightly inconvenient, but one got used to it.

On the screen, Glover Johnson displayed as sitting in his office, in the WARSEC Vaasa Headquarters, in Finland. Glover was a short 38-year old black man with an impressive chest circumference, giving away the fact that he spent at least two hours daily at the gym. As usual, he was wearing a suit. This time, it was a black suit, with a light blue shirt, but no tie.

Ralf greeted him: "Hi, Glover, when is the baby coming?"

"Still on October 12th. So far no changes."

"Good. What did you want?"

"Two things," Glover declared. "For the manufacturing of the Forward class ships, it seems that Tatjana's team has come up with a good solution, to manufacture ships faster and cheaper."

Tatjana Aydermir was the WARSEC production director and was supervising the manufacturing of aerospace shuttles and spaceships on the Moon. She had been working closely with Thierry Diakité, a talented robot engineer, to find a way to manufacture the spaceships of the Forward class as cheaply and as quickly as possible. This first class of interstellar spaceship would be used for the Alpha Centauri mission, hopefully launched before the year 2100.

Ralf felt a little thrill. War in Morocco had been averted, and now he was back in business, planning the coming interstellar exploration. He looked at Glover through the webcam and said:

"Yes, I am vaguely aware of it. I met Tatjana and Thierry on the moon."

Glover went on: "However, their solution requires a small change in the design of the ship."

"Meaning?"

"We would not be able to start production before February 2098," Glover replied. "But the gain of speed is such that we should still have ships operational for 2099. It would be great if you could come down to Vaasa, to make a formal decision by the end of the week."

Ralf was, in a way, happy to have been given a good reason not to stay longer in the orbital station. After a short reflection, he said: "OK. I will come down to Earth tonight. I will take the ESA flight to Toulouse. I should reach Vaasa by tomorrow afternoon."

"Good," Glover said. "Then, I don't know if you have read my emails, concerning the Space Bear."

"No, I haven't."

"The atmosphere entry went fine, and the test flights in the atmosphere are beyond expectations. The Airbus chief engineer contacted me."

"Meaning?"

"It should be certified by the FAA at the latest in April next year. Since the orbital station will open about that time, it could be wise to have two dozen exemplars manufactured already by then. I feel it will be a best seller, this plane. The Ryanair vice president for procurement sent me a firm promise of an order of 24 exemplars."

"I know," Ralf said. "And the EU Air Force general even more. He talked of a first order of 200 exemplars."

On the screen, Glover smiled: "That's great news! It will finance the construction of a few more Forward class ships."

"Glover, don't you understand what it means?"

"Yes, it means that all the armed forces in the world are gonna down-size their navies and increase their space transportation. I don't care, the few friends I have left in the US navy are all in the submarines."

Before joining WARSEC, Glover Johnson had been a senior officer in the US navy. Originally from the submarine branch, he had mostly worked with the safety of onboard compact fusion reactors. He had written a book on how US navy nuclear safety standards could be applied to the deployment of compact fusion reactors in space and had eventually reached the rank of rear-admiral, even being detailed to NASA for a few years.

To Ralf's dismay, Glover seemed to predominantly interpret the large order of the EU Air Force as a sign that the armed forces of the world would downsize their amphibious fleets and invest in space transport. After all, suborbital transportation capability implied a faster way to deploy soldiers anywhere in the world. It made sense, but it was not the point Ralf was trying to make.

"You don't have moral issues having a UN-backed

consortium selling transport aircraft to armed forces around the world?" Ralf wondered.

"Of course not," Glover replied. "They would get those shuttles anyway. If not from us, from somebody else."

Ralf did not answer.

"Listen, Ralf," Glover added, "It's like in Sun Tsu's Art of War. Take the resources of your enemies. You don't like armed forces, do you? Just think that you are taking their money. They are never going to use these aircraft for military purposes anyway. By the way, you have seen it: the war with Morocco has been averted."

Ralf did not insist.

Later that day, he reflected over what Glover had told him. He was partly right. UN member states were not willing to increase their contribution to the WARSEC budget, but they were more than eager to get suborbital transportation capability. Selling them aerospace shuttles was an indirect way of collecting money from the UN member states.

Besides, one had to be serious. Wars belonged to the past. Even in the recent tricky situation between Morocco and the European Union, the UN secretary-general had managed to work out a diplomatic solution.

That afternoon, as Ralf was wandering in the orbital complexes, he wished that the hotels and restaurants had already opened in the commercial rings. He could have used a proper lunch.

In the evening, he boarded an Albaspace belonging to the European Space Agency and smiled as he floated his way into it.

The long, thin, windowless aerospace shuttle had been manufactured by V-Space, the sister company of Vahlroos Corporation. With its four CUBIC-R engines over the curved delta wings and its scramjet at the rear of the fuselage squeezed below the overarching bent aileron, the Albaspace was undoubtedly the best aerospace shuttle in the world. Smoother and faster than the Space Bear or the Space Hound WARSEC Ventures was trying to certify. In suborbital flight, it could travel anywhere in less than an hour. The US president had adopted it as Air Force One, the EU president as EU Flight One.

It was, however, an expensive and exclusive plane and meant for VIPs only. The middle classes would never be able to afford to travel to the orbital station aboard an Albaspace and WARSEC Ventures' planned aerospace shuttles were needed to make space democratic.

Michael Vahlroos, the CEO of V-Space and Vahlroos Travel, had seen the whole of WARSEC Ventures as unfair competition to his Albaspace. He had refused to join the enterprise. That made Ralf smile even more. When it came to the orbital station, Michael had had a completely different approach, and had even become the main stakeholder of the station, after WARSEC. Vahlroos was to open several hotels and a space attraction center, not to mention a Space Spa and a Space Casino during the next extension wave. There had even been talks of expanding their activities to the moon.

And there he was, boarding the aerospace shuttle manufactured by the company with which he was both competing and partnering.

As he floated through the Albaspace's airlock, Ralf spotted editions of the two European weekly satirical newspapers still actually printed on paper: the French-language *Canard Enchaîné* and the English-language *Chained Palmiped*. He took the English-language paper and went to his seat.

He browsed through it once the windowless shuttle had undocked from the station.

One headline read '*Your Majesty President*'. It referred to the newly sworn-in president of the UK. Ralf had completely forgotten about it. In June earlier that year, the subjects of the United Kingdom of South Britain had been called to a referendum to vote on the future constitutional form of their country. The result had been the establishing of a British Republic called the United Commonwealth of South Britain, and still referred to as 'UK'. The British president elect was to be sworn in the following day, on 19 September, and become the next British head of state. King Eamon would be remembered in history as the last king of England. King Eamon, whom Ralf knew as plain Eamon, was a medical doctor and a psychiatrist, and he had expressed interest in joining WARSEC. Ralf knew already that Eamon Windsor had been accepted as a senior medical officer.

Another headline was titled '*You smoked me, so I smoke you*'. The article told the story of Moroccan diplomat Hassan Benkirane being caught with two tons of cannabis in Paris in the crown prince's private jet. The analysis of the cockpit voice recorder seemed to show that the prince himself had wished good luck to the diplomat. That bade ill.

It was the first time Ralf had read about the cockpit voice recorder, and it was bad. He had always hoped that the prince had been innocent and that a short police interview of the crown prince in Geneva would just sort things out.

The only thing to do was to hope for the best. Hira Dorjee-Sherpa was now in Casablanca anyway. The Europeans would not attack as long the UN secretary-general was in Morocco.

A few hours later, the Albaspace started its atmosphere re-entry, and it was shaking.

Ralf could feel how the shuttle was now performing S-turns to lose momentum. Eventually, the screens in the cabin started showing the view from the aircraft again. It was a beautiful night with a starry sky.

Suddenly there were violent flashes on the horizon on one of the screens. It was the screen showing the spacecraft's starboard. On another screen, there was a map. They were flying 90 km (56 miles) west off the coast of Morocco.

The frequency of flashes increased.

Ralf thought for a moment of the secretary-general, who was in Morocco, of all the innocent Moroccans people who were in their homes that night and would wake up in a bombing hell.

He cried silently.

05: SMOKE AND FIRE
(19 SEPT 2097)

"*Lieutenant Guaino! Qu'est-ce que vous foutez?* ['Lt. Guaino, what the hell are you doing?'] 500 of our paratroopers will jump over the airport in 35 minutes. We must take it now!"

Aisha had heard it in her back-up radio set. It was Major Poisson, from the 2nd Foreign Parachute Regiment, who was yelling on the wireless.

It was 7:55 on Thursday 19 September. The first sun rays showed themselves in the east. Above the horizon, Venus and Jupiter were still visible, but they would soon disappear under the brightness of the rising sun.

Many things had gone wrong that night. The legionnaires had left their camouflaged trenches a bit before midnight and arrived in the vicinity of the military airport at two in the morning.

Aisha's squad had opened a breach in the fence and cleared

the mine field. With the paratrooper platoon, they had crawled their way between the main runway and the taxiway.

At 3:45, they were in position, lying by the taxiway, camouflaged, 120 meters (400 ft) away from the main hangar they were supposed to storm.

At 4:00, the lieutenant had asked for permission to engage. It had been denied. The invasion had been cancelled. No explanation had been given.

Lt. Guaino had had his platoon crawl back the way they had come from, in order not to be surprised on the military airfield by the Moroccans at sunrise.

At 5:30, they had been one kilometer (0.62 mile) away from the airport, when they had suddenly seen some flashes far away in the west.

Then, they had heard some sirens and seen some activity at the airport. A moment later, eight fighters and twelve attack helicopters had taken off from it. They were never to come back.

At 6:05, they had eventually been told that the invasion was to take place after all. There had been a misunderstanding. The assault on the airport should not have been cancelled. The rest of the parachute regiment would jump as planned over the airport at 08:30.

The five platoons of paratroopers and their supporting engineers had moved back to the airport. Lt. Guaino's assault team had to crawl their way back between the runway and the taxiway again.

However, dawn was coming, and they did not dare cross the last taxiway to retake the position from where they were supposed to attack.

Aisha considered an alternative route to the initial plan. She crawled silently to Lt. Guaino and whispered:

"Sir, it's too risky to rejoin our previous position, and the main hangar is a whole 300 meters [980 ft] away. Better go over there to the left. The first building is only about 100 meters [330 ft] away. From there, we could progress to the hangar and the control towers."

The lieutenant shrugged and looked at Aisha as if she was a retard: "Are you stupid, sergeant? These houses will be the job of 2nd platoon. We have to take the main hangar and attract their fire. Otherwise 3rd platoon won't be able to outflank them."

The very idea of attracting anybody's fire sounded like a very bad one. Aisha tried again: "But, lieutenant. If we run straight, we will be spotted and slaughtered."

This did not frighten the paratrooper officer who simply replied: "Listen up, sergeant. They don't expect us, okay? They are certainly not waiting for soldiers coming from inside the airport."

Aisha gave up and just said: "All right. I will prepare the mortarmen to set up a smoke screen."

"Sergeant, do you have a brain at all?" Lt. Guaino whispered, very irritated. "If we use smoke, guaranteed we will attract fire before we reach the hangar. First squad, over here."

The eight paratroopers of the 1st squad crawled to the lieutenant and listened to his instructions. Whoever he was, Lt. Guaino was certainly not a good tactician, Aisha thought. She called to herself the two mortarmen of the remaining paratrooper squads and had them lie beside Torbjørn Eriksson.

"Listen up," she whispered, "Load your mortars with smoke grenades. You hear a shot, you fire your smoke rounds. You at 70 meters [230 feet], you at 140 meters [460 feet] and you at 210 meters [690 feet]. Understood?"

"*Oui, sergeant,*" the mortarmen replied.

She then crawled to Jean-Claude, who was angrily pointing his middle finger to the back of the paratrooper lieutenant. She whispered to her machine gunner:

"Rheinfeldt, calm down. Get your machine gun ready. Be ready to give suppressing fire on the right."

The bald Luxembourger acquiesced.

She then crawled to Tran, Nguyen, Gonzales and Kowalski to give them the rest of her instructions.

"*Lieutenant Guaino, c'est quoi ce bordel? Il est huit heures cinq, putain!*" the major yelled on the radio again ('Lt. Guaino, what the fuck is happening? It's 8:05 for fuck's sake!').

Suddenly, the eight paratroopers of the first squad stood up and started running across the tarmac, straight toward the hangar.

They had made sixty meters (200 ft) when a burst of

machine gun crackled.

Blood splattered, and the eight paratroopers fell. All of them.

The lieutenant lay there with wide eyes and open mouth.

While the lieutenant lay helplessly, the three mortarmen had already fired their smoke grenades. Jean-Claude was now returning fire, while Aisha and her A team were throwing additional smoke grenades at close range.

"B-teams: smoke and fire, smoke and fire," Aisha yelled. "Mortars: smoke, machine guns: fire. A-teams on me. Through the smoke."

She stood up and ran straight into the smoke without looking behind her.

As she ran, she saw Jean-Claude's tracers flying dangerously close to her. *Quel con le Luxembourgeois* ('What a Luxembourger idiot!')

She arrived at the fallen paratroopers. Four were dead. Three were wounded. One was pretending to be dead.

She took cover behind a dead body. The smoke was now very thick, and her eyes were itching. The next moment, her squad was with her. She crawled to the wounded mortar man, ignored his screams and took his 51-mm individual mortar as well as his six smoke rounds.

"Kowalski," she said, "You take the machine gun."

Using the mortar, she placed extra smoke in front of her and on her left, where the enemy fire was most likely to come from. To the side, she could see the tracers of the paratroopers and Jean-Claude providing covering fire.

"The paratroopers are hiding," Corporal Tran said. "They have not followed us."

"We need to push for the first house, anyway, or we are dead," Aisha replied. "The smoke is thick enough. Get rid of your packs. Take only the ammo. Gonzales, you carry the mortar for me. Let's go."

They resumed their charge, this time toward the closest house, together with the paratrooper who had been pretending to be dead. Aisha ran as fast as she could.

Behind her, Kowalski was swearing in Polish: "*Zdrowas Maryjo, laski pelna, Zdrowas Maryjo, laski pelna.*" He sounded pretty pissed.

It took her seventeen never-ending seconds through the itching smoke to reach the first building. There, she took a grenade from her combat jacket, unpinned it and threw it into the house, but forgot to take cover, as she was panting like a rhinoceros.

She was stunned by the shockwave. One of her earplugs fell out.

As she was struggling on the ground, looking erratically in her pocket for a new pair of earplugs, she saw Corporal Tran and Private Gonzales, storming the building.

The crackling of their assault rifles in the confined building added excruciating pain to her ears.

Her radio, Damian Kowalski, was standing aimlessly at the edge of the building and the paratrooper who had played dead forced him to take cover.

"You know, when your time is up, it's up," Kowalski said to the irritated paratrooper.

Aisha had put her new earplug in, and she was now hearing people talking normally, as the noise of the firing and explosions in the background was filtered away.

She led Kowalski and the paratrooper into the building.

There were four dead men inside, all unarmed.

Aisha ordered Kowalski to put the machine gun at the window to cover the military camp and Nguyen to stay in standby in the door way with his recoilless anti-tank rifle.

Corporal Tran, who had been standing at one of the broken windows giving on to the hangar, whistled and signaled Aisha to join him.

"Sergeant," he said, "Behind the hangar, I think there is an armored vehicle. The machine gun fire must have come from there."

"Can Nguyen hit it with his bazooka?"

"No, it's behind. Use a mortar round."

Gonzales, who had picked up the 51-mm mortar, came to Aisha and handed it over. The 51-mm mortar could be used indoors through a window, and she aimed behind the hangar.

"Fifty to seventy meters [164-230 ft]," she said. "Three high-explosive rounds."

With Gonzales' help, she fired all three rounds in just six seconds. The first explosions occurred shortly after that.

Suddenly two anti-aircraft vehicles appeared from behind the hangar.

Tran ran to Nguyen and had him aim his anti-tank weapon at the one on the left, while Kowalski was opening fire with his light machine gun at the one on the right.

Two seconds later, the vehicle on the left disappeared in a fireball, hit by Nguyen's rocket.

But the other vehicle was now pointing its 40-mm gun at the building, and all the legionnaires ran to the other side of the building and plunged to take cover.

Aisha was expecting to die.

She heard an explosion.

It was not the characteristic sound of 40-mm rapid fire.

The two other A teams of paratroopers were finally there. They had fired with their two anti-tank weapons at the vehicle. Aisha's B team had also joined them: Corporal Singh, Private First Class Eriksen and Private First Class Rheinfeldt. Lieutenant Guaino was nowhere to be seen.

She put one A team of paratroopers in charge of the defense of the captured building, and she led the charge to the main hangar, fifty meters (164 ft) away.

When they stormed it, they saw a dozen mechanics raising their hands. Jean-Claude Rheinfeldt opened fire with his machine gun and hit two mechanics in the heads, their brains splashing against the helicopter undergoing maintenance.

He stopped firing only because Torbjørn had grabbed his machine gun. The Luxembourger and the Norwegian were now punching each other in front of the remaining Moroccan mechanics, who were unsure what to do.

Aisha asked them in Arabic to gather against one of the walls, while she asked her A team to inspect the rest of the hangar. Tran, Gonzales and Nguyen checked around. It was clear.

Corporal Singh managed to stop Rheinfeldt and Eriksen fighting, though the Norwegian now had a black eye.

Aisha was contemplating the control tower, forty meters (130 ft) away. She asked the nearby paratrooper sergeant to place some more smoke. As the smoke screen rose in front of her, she caught a glimpse of Moroccans soldiers fleeing from the tower.

"You and your team, you stay at the hangar in support," she said to the paratrooper sergeant.

"My squad: forward to the tower," she yelled.

The mountain engineers made a dash for the tower, through the even more itching smoke. Once there, Singh threw a grenade through the door. This time, all had taken cover properly.

The grenade went off. Aisha hated explosions in confined areas. They were always too noisy, despite the earplugs.

Corporal Tran led his A team upstairs in the tower.

"Clear," he said.

When Aisha arrived at the top of the control tower, she could see what a bloody mess it was. Three air controllers lay dead in a pile of glass fragments. They were all unarmed.

"Oops," Rheinfeldt said. "My mistake: the fire did not come from there, obviously."

He laughed.

Aisha was too exhausted to be judgmental and just ordered:

"Rheinfeldt, Kowalski. You stay here with your machine guns, and see if you can provide fire support. Kowalski, you have the radio. You tell me if you see anything suspicious. The rest of us, we form a defense perimeter around the main hangar. But first, we get back our packs."

The squad started to go down the stairs.

"Sarge," Rheinfeldt said, "I'm low on ammo. If you could get me some more."

"Sure, private," Aisha replied.

"Sergeant," Kowalski added. "I think the situation is pretty much under control, looking from here. 2nd platoon has taken the other buildings at the other end of the taxiway. 3rd platoon is holding a line of fire against the camp from the runway. 4th platoon is coming in reinforcement toward us. 5th platoon is digging trenches to put their 60-mm mortars."

"Don't stay too long by the window," Aisha told him as she went down the stairs.

They made it to where the paratroopers had fallen. Only the four dead were left. The wounded had been transported somewhere else.

As they picked up their rucksacks, they were met by the 4th platoon of the parachute company, and with them were some combat engineers from the 3rd platoon, including Lt. Hoffman.

"The paratroopers said that you led the charge," the engineer lieutenant said to Aisha. "Second time, after Kirghizstan. Keep up like that, and we will make you an officer."

As they were standing, they heard the sounds of jet engines flying at low speed. They raised their heads and saw two huge cargo planes coming low over the runway. Their cargo back doors were open, and paratroopers were jumping out of them, two by two.

They blenched, as they heard some mighty explosions coming from the military camp. These were bombs falling. They then saw some AF5 Dachshunds roaring at full speed above the ground. They were providing close air support while escorting the transport plane.

There were seven of them.

"Only two cargo planes and seven fighters," Lt. Hoffman noted. "What the hell has happened? There should be five heavies."

"That's only one company jumping," a paratrooper standing nearby said. "We were waiting for a whole battalion."

The jump was a mess.

Aisha saw how some paratroopers got entangled in one another's parachutes and fell too fast to the ground.

At that moment, she felt happy to have failed to become a paratrooper, back at Legionnaire School. She preferred being a mountain engineer.

Aisha made it back to the control tower, carrying Kowalski's rucksack as well as extra ammo for Rheinfeldt. As she reached the control floor she heard Jean-Claude say:

"Keep low, sergeant. There is a sniper somewhere."

"Are you OK?"

"I'm wounded. In the shoulder. Kowalski is dead."

"Dead?"

"He would just stand at the window, not taking cover," Jean-Claude said.

Aisha sat down beside Jean-Claude.

"'*When your time's up, it's up*'," she said, "That's what he was always saying. It's no good being a fatalist."

"It's no good at all," Jean-Claude Rheinfeldt admitted.

Aisha noted a penis and a clitoris drawn with blood on the

floor. She pointed it to Jean-Claude.

"That's my trademark," he replied. "A tribute to Kowalski. What's the hold-up with the paratroopers, by the way? Only two hundred jumped. It should have been many more."

"I don't know, Rheinfeldt," Aisha said. "I guess we're gonna get *Arnhemized* or *Dien-Bien-Phued*."

"*C'est pas une situation d'avenir*," he commented to himself ('We have no great future ahead of us').

Aisha was exhausted. They had been up all night, crawling back and forth on the airport, before making an assault in daylight, while they should have struck at night with thunderclap surprise.

She had lost the first man under her command. She did not even care. She was in the EU Foreign Legion invading her own country, and it did not even bother her. Rheinfeldt had been right: Exhaustion and weariness were the best medicines against doubts and bad conscience, but also against fear and human feelings.

All she wanted was for it to be over. She wanted to be back in France. She wanted to climb with her boyfriend. She wanted to do some mountaineering and skiing.

She was tired of fighting. If she made it back, she would ask to be transferred to the support company of the regiment. This was the company that would only build bridges and install field cable cars. They were never deployed overseas, and they did more mountaineering than the regular combat engineers.

She thought briefly of her father, in Casablanca. When they had been crawling in the night, they had seen quite some bombing far in the west. She wondered if he was OK. He must be. He was in Casablanca. The UN secretary-general was in Casa. The EU Armed Forces would never hurt UN personnel.

Jean-Claude Rheinfeldt was holding his *Dag Hammarskjöld* medal he had been awarded the previous year by the UN secretary-general.

"You brought your medal with you?" Aisha noted. "I did not know you were a sentimentalist."

"Did not want the guys of 1st company to steal it," Jean-Claude replied, "I'm gonna get a purple heart, now."

Jean-Claude had spread blood inadvertently on the medal's round crystal and blue ribbons. The face of the second UN secretary-general was now stained with bloody fingerprints. Aisha now remembered the story of Dag Hammarskjöld. The Second secretary-general of the United Nations had perished in a plane crash in Africa in the 1960s. His plane had been shot down by white mercenaries working for some mining companies.

Then, she suddenly had a moment of huge anguish. A UN secretary-general had been murdered before and, she had understood, with the complicity of some great power. Could it happen again? Was Mrs. Hira Dorjee-Sherpa really safe in Casablanca? If not, could they also kill her father?

She was just thinking, empty-hearted.

She was not feeling anything.

She wondered about Éric, her boyfriend. Had he been deployed with his Alpine rangers somewhere?

What about Samir and Sanne in Cambridge? What did they think about it?

That did not matter anyway. For now, the only thing she knew was that she was stuck in a shithole called Khouribga.

06: A Jolly Little War
(19 Sept 2097)

That night in Cambridge, Samir Benyamina had not slept well. There was a stench of sewer in his little student flat. It came from the pipes under the sink, and he had not been able to fix it yet. Student flats in Cambridge, were, surprisingly enough, in even worse shape than the slavants' containers.

At least, he was not sharing the one-room apartment with anybody but his girlfriend. And the rent was cheap. If one failed to get a hand on one of these student flats, there was no other way of finding housing in Cambridge for a decent price.

His girlfriend, Emily Chapman, was working as a nurse at Addenbrooke's hospital, and he was himself working part time as a cook at *The Honourable Schoolboy*.

And yet, in Cambridge, it was difficult to afford anything other than a student room with a low income and a half.

Emily, an athletic red-haired and blue-eyed English girl, had been in a bad mood. Most of the medical staff from the E.R, where she was working had been requisitioned by the army. She had now spent thirty-six hours in a row at the hospital and she had complained that the sewer stench was still there when she arrived at the flat in the morning.

"I'm also working a lot," Samir defended himself. "I now have the spare parts. I will fix the pipes tonight. Please bear with me."

"Still," Emily said as she was taking off her clothes and going to bed, "You work less than me. You should also have gone to the anti-war demonstration with Sanne."

"I'm busy," Samir replied. "Besides, the war has been avoided. When I last checked yesterday evening, the Moroccan crown prince was *en route* to Geneva to be interrogated by the Swiss and EU police. The EU had agreed to call off the attack on Morocco."

"Do you think he is really the brain behind a drug trafficking network to Europe?"

Samir looked a short while at Emily. He was an athletic man of average height with curly black hair

"I know he is," he finally said.

"How do you know?"

"I'd rather not say."

Samir gave Emily a kiss, grabbed his backpack and went out. The community college was a fifteen-minute bicycle ride from his student home.

Community colleges were said not to be as fancy as

universities. As far as Samir was concerned, the main difference was the following: at university, courses started at 9:00 at the earliest. In a community college, they started at 8:00. And it sucked.

He had spent two years as a slavant working first in an elderly home and then in the endocrinology department of Addenbrooke's hospital. Like all young Europeans, he had done his two years of European Service, but only the slavants (made of the contraction of slave and servant) serving in the healthcare branch had real hour constraints.

He had endured it for two long years and now, when he finally was a student, he still had to get up early.

On that morning, Samir had his first class in artificial intelligence history. This was one of the minor courses of his program in robotics. After introducing himself, the teacher went through a long list of literature.

Damn it, how would he find the time to read that, work part-time, and still do some climbing with his friends? He would have to look for book summaries online. He was half asleep as the teacher was talking, and he noted that all the students in the classroom looked equally tired. One should not start class at 08:00. That should be a universal rule! He was taken out of his thoughts by the insistence of the teacher on one question. He had written '2048' on the whiteboard.

"2048. Why is it a key date when it comes to robot history?"

Nobody answered.

"OK, since you still all seem to be asleep, I will tell you. In 2048, member states of the International Labor Organization, I-L-O, agreed to sign a series of treaties to tax robot labor."

The teacher wrote 'ILO' on the whiteboard and went on:

"Of course, these laws do not apply in the high seas or in space, because it's international territory. Some rich entrepreneur tried to launch a floating island where companies would be able to use his robots to manufacture clothes without being taxed. He went bankrupt. Bad idea to have robot manufactories in the high seas. What about space?"

Nobody answered, and the teacher wrote: '*Moon: WARSEC Ventures*'.

"Come on! You know what WARSEC is? The World's Agency for the Regulation of Space Exploration and Colonization? It was created two years and a half ago."

The teacher went on and wrote 'Boeing, Airbus, Comac, Bombardier, Lockheed'.

"Well," the teacher said, "All those aerospace companies, they came together with WARSEC and formed a joint venture to open a factory on the moon. The UN Agency WARSEC, owning the resources of the moon, uses the know-how of these private companies to manufacture cheap aerospace shuttles. That's their plan. Currently, they are testing prototypes for their two shuttles: the Space Hound and the Space Bear. Mass production may start as early as next year. So why is it cheap to produce on the moon?"

Nobody answered.

It was a stupid question, but Samir finally raised his hand. He needed to wake up.

"They use minerals from the moon, available for free. Only high-tech components are imported from Earth, at a low cost, using the space elevators. Most importantly, they make intensive use of robots, which are not taxed there."

"Very good," the teacher said. "So, in fact, you can say that WARSEC, a UN agency, is doing social dumping to bypass rules set by the ILO, another UN agency. In WARSEC's defense, without that, it would not be possible to promote cheap travel to space. They have been clever enough to associate all the private companies who wanted to. Only V-Space, from the Vahlroos corporation, has refused. But back to the 2048 ILO treaties on robot labor. Why would they have been passed?"

Nobody answered.

"Do you think companies using robots would just let this happen, without lobbying their governments not to?"

The class remained silent.

"It's a tricky question. But in fact, they did. It was a face-saving approach for them, to stop investing in artificial intelligence and robots. In fact, artificial intelligence has never been as good as everybody believed it would be, back in the 2020s. The more complex the algorithms, the more AI engineers you need, and they don't grow in trees."

A few students laughed.

"The more algorithms, the more complex a system becomes. The more complex a system becomes, the less understood and predictable it becomes. In the end, the more people you need to mitigate these risks. Chaos theory. Do you know the book *Jurassic Park* by Michael Crichton?"

Nobody answered.

"Read it, it's a good book. What Ian Malcolm says in that book about keeping dinosaurs in a park can apply to artificial intelligence. Of course, there have been a lot of terrible business ideas behind the very moderate success of AI."

On the whiteboard, the teacher wrote 'Self-driving car'.

"What was wrong with them?"

Samir rose his hand:

"Self-driving cars were very expensive cars from the beginning meant for wealthy people. But rich drivers don't want to be driven from A to B. They want to drive over the speed limits and break the rules. The AI would force them to comply with the rules. Rich people did not like it."

"Good point, student whose name I don't know," the teacher said. "Also self-driving cars have never proved fail-safe. To be allowed to drive them, you need an extension of your driving license that states you have an advanced understanding of driving systems."

"Remember," the teacher added, "Artificial intelligence can follow the rules. It cannot understand them. Artificial can identify patterns and reproduce them, but it cannot understand why the patterns are like they are. And by the end of your bachelor's in robotics, you will know what I mean by that."

At the break, Samir saw on his smartphone that he had a lot of messages on his chat applications. There was a message from his father in Paris whom he deeply disliked.

"*Dans ta gueule Maroc! 2040 est vengé!*" ('In your face, Morocco! 2040 is avenged!').

Samir's father was Algerian and had migrated to France after the Qatari Flu in 2074 when the EU needed more manpower. Samir's grandfather had been a war hero in the 2040 Summer War when Algeria had tried to liberate Western Sahara from Moroccan rule. His father loathed Morocco.

Why was his father writing this? The war had been averted. Or?

On another group chat, there had been an exchange of messages:

> » *Sanne vdM: "Seems the EU murders people in Switzerland. We are at war."*

Sanne van der Maas was now doing a master's in economics at Cambridge University. Samir had met her during his civil service. He had been changing the diapers of senile English men, she had been helping English kids with mathematics.

> » *Amina D: "EU at war with Switzerland?"*

Amina Dörflinger was a Swiss student in geology in Cambridge, now in the third year of her bachelor's degree. She was an elite climber and had won a bronze medal in lead-climbing at the 2096 Summer Olympics in Riga. She had now stopped competing, but Samir, Emily, and Sanne were still climbing regularly with her at the gym.

> » *Sanne vdM: "The Moroccan crown prince was shot dead after landing in Geneva. The murderers were arrested. Unclear who they are. Swiss and leftist papers suspect they were EU spies."*

Samir typed: *"Was it James Bond who killed him?"*

To which, Sanne replied: *"Not funny. We are at war with Morocco."*

> » *Amina D: "Who cares?"*
> » *Sanne vdM "Irresponsible geologist! I'm gonna check with Ralf Åhman what he knows."*

Sanne van der Maas had been the only survivor of the failed Martian colony. She had been born on Mars in 2076, at the start of the colony. In 2094, her evacuation to Earth had been organized by the United Nation Office for Outer Space Affairs, which had now become WARSEC. As a result, she knew a lot of fancy people, including Tintin Mutombo, Anatoli Govorov, and Alice Fù, the three brains behind warp propulsion.

She also knew Ralf Åhman, the director of the World's Agency for the Regulation of Space Exploration and Colonization, or WARSEC.

In the corridor of the community college, there was a TV.

Students had gathered around it. 19 September 2097 was the day when the first president of the UK was to be sworn in and take over after King Eamon, the last king of England. Eamon Windsor, who was professionally a psychiatrist in his thirties, had formally applied to become a medical officer at WARSEC.

Then, the news shifted to the war in Morocco. EU president Eugénie Bonavita was assuring her fellow European citizens it was nothing else than a '*jolly little war*' that would be over within two days.

The text *Jolly Little War* remain stuck on the low left corner of the screen.

As he was sitting at the rear of the direct flight from Toulouse to Vaasa, Finland, Ralf Åhman was furious. The EU had attacked Morocco despite their pledge not to. The UN secretary-general was still in Morocco, but they had attacked nonetheless.

He still remembered seeing the bombing of Morocco from the sky, as the ESA Albaspace had been taking him to Toulouse. It had been a horrific sight. He hoped that Mrs. Hira Dorjee-Sherpa was safe.

Ralf was suddenly ashamed of being European. His paternal grandfather had migrated from Eritrea to Europe in the 2010s, and he had passed away only recently. What would he say? His father, as healthcare personnel, had given his life in 2073 to protect European lives against the Qatari flu. But the EU was now bombing a country, allegedly because of some cannabis smuggling affairs, but in practice to control the phosphate mines. That was outrageous.

The whole conflict gave a bitter taste to his own projects, and he hated it. The WARSEC Ventures' two first aerospace shuttle prototypes, the Space Hound and the Space Bear, had turned out to be above expectation. These two shuttles had been developed to make travel to space affordable. Yet, Ralf's biggest customer was likely to be the EU Air Force, with an order of 200 Space Bears. The same air force that had been bombing Morocco.

Ralf hated himself for being so naïve. He needed funding to finance the construction of the first interstellar exploration warp-ships. The plan had been to earn additional income by making space travel cheaper and encouraging space tourism within the solar system. Instead, he was making war easier. How ironic for a UN diplomat!

As the plane made its final approach to Vaasa Airport, Ralf caught a glimpse of the huge and ugly arena nearby. The mayor of Vaasa was really suffering from megalomania. That the UN agency WARSEC had moved its headquarters to his city had not helped. The mayor believed that Vaasa could become a new New York City.

As soon as he jumped off the plane, he saw that he had missed calls from his mother and his ex-partner. They were certainly worried, but what would he tell them?

He worked at the UN but had no more information than anybody else. His mother was in Scotland. She had left Sweden to return to her home country after his father had died. His ex-girlfriend and their two children were in Norway. None of them would be hit by a Moroccan bomb anyway.

At the arrival terminal, Glover Johnson, his global safety director, was waiting for him.

"Hi, Glover," Ralf greeted him.

"Hi, Ralf," the athletic black man replied. "Come, it's a mess. Everybody at WARSEC is worried. Might be good if you could do a little speech."

Glover Johnson led Ralf hastily to the parking lot. As he started the car engine, he said:

"I suppose we will want to postpone the decisions we talked about yesterday. At least until we know what has happened to Hira, and how it stands for the UN."

"Agreed", Ralf said as the car drove away.

He hoped they would soon hear from the secretary-general. Glover was to go on paternity leave by the end of the year, and if some decisions could not be taken before, the whole interstellar exploration project might be delayed. Not that it was as serious as a conflict between the EU and Morocco, but still.

"By the way, when do you go on paternity leave?" Ralf eventually asked his global safety director.

"Baby is due on October 12th. I will take seven days off.

Then I will be on leave from December 1st to the end of March. Laura has volunteered to do two cargo cruises during that time. She does not want the baby to harm her career."

Glover's wife was a merchant vessel captain at Maersk, the Danish shipping company.

"Is she going to look for a job in Finland?" Ralf wondered. "There are a few naval companies here."

"We will see," Glover said as he pulled over.

They had arrived at the nearby WARSEC premises. Ralf felt his smartphone vibrate. He took it and checked. He had received a message from Sanne van der Maas. He was in no mood to check. But had also received a message from Esko Punainen, a friend of his who was working as an EU diplomat. He was currently based in Kirghizstan.

His message read: "*Hi, Ralf. All international phone lines to Morocco cut. Kirghiz ambassador to Morocco reported to Bishkek by satphone: 'Diplomatic districts not bombed. European soldiers patrolling the streets.' Assume UN secretary-general is still alive. / Esko.*"

Before getting out of the car, Ralf took a deep breath. This was the first slightly positive piece of information he had got.

Glover wanted him to give a speech for the WARSEC employees. At least, he would be able to convey some glimmer of hope.

07: OPPORTUNITIES
(19 SEPT 2097)

It was seven in the morning in New York City when Sophie Couillard was drying her blond hair in Michael Vahlroos' bathroom.

"Damn it," he cursed, "the ebutler is broken. It won't answer to my voice. It won't open the curtains."

As she switched off the hairdryer, she heard Michael clap in his hands. No computer voice would answer him.

"Have you seen my tablet?" he asked from the living room. "I can steer the curtains from the tablet."

"No, I haven't," she said, putting her bra on.

"I can't open the curtains."

"Why don't you use your arms?" she replied, applying mascara around her blue eyes.

She went out of the bathroom. Michael was moving restlessly around the living room. He was still naked. He loved his body, she thought. Not that there was anything extraordinary.

Everything was below average, but at least he was not fat, though there was no muscle either. His body hair also showed he was really blond. She suspected he saw himself as much more attractive than he really was. So did all the super-rich. He was, after all, the minority owner and CEO of the Vahlroos Corporation. Besides, he was a very religious evangelist and believed himself blessed with everything God had in store for him. Sophie did not mind, except that his faith made him a bad lover. He would only act with his lower front, which was far from exceptional, and never with his tongue.

On the other hand, in her case, occasional bad sex was better than no sex at all. Sophie Couillard was the general manager of V-Space, one of the Vahlroos Corporation subsidiaries. She was based in Burkina Faso, where V-Space's R&D department and main factory were located. She had climbed up the company's ladder after being the project director of the Albaspace, the world's bestselling aerospace shuttle. Beside her current position, she had recently been appointed as a director of the board of two other of the Vahlroos Corporation subsidiaries: V-Fusion, which was manufacturing compact fusion reactors and Vahlroos Travel, about to capitalize on space tourism.

Michael Vahlroos was her boss. Yes, she was occasionally sleeping with her boss. And so what? If she could find anyone else, she would take him. Intelligent and shy men were scared by her tall and athletic figure. Athletic and sexy men were scared by her intelligence. What was she supposed to do about that?

Michael was still walking around in the living room, back and forth, to and from his room, looking for his tablet. He eventually resigned himself to using his arms to open the curtains. He stood naked in front of the bay window of his loft apartment.

All of New York City was below them, and on the horizon, one could see the giant dykes that had been built to protect the metropolis from the rising sea level.

"Why don't you put some clothes on?" Sophie asked him.

"Where is the remote control?" he asked. "I want to check the news, I have not been able to check it."

"I don't know. This is your flat… Have you checked on top of the speakers?"

She went to the bedroom to get dressed. She heard a sound. He had found the remote control and switched the TV on.

"Yes! Yeees! Yees!" Michael screamed.

"What's happening?" Sophie asked as she was buttoning her shirt.

"EU has declared war on Morocco! I knew it, I knew it!"

"What's so great about it?"

"I bought some stocks at Lockheed and Thales. The EU Armed Forces will run out of ammo soon and will need to resupply. My stock will be rising today."

"Ah… Good for you."

"Even better: The UN secretary-general was in Morocco: she has been captured by the European Armed Forces."

"What's good about that?"

"Don't you understand, Sof'? This is God's revenge against the UN, and all the trouble they have made, creating WARSEC and putting more regulations in our way. That will calm them down. We are blessed. I am so blessed. God is with me."

"If you say so," Sophie said, not really caring. His religious beliefs were just like an incurable disease. One had to learn how to live with them.

"Today, at the board of directors, it will help us win some points."

Sophie had put her trousers on and was now back in the living room. Michael Vahlroos was still naked.

"If we want to make it to the board of directors, you may want to get dressed…"

They arrived at the Vahlroos Tower shortly before 9:00 and went directly to the 56th floor, where Betalpha Inc. was headquartered. It was the official name of the Vahlroos Corporation, encompassing Vahlroos Construction, Vahlroos Property, Vahlroos Investment, V-Fusion, V-Lab, V-Space and now Vahlroos Travel.

After his parents had died in the Big Two, a devastating earthquake flattening San Francisco in 2081, Michael had inherited Vahlroos Corporation, a real estate company. Back then, he had been working as a nuclear engineer at Lockheed, but after taking over, he had made the company thrive and grow fast. He had founded V-Fusion and successfully commercialized the first compact fusion reactors, which had been deployed in all the navies of the world. Even merchant fleets had started to use compact fusion reactors. CFRs also powered the orbital station. He had then founded V-Space, which had successfully produced the Albaspace.

He had more recently founded Vahlroos Travel with the ambition to be the first player in the space tourism industry.

As the elevator surged past all the floors of his corporations, Michael whispered to himself:

"I'm so blessed. I'm so blessed. I love Thee, God."

They arrived just in time for the start of the meeting of the board. The meeting room was located on the 56th floor of the Vahlroos Tower, where the holding entity controlling the Vahlroos Corporation, Betalpha Inc., was quartered.

Michael Vahlroos greeted everyone and immediately took the floor in front of a white canvas screen hanging against the wall. The low morning sun in the east-southeast lit him in the eyes through the long and large meridional window bay. Sophie lowered the blinds for his sake.

The directors were all sitting around a long table. They were all grey-haired, mostly white, males.

Jim Pattisson, the potbellied chairman of the board, still had his white trucker moustache. "The world is at war, it seems," he started. "Good or bad?"

"Thank you for asking this very relevant question, Jim," Michael replied. "Overall it's good. First of all, Vahlroos Investment had taken some positions that are soaring as we speak. War is sometimes good business."

Michael paused and smiled.

This did not pacify the chairman, who added:

"The UN secretary-general has been captured by the EU Armed Forces."

"It will be an occasion for the UN to learn humility," Michael replied, "To accept that idealism is off-topic in this real world."

"What do you mean?" the chairman asked.

"They have enforced too many regulations in space, which are the very reasons we have not joined WARSEC Ventures and their manufacturing on the moon. Now, what is this war about? It's about phosphate. Morocco has all the remaining reserves of phosphate on this planet. Without phosphate, no fertilizer. Without fertilizer, no food. At least not enough food to feed 10.5 billion people."

"Will it change their views on space regulation?" the chairman asked.

"They cannot keep claiming that the UN owns all extraterrestrial resources only allows private corporations the right to extract these resources in exchange for a fee. They will have to let private corporations boldly go where no one has been before and yield extraterrestrial resources over there."

"Nothing seems to indicate this."

It was Sonny Baldwin who had spoken, the only Afro-American director of the board. Michael liked black people, he even had his V-Space factory in Burkina Faso. However, he disliked Sonny intensely. He took a deep breath, smiled, and said:

"It will happen. Anything else would not make sense. We currently have a case before the Federal Court, and we expect the US government will be obliged to ask the International Court of Justice to evaluate the validity of the Vienna treaties. The timing is right. The ICJ will give us justice, and WARSEC will have to let us exploit space resources for free."

"What about the UN secretary-general?" Sonny went on. "Isn't it bad for Vahlroos Travel? What if the opening of the orbital station is delayed? We had been expecting the return on investment by 2100. Might that be off the table?"

Michael needed a short time to think before replying:

"Thank you for asking this question, Sonny. So far, we have no information that the EU soldiers have hurt Mrs. Hira Dorjee-Sherpa. I believe the war, overall, will be over within three days. It should not have any impact on WARSEC or on the current construction work on the orbital station. Its opening to commercial activities is still scheduled for May 2098, next year."

"Will the Vahlroos Travel's businesses be ready by then?" the chairman asked.

"Yes," Michael replied. "I was in the orbital station four days ago. We will be leasing two hotels, one to Radisson and one to Sheraton, and also have our own, a more low-cost hotel. Ryanair is to open cheap lines from Europe, and they have already signed a letter of intent to channel customers to our hotel. We will have a space casino, though its activity may be limited at the beginning, but most importantly, we will have the space attraction center, with a whole set of activities in weightlessness. There will even be a place where nerds can play Quidditch in 0-G with special broomsticks designed by our V-lab. Nerds are always a good way to make money."

"I like Harry Potter," Sonny Baldwin said. "What about V-Space? I guess the Albaspace will meet heavy competition from the aerospace shuttles manufactured by WARSEC Ventures."

Sophie was about to answer, but Michael did not give her the time to.

"Thank you for asking this question, Sonny," he said, "So, as for V-Space—"

"Thank you, Michael," Sonny interrupted him. "V-Space's GM is here. I thought we could let her answer that question."

Sophie smiled and thanked Baldwin by nodding her head. Michael often behaved like a male supremacist, and everybody usually let him. She took the floor.

"I have prepared a little presentation. Let me just synchronize my smartphone with the projector."

She tapped quite a few times on her touchscreen, and she could see how some directors looked impatient. Eventually she began projecting a presentation on the canvas screen behind her.

"As you know, last week, WARSEC Ventures tested two new prototypes. We start with the Space Hound, as you can see in this picture. Initially a project by Boeing, its prototype is currently going through intensive tests on the moon. It is smaller than the Albaspace but has vertical take-off and landing capability, meaning it can land on the moon. It can also take off from a large mansion or estate and can reach any place on earth within one and a half hours. However, it has no scramjet, only CUBIC-R engines. It can take only 60 passengers and is more noisy and shaky than our Albaspace. It may compete with existing private jets, but not with the Albaspace."

"What about the Space Bear?" Sonny asked.

"That's my next slide," Sophie went on. "The Space Bear, originally a project by Airbus, is currently being tested in Toulouse. Could be certified by the FAA as soon as March next year.

VTOL and can also land on the moon, and take off from smaller airports. As you see, it is massive, more than 80 m (262 ft) long. Ryanair plans to acquire some, and there will be room for almost 700 passengers in their version. However, again, no scramjet, so it is slower. It takes two hours to reach any position on the planet. We, however, know that the EU Armed Forces have expressed their intent to acquire some, as it will give them the ability to send their troops anywhere in the world. The US

Air Force and the Chinese Air Force may soon follow."

"They are manufactured on the moon, aren't they?" The chairman asked.

"Indeed," Sophie answered, "WARSEC Ventures manufactured the prototypes on the moon, and plan to have their mass production there. They will be fifty percent cheaper to produce than our Albaspace, but in terms of pricing, they will be only twenty-five percent cheaper, according to our competitive intel. WARSEC still wants to take home a fat margin. Their purpose is to raise money for their interstellar exploration."

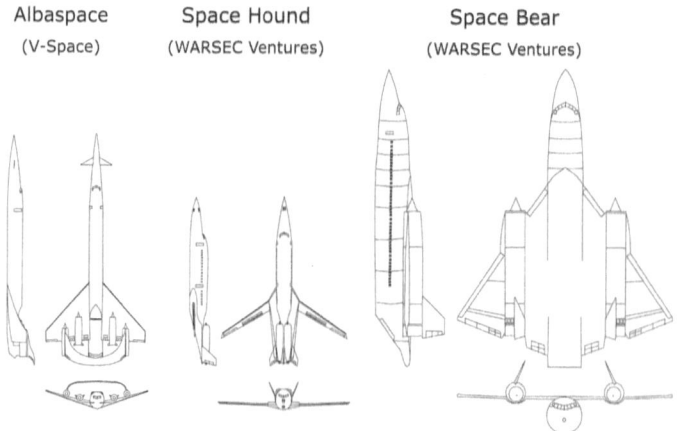

Figure 4: The Albaspace, manufactured by V-Space and the Space Hound and Space Bear, both manufactured by WARSEC Ventures.

"What will be the impact on our sales?" Sonny Baldwin asked.

"No panic," Sophie answered. "The introduction of these two aerospace shuttles will first start an overall market growth, especially with the opening of the orbital station to commercial activities. Although we will lose some of our 95% market share initially, the impact in actual volume will be marginal. In fact, we believe we will benefit from the market growth over the next five years. Wealthy tourists will still prefer to fly up to the orbital station onboard an Albaspace rather than a shaky Space Bear. According to our analysts, it's more the market for regular aircraft that may see a contraction, and this is not our problem."

"You said we will benefit from the market growth over the next five years. What about then?" the Chairman asked.

"By then, we will have a new competitive advantage," Sophie replied. "You see, now, aerospace shuttles have to dock into EM-drive modules in orbit to transit to the Moon, if they do not want to take three days to get there."

EM-drive stood for Electro-Magnetic drive, a system which could propel a spacecraft in orbit using only electromagnetic waves. As it relied solely on electric power, it was more efficient than traditional chemical propulsion.

Sophie went on: "Within two years, we will have launched our Albaspace Neo: it will have vertical take-off and landing capability, and will therefore be able to land on the moon. It will also have an EM-drive powered by an onboard new generation CFR."

"Have the FAA and the EASA approved it?" the Chairman asked.

"They will have by February next year," said Michael. "Before becoming a CEO, I was a nuclear engineer, and I have never seen a compact fusion reactor so safe."

"Good," the Chairman said, "So in five years, we'll still have the best aerospace shuttle in the market."

"Yes," Sophie said, "You can see it on these graphs with the projected market growth, market share, and revenue."

The graphs on the screen showed indeed that V-Space's market shares were expected to decrease significantly, but also that the total market size was expected to increase considerably. As a result, the projected sales remained relatively steady.

"What about the V-liner? Any news on it?" Sonny Baldwin added. "I mean, Tintin Mutombo, the warp specialist, now works at WARSEC. Thierry Diakité, your best engineer, has also gone over to the competition."

Sophie looked at Michael.

In September 2094, after the first successful faster-than-light travel by the *Alcubierre* spaceship, manufactured by the Chinese, Russian, and Japanese space agencies, Vahlroos Corporation had decided to develop a competing warp ship that would also have atmosphere entry capability.

The loss of the two key African engineers had been Michael's fault, and he had refused to reconsider his initial idea and go over to a more realistic approach, as proposed by both Tintin and Thierry. Michael would not answer, though.

"It is true that the project has been slightly delayed," Sophie admitted.

"The warp propulsion director was fired for sexual harassment, and you have no Tintin." Sonny went on. "I mean, you lost a Nobel Prize in Physics. How are you gonna continue?"

Sophie looked at Jim Pattisson, the chairman of the board. She had shown him her strategy, and he had endorsed it, but he was now remaining silent as she was cross-examined by Baldwin. She finally said:

"This has been a tough time. However, the overall consensus is that the resulting delay is good for V-Space."

"How so?" Sonny asked.

"As you saw," Sophie replied. "Regarding the product life cycle, we are good with the Albaspace. Now, in four years, there will be a new exotic matter available for industrial use. With the green matter, a spaceship can't go over warp 10. With the purple matter, a spaceship would be able to reach warp 40. We will launch the V-liner when it is available. By that time, it will mean that it will be possible to travel everywhere on Earth within twenty minutes only. But also, to the orbital station and to the Moon. Not to mention Mars, when tourism opens there."

The directors were looking attentively at Sophie. She continued her exposé:

"The Albaspace Neo will take six hours to the orbital station and twelve hours to the moon. It would take sixty days to Mars if it flew there. The V-liner will take only twenty minutes to any of these locations, including the take-off and landing maneuvers. We will have simply the best spacecraft in the world."

The directors looked impressed.

"I also want to add," Michael Vahlroos said, "that if the UN changes its stance on space regulation subsequently to the current conflict, and most of all, my suing them, the whole market of space mining will open up. And we will be the only ones to provide a warp-ship with atmosphere entry. And, believe me, we will keep this advantage for decades."

08: KHOURIBGA (19 SEPT 2097)

In Morocco, the situation at Khouribga had worsened for Aisha Barjaoui and her men. Despite the bombing of the nearby military camp by the air force, the legionnaires had failed to break through it. 4th platoon had had two squads wiped out, and another squad of Lt. Guaino's platoon got decimated, when the paratrooper officer ordered them to charge 400 meters (0.25 mile) with no cover.

When Lt. Guaino had stood up to send his next squad to the assault, he had been hit in the buttock by Corporal Tran's suppressing fire. The lieutenant had cursed a lot, and Aisha did not know what to think. In Kirghizstan, Tran had once shot through her jacket with his pistol as he was aiming at an insurgent two meters to Aisha's right. Back then, he had been hanging on a rope in a harness. However, Aisha was not certain it had been totally unintentional this time.

The remaining squad of Lt. Guaino had nonetheless proved

grateful and offered Tran a bottle of Ricard. For some reasons unknown to Aisha, many paratrooper legionnaires were also carrying bottles of alcohol, on top of their regulatory equipment.

Aisha's squad of mountain engineers had also suffered casualties. Damian Kowalski had been killed, and both Jean-Claude Rheinfeldt and Corporal Singh had been wounded. Their morale had taken a knock, and Aisha wondered how officers could even consider a frontal assault on the military camp without tank support, or at least more substantial air support.

Besides, they had not received the expected reinforcements. Out of the three promised parachute companies, only one had landed. A paratrooper had told Aisha how they had been attacked by Moroccan fighters off the coast of Morocco. One of the cargo planes had caught fire, and some of the paratroopers had managed to jump out of it before it crashed into the sea. Two other cargo planes had been damaged and diverted to Casablanca. One of the cargo planes had made it to the phosphate mine ten kilometers (6.2 miles) away, where the rest of the force was fighting.

In the end, Major Poisson, the commanding officer of the legionnaire paratroopers, had decided that the best was for them to wait for reinforcement, so they dug foxholes and trenches.

The airport's main hangar had been transformed into a field hospital. Large flags of the Red Cross and Red Crescent had been stretched on the roof, and a few medics were providing care to the wounded. Moroccans prisoners of war were also kept in that same hangar.

By the end of the morning, nobody knew what had happened on the coast, except that three landings had occurred in Rabat, Casablanca, and Western Sahara. The wireless communication channels were all jammed by the Moroccans. Had the European invasion been successful? Why had there been an order followed by a counter-order? How long would they have to hold the airport and wait for reinforcement? No legionnaire knew.

What they were sure of was that the Moroccans in Khouribga had received reinforcement. By 12:30, they had started shelling the airport with 120-mm mortar rounds. The explosions were terrible and, before long, the airport was covered in thick clouds of dust.

Luckily, the Moroccans were careful not to hit the hangar that had been turned into a hospital and Aisha decided to go there to rest a bit.

Jean-Claude Rheinfeldt had a bandage on his shoulder and was sitting close to Lt. Guaino, who was lying on his belly.

"You like killing your own men, don't you, Guaino?" The Luxembourger legionnaire asked. "I am said to have an IQ of 90, but even I would not be as stupid as you. Do you have an IQ below 80? I thought 80 was the minimum to enter the army."

Jean-Claude spanked the lieutenant on his bloody buttock and the paratrooper screamed in pain.

"Fuck you, trooper!" the lieutenant yelled.

"Fuck you, lieutenant," Jean-Claude screamed back and punched the Lieutenant in the face. "You lost two fine squads, asshole."

Other wounded men were looking at Rheinfeldt.

"What's going on, legionnaires?"

It was Major Poisson, who had installed his CP in the hangar. Lt. Hoffman and Sgt. Uwilingiyimana from Aisha's engineer platoon were soon there. Uwil crouched next to Rheinfeldt, who was now crying. Aisha had never thought Jean-Claude able to cry. He must have been exhausted.

"Move that man away from my lieutenant", the major commanded Aisha.

"*Mon commandant*, tanks are coming."

It was Capt. Léger, the commanding officer of Aisha's engineer company.

The major turned to Aisha's captain and asked: "Are they ours?"

"It's half past two," the captain replied. "112 kilometers in eight hours, it's very unlikely."

The major was more optimistic:

"112 kilometers in eight hours is possible, provided the Moroccan army has collapsed."

"Given the 120-mm shelling, I don't think it has collapsed,"

Lt. Hoffman objected.

"Let's check that out," the major said.

"Barjaoui," Lt. Hoffman said. "Take your squad and follow me. Uwil, come with us."

Sgt. Paul Uwilingiyimana carried Jean-Claude five meters away from the wounded paratrooper lieutenant, while Aisha assembled the rest of her squad. They all followed the lieutenant out.

There were four tanks and six armored vehicles approaching from the town of Khouribga, northeast of the airport. Lt. Hoffman led his platoon sergeant and Aisha's squad along the taxiway toward the town and commanded them to take cover in the ditch by the side of the runway.

The tanks were still more than a kilometer (0.6 mile) away but there was no doubt they were Moroccan tanks. Finally, two of the tanks and one armored vehicle moved forward toward them, while the other vehicles kept some distance in support.

"Let them come close," the lieutenant said. "They have not seen us. When they are on us, Nguyen, second tank. Uwil, bomb the first. Barjaoui and Eriksen, smoke grenade. The rest on me."

The first tank was now passing by them, followed by the armored vehicle, itself followed by the second tank, with fifteen meters (49 ft) distance between each vehicle.

Nguyen suddenly raised his anti-tank weapon and fired at the second tank, hitting the turret, which disappeared in a ball of fire. At the same time, Aisha threw a smoke grenade while Sgt. Uwil simultaneously made a dash for the first tank and stuck an explosive charge on the engine.

As Uwil was running back to the ditch under the still thin cover of the smoke, he was hit in the shoulder and buttock by firing from the armored infantry vehicle behind.

The first tank finally exploded.

The smoke screen was now thick enough and Lt. Hoffman led the charge against the armored vehicle. The next second, he was climbing on the vehicle's turret, opening the hatch and emptying his mag in it.

Corporal Tran was also there, casting a teargas grenade into it.

Gonzales opened the rear door of the vehicle and retrieved four prisoners out of it.

The lieutenant and Tran jumped into the vehicle. The lieutenant's head came out.

"Barjaoui!" he screamed. "You keep these prisoners and check on Uwil. Eriksen: smoke corridor to the east. Gonzales, come back here and help with the turret. Nguyen, we need you with the bazooka. Listen up, folks, we have a working 40-mm Gatling gun. The other tanks won't know it because of the smoke... We're gonna outflank them and surprise them."

Pointing her pistol, Aisha told two of the prisoners to lay

face down on the ground, and asked the two others to bring forth the wounded sergeant, while she helped Eriksen to place the smoke.

Shortly afterward, a mortar round fell some hundred meters away. It was from the paratroopers' support platoon, entrenched in foxholes half a kilometer behind them. They were aiming at the remaining vehicles with their three 60-mm and two 81-mm mortars.

This did not disturb the prisoners, who were quick to bring back the fallen tall Rwandan sergeant. Aisha was relieved to see that Uwil was only wounded. She gave her emergency kit to the prisoners and asked them to stop the bleeding, while Torbjørn was firing the last of his remaining twelve smoke grenades, using his 51-mm mortar.

As the smoke screen started to rise and grow thicker to the east, Aisha could see that the other two tanks and five armored vehicles were moving toward them as mortar shells fired by the paratroopers behind were exploding around them.

John Nguyen, who had now climbed on Lt. Hoffman's captured vehicle, fired another rocket with his recoilless rifle.

A third tank went up in flames.

Lt. Hoffman's vehicle was now dashing eastward through the smoke corridor, while tracers of 40 mm were flying just where it was before.

Aisha helped Torbjørn reload his 51-mm mortar with high

explosive rounds and aim at where the other armored vehicles were supposed to be.

Because of the smoke screen, she could not be sure of what was happening.

She could hear Torbjørn's 51-mm rounds explode, as well as some 60-mm and 81-mm rounds fired by the paratroopers' support platoon.

She heard twice the sound of a rocket explosion fired by a recoilless rifle.

Most of all, she heard the characteristic sound of a high speed 40-mm Gatling gun.

Then it turned silent, and as the smoke started to dissipate, she saw that there was only one armored vehicle standing intact, about 700 m (2,300 ft) away. Using her assault carbine sight, she was relieved to recognize Nguyen standing on it with his recoilless rifle.

"Unbelievable," she said to Torbjørn. "They have made it."

In the next instant, Lt. Hoffman's captured vehicle disappeared in a huge explosion.

It was followed by a series of other mighty explosions. Dust was blown away by the shockwaves and swirled in the air, adding to the ambient smoke screen.

"What the fuck?" Torbjørn exclaimed.

Aisha looked up.

Eight large drones were flying at low altitude and firing rockets.

Under their wings, she recognized the four black stars arranged in as the atomic structure of a diamond: the insignia of the EU Air Force.

"Our own air force is killing us!" she screamed.

She took her radio set and tried to call.

"The frequency is jammed," Aisha told Torbjørn. "I cannot make contact with anyone."

The drones were now coming back for a second pass over the airport, firing with their rocket pods.

A few hundred meters away, Aisha recognized Capt. Léger, running from the control tower and waiving a white flag for the drones.

The drones kept on firing, and the captain disappeared in a rocket explosion.

Aisha started removing her combat vest and her jacket.

"What the fuck are you doing?" Torbjørn asked.

"Something is wrong with these drones. They should have aborted the attack. The radio frequency is jammed. We need help. The Moroccans must have communication landlines. If I run to them without my uniform, they may let me come through."

"OK, I will come with you," Tobjørn said.

"You needn't," Aisha replied. "I speak Arabic, you don't."

Aisha asked one of the prisoners to come with her and have the others promise they would take care of her wounded platoon sergeant.

Aisha had only kept her bra and her military trousers.

She noted that Torbjørn had only kept his underpants and was barefoot.

What an idiot!

There was no time to argue: Some drones were now coming for a third pass while the remaining ones were bombing the town of Khouribga.

"The Moroccan positions are 300 m away. One minute's sprint if we are lucky," Aisha said. "When the drones have flown over us, we run."

As the four drones were now firing their Gatling guns at the airport, Aisha started running with one prisoner toward the military camp.

She ran as fast as she could, waiving her white undershirt.

The prisoner had difficulty keeping up, but Aisha did not care.

Behind her, Torbjørn was yelling: "*Arsla* på*! Arsla* på! Arsl*a* på! Arsl*a* på!" ('Move your ass, faster!')

Torbjørn ran past Aisha and he was first to reach the Moroccan military post. He collapsed in the arms of one of the Moroccan soldiers, still yelling: "*Arsle på! Arsle på! Arsle på! Arsle på!*"

"Don't pay attention to him, he is only Norwegian," Aisha said to the Moroccan soldiers in Arabic when she reached them. "The drones have gotten crazy. They fired at everything that moved."

"Thank you, we have noticed, Mrs. Obvious", a Moroccan sergeant replied.

"Can you shoot them down?" Aisha asked.

"You have annihilated our air force and destroyed all our anti-aircraft defense in the area. How do you want us to shoot them?"

"The land phones still work? Can I make a call to France?" Aisha wondered.

"You have cut the international phone lines," a soldier replied. "But if you want to call your army, you can just make a call to Casablanca. Your army is occupying it. We have a land phone."

Aisha remembered from *Bollox news* that the UN secretary-general was staying at the Radisson hotel in Casablanca. She was certain the European military would have occupied it, first thing after landing in Casa. Using a still working online directory, she found the number and gave a call.

"Allo?" she said. "Do you have a European officer nearby? This is an emergency; Europeans are being slaughtered by the EU Air Force."

A moment later, she was talking to a captain from the

Parachute Marine Regiment.

"Squad sergeant, 2nd Foreign Engineer Regiment, *mon capitaine*. I am in Khouribga with my outfit and the 2nd Foreign Paratrooper Regiment, *mon capitaine*. We are under attack by EU drones killing EU legionnaires. Our radios are all out. We need help now."

"*C'est une blague, sergeant?*" ('Is that a joke, sergeant?').

"*Non, mon capitaine.*" ('No, Sir.').

"*Écoute, je vais voir ce que je peux faire.*" ('Listen, I will check what I can do.').

Aisha did a quick calculation. There was air cover flying over Casablanca a hundred kilometers (62 miles) away. EU Fighters could fly at Mach 17 with their scramjets and were in theory less than half a minute away unless they wanted to save on their fuel. They should be here in no time.

Meanwhile, the eight drones continued to strafe the airport and the town at regular intervals. Some paratroopers from the heavy weapon platoon had managed to shoot down one of the flying machines, but these drones were built like Dachshund fighters and could endure substantial damage and still keep flying. One drone was almost missing a wing and was still able to fire rockets at the airport.

Three minutes had gone, and still no support.

Suddenly, four AF5 Dachshund Fighters from the EU Air Force showed up and engaged the drones.

Unfortunately, the drones were effectively programmed to elude air-to-air missiles and the fighters had to engage them in a dogfight.

One fighter was shot down immediately, while a second fighter was shot down after gunning down the first drone.

Six drones were left, but only two fighters.

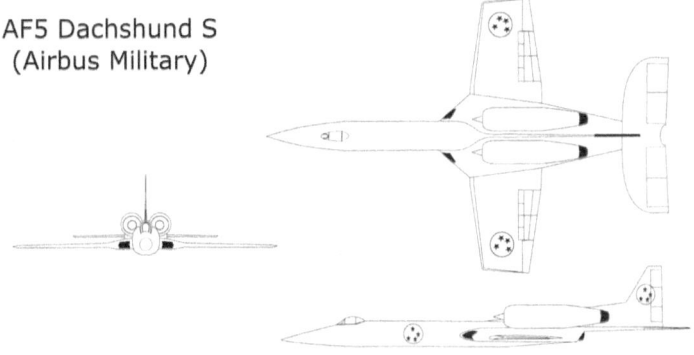

AF5 Dachshund S
(Airbus Military)

Figure 5: AF5 Dachshund with its two CUBIC-R reactors and scramjet. It is stealth and equipped with an internal bomb bay and two 25-mm Gatling guns. Here with the insignia of the EU Air Force.

Luckily, one of the fighters seemed to be quite agile and managed to gun down one, two, three and four drones, while being properly covered by his wingman.

While he was downing his fifth kill, he was hit by the last drone. The pilot managed to bail out.

The last drone was eventually gunned down by his wingman, who quickly flew away.

The airport was covered by a huge cloud of dust, and it was difficult to assess the situation.

"And now what?" a Moroccan major asked Aisha.

"I would like to call for a truce," Aisha replied, "to check on the casualties."

"Do you have a mandate for that?" the officer replied. "As far as I can see you are just a female soldier in a bra. Where are you from? You look North African to me."

"I'm French with Algerian origins." Aisha lied, putting her white undershirt back on. "If you drive me back there with a white flag, I can try to negotiate a truce."

A moment later, Aisha and Torbjørn, still in underpants, were sitting on a jeep driven by the Moroccan sergeant who had been manning the outpost. They were holding a white flag.

They drove first to where the armored vehicle captured by Lt. Hoffman and her squad's A team had been blown apart by the drones.

The sight of it was dreadful. The wreck was still burning, and Aisha could smell the scent of grilled meat. Fifty meters

(164 ft) away from the wreck, she recognized the hand of Private Nguyen.

That was all that was left of his body. Lieutenant Hoffman, Corporal Tran, Private Gonzales and Private Nguyen were dead.

They drove forward to where they had left Sgt. Uwil and the three prisoners. The two tanks were smoking beside them.

One of the prisoners had taken Aisha's assault carbine and was pointing the gun at the jeep. The Moroccan sergeant managed to calm him down.

Another prisoner was crying while the third one was trying to comfort him.

Or were they still prisoners? Perhaps the roles had changed, Aisha noted.

She ran to Sergeant Uwilingiyimana, lying beside the ex-prisoners.

"I'm fine, Aisha," he said. "How is the lieutenant?"

Aisha shook her head.

"Dead?"

Aisha nodded.

"And Tran, Nguyen and Gonzales?"

Aisha shook her head again and made some effort not to cry.

"The Moroccans are ready to negotiate a truce for us to take care of our wounded," she said, changing the subject. "We are driving to the hangar with white flags. I hope the legionnaires accept."

"OK, if you put me on that jeep, I can support you," the sergeant said.

Aisha put her military jacket and her combat vest back on.

"Incredible!" Sgt. Uwil exclaimed. "Everybody here has been burned by explosions, but you are completely sunburnt."

He was talking to Torbjørn, who was still standing in his underpants. His skin had turned crimson.

"Come on, legionnaire. Put your clothes on, put a fucking hat on your head, take a salt pill and don't forget to drink," Sgt. Uwil said. "Sgt. Barjaoui. Help that fucking Norwegian out."

The natural authority of Sgt. Uwilingiyimana helped Aisha pull herself together, and while she was helping Torbjørn to put back in his clothes on, the platoon sergeant was still commenting:

"White people call us colored people, but by looking how this white Norwegian turned into crayfish red, I think they ought to call themselves the multi-colored ones."

A moment later, they were at the hangar with their white flag, and they were told no officer was standing, except for a medic sergeant. He accepted the truce immediately. Aisha sent the Moroccan sergeant to tell his major.

09: HONOR AND FIDELITY (19 SEPT 2097)

Aisha soon realized that the situation was far worse than she could have imagined. Out of the 406 paratroopers and combat engineers who had seized Khouribga airport or jumped on it, only 34 were standing. None of them was an officer. While a few were checking on the wounded legionnaires, most of them just stood aimlessly waiting for orders.

Around them, wounded men, and a few women, moaning or screaming in pain.

The Moroccan major was looking at the wounded European legionnaires as if they were dead men.

The Moroccan captors did not seem willing to make any decision regarding them either. Aisha was angry at all of them. Yes, they had been bombed pretty heavily, now it was about saving lives.

"Major," she said in Arabic. "There are plenty of wounded lying all over the airport. We need to do some triage. How many jeeps can you lend us? How many men could you spare us to assist the wounded?"

"You want vehicles from me?" the major yelled. "Your air force did that, not mine. Your country invaded mine, not mine yours."

"There is nothing we can do about it," Aisha went on in Arabic. "Our quarrelling here and now cannot undo what has been done. What we can do is save lives. The town has been bombed pretty thoroughly. I can try and call the EU HQ and get some more medical supplies here."

"Can you?" the major wondered.

"I can try if you put me through with the landline again. In the meantime, if you can lend me a few cars and a few men…"

The major remained silent, and Aisha could hear some wounded screaming and moaning.

"*Min-fadlikum*," she added, begging.

The major looked one more time at all the wounded soldiers and finally said: "You get three pick-ups and nine men, not more. Follow me to the phone."

Aisha turned to the legionnaires and yelled:

"Listen up! Three medics stay here at the hangar. The rest, *15 binômes*, 15 pairs, spread out on the area and check for wounded. The Moroccans will come with three jeeps and help bring everybody in front of the hangar. I will check for medical supplies."

She followed the major in his jeep back to the land phone and started to negotiate with the EU Armed Forces, in Casablanca. Luckily, the surviving Dachshund pilot had given an account of the situation in Khouribga seen from the sky, and they eventually believed she was really negotiating a medical evacuation. It still took her twenty minutes to be put through the medical evacuation HQ. The Europeans were ready to send six helicopters in rotations to bring medical supplies and repatriate the wounded. The Moroccan major refused: if any EU aircraft flew over Khouribga, it would be shot down with the new anti-aircraft batteries they were to receive as reinforcement. Was the major not interested in having more medical supplies for the town? He did not trust the Europeans.

Finally, a deal was struck. The Europeans would send twenty trucks with medical supplies, a doctor, and a few medics, as soon as they had negotiated a truce with fighting Moroccan forces thirty kilometers west of Casablanca. The Red Cross and the Red Crescent had to be involved as well. If she could try to make some calls to the Moroccan side on her end, it would speed up the negotiations to secure a truce.

Aisha took a few deep breaths. Diplomacy was not her thing, and she just wanted to punch everybody.

"My name is Capt. Kenneth O'Malley and my EU personnel number is 2068-07-13-4587-9461."

The pilot who had bailed out had been captured and was

now brought forth by some Moroccan soldiers. The short, broad-shouldered, blue-eyed officer was standing in his flying suit. The Moroccan major had his pilot helmet removed and Aisha saw that he had ginger hair.

In Arabic, the major asked the sergeant to put the helmet back on his head, lest the ginger pilot get sunstroke.

"You have long ID numbers in Europe," the major finally said. "By looking at your insignia, you are from the 1st Attack Squadron. I'm from the air force as well."

"My name is Capt. Kenneth O'Malley and my EU personnel number is 2068-07-13-4587-9461."

"Cut the bullshit, captain," Aisha said.

Both the EU captain and the Moroccan major looked at her with wide-open eyes.

"Don't you hear the screams of the wounded, captain?" she went on. "I do. Given the situation, we are nowhere near getting any outside help. There may be a hundred wounded or more here. I need your help, sir."

"How could I help, sergeant?" Capt. O'Malley asked.

"Ten to 20 kilometers to the south," she went on, "there should be about two hundred legionnaires in the phosphate mine. Go to them, and ask for their assistance. We need their medical supplies. We need them to volunteer and come here to help with the wounded."

"How do I get there?"

"Major," Aisha turned to the Moroccan officer. "Would you

have another vehicle?"

"You're joking, sergeant," the major said. "I can lend you a moped. My sergeant will drive your captain."

"*Shu-kran Zhazilan*," Aisha answered ('Thank you very much.').

As the air force captain vanished on the luggage rack of a moped driven by the Moroccan sergeant, Aisha tried to convince the major to call his own superiors, to negotiate a truce at the front line. After one hour of repeated calls and promises of medical supply to the Moroccans, no agreement had been reached. It seemed that the chain of command of the Moroccan Army had been broken and no one wanted to make a decision.

The air force captain came back on the moped's baggage rack. He had kept his pilot helmet on. Aisha was dismayed at seeing he had not even brought back a single first aid kit.

"And?" she said.

"Your legionnaire friends are a band of assholes!" the air force captain yelled.

"What happened?" Aisha wondered.

"They refused to help," Capt. O'Malley said. "They said they need all their force to defend themselves against the Moroccans. They refuse to give a single first aid kit."

"They even fired warning shots at us," the Moroccan sergeant added.

Aisha's heart sunk. She wanted to punch someone.

She took a deep breath and went back to the phone.

She finally reached a Moroccan officer who was willing to accept a truce at the front, but he also wanted some medical supplies for his own regiment. Aisha ended up making calls to the EU medical evacuation HQ and the Moroccan army. They eventually came to an agreement.

"The European trucks will be here in three hours," she said eventually.

It was four in the afternoon.

The Moroccan sergeant drove Aisha and the air force captain back to the airport's hangar. It was the only building standing at the airport. All the others, including the control tower, had been flattened to the ground.

The wounded had been lined up in front of the hangar. Many were moaning.

"It's not good," Torbjørn said. "At least 150 dead and more than 200 wounded. No morphine. No bandages, we have been using clothes. A good thing that we legionnaires drink a lot. The alcohol has been used to disinfect the wounds. For the burns, we have been using water and salt. We could have used more water, though."

Aisha climbed up on top of the Moroccan jeep.

"Listen up, all," she said loudly, "In three hours, there will be a Red Cross convoy coming here with a doctor, medics, and medical supplies. In five hours, you will be in a field hospital in

Casablanca, and evacuated to Europe."

A few wounded cheered.

"In the meantime," she added, "We will have to make do with no morphine, no bandages, barely enough water, and worst of all no alcohol. So, suck it up and shut up!"

A few legionnaires laughed, and she got down from the jeep.

Torbjørn took Aisha aside and said: "Captain Léger is still alive. In pretty bad shape, but still alive. He wants to talk to you. He is over there, close to Sgt. Uwil."

Aisha walked along the row of wounded and saw her captain. His clothes had been torn off. His face, left shoulder and arm were badly burnt. The clothes that had been used as bandage around his stomach and legs were stained with blood. Besides him, Sgt. Uwilingiyimana seemed to be sleeping.

"Captain," she whispered as she crouched beside him, "You wanted to see me?"

The captain opened his eyes.

"Aisha? Listen up, sergeant. What I am going to ask you is not a regular order. You don't have to obey me."

"*Mon capitaine*?"

"What happened today… The European government will certainly try to cover that up. And we owe them our fidelity. Yet, we owe ourselves our honor, and I cannot betray the legionnaires who died today for nothing."

"*Non, mon capitaine*," Aisha replied ('No, sir.')

"Listen, Aisha," Captain Léger said, "In each of the drones, there is a black box. Contrary to what the name suggests, these black boxes are actually orange. The Europeans should not recover them. The UN should. Otherwise, there will never be an international investigation, and they may even try to cover the whole thing up."

"The UN secretary-general is in Casablanca, as far as I know," Aisha said hesitantly.

She went back to the Moroccan sergeant, took him aside and told him her idea. The sergeant would first need to discuss it with his major. That was fine as far as Aisha was concerned.

The sun was disappearing behind the horizon when the Red Cross convoy finally arrived at 19:08. It took almost an hour to load all the 213 wounded, after giving some additional care to the most critical ones, and it was almost night when the convoy started.

Aisha Barjaoui and Captain O'Malley sat in the front truck.

"You have a big rucksack," the captain noted.

"Climbing equipment, mines, and so on," she replied. "I won't leave it here. I was lucky it was not destroyed, and some of the climbing equipment is my private stuff."

She had lied. In fact, she had got rid of all her mines and explosives to make room for four orange boxes that had been retrieved by the Moroccan soldiers. They had kept the other four. Aisha had taken it upon herself to smuggle half of the black boxes to some UN officials in Casablanca. European soldiers were to not lay hand on them, else the European Union would attempt to cover up what had happened with the drones at Khouribga.

It took them one hour to reach the front line at Berrechid, 40 km (25 miles) south of Casablanca. There, the Moroccans did not want to let the unscathed legionnaires go through the checkpoint. Aisha had to negotiate for another half an hour until the officer agreed to let them through.

Finally, they were met by some EU military police, who led the convoy toward Casablanca.

As they approached the Moroccan city, they could see that parts of it were burning, and the Military Police motorcycles had them first turn right on the A5 motorway and then turn left on the road 315. Her parents' house was nearby.

She started to say something but stopped.

"What is it, sergeant?" the air force captain asked.

"The whole *Cité Djemaa*..." she said. "It has been flattened to the ground...Why did they bomb that district? There were no military living there."

"Standard invasion warfare," Capt. O'Malley replied. "If you want to invade a country, you violently bomb the poor district lying close to the richer neighborhood. That way, the rich people who have a lot to lose will immediately support the invaders, so that the conflict stops as fast as possible. That was what I was taught in a seminar at the *École Militaire* in Paris."

A moment later, the convoy reached the harbor. The wounded were transported in a hospital boat from the EU Navy, and the air force captain went with them: he was to be flown back to Europe from the EU Navy carrier. Meanwhile, the three dozen still standing legionnaires were quartered in a warehouse, where they were given water and military rations.

"Sir, we have had a horrible day, and you want us to eat that food," Aisha said to an MP officer. "I'm pretty sure that the hotels here have some good food left. Let me do a tour. My legionnaires deserve that."

"Legionnaires and looting are never a good combination," the Military Police officer replied.

"Listen, sir. I'm from Casablanca. I have some contacts here. Besides, we have some cash, from the dead legionnaires. I assure you there will be no looting. I will only take private Eriksen here."

"You are the sergeant engineer who negotiated the truce and the evacuation of the wounded?" the officer asked.

"Yes, sir."

"Then I trust you. You deserve better food than that, after all."

Aisha took Torbjørn to the nearest jeep, and they drove at full speed to the Cité Djeema. They stopped on 24th street. She looked at the collapsed building. It was there she had grown up, in a little flat on the fourth floor. She jumped out of the jeep and ran to what was left of the building. All around, she could hear people crying.

She recognized a former neighbor who was walking by. She had been trying to recover some pictures from her apartment, which also had been blown apart, but in vain. Everything had burned. Did she know anything about her father? He was probably dead, the neighbor replied. Like everybody in these collapsed and burned buildings. All the buildings had been blown up even before the air sirens had started. The neighbor had been lucky to have spent the night with a richer man in a richer neighborhood. There, no bombs had fallen.

Aisha suddenly hated the European Union and the EU army. She thought about her rucksack and the orange black boxes. She had to meet the UN secretary-general now. She went back into the jeep and drove at full speed to the Radisson hotel.

She noted it was guarded by parachute marines, the elite of the European Army.

"Torbjørn, you stay here," she commanded.

She jumped out of the jeep, took her rucksack, and walked resolutely into the hotel.

"Hey, sergeant, where do you think you are going?" a

parachute marine asked.

"To the kitchen. I have thirty legionnaires pissed off and hungry. I would not mess with them if I were you."

"Legionnaires? You are the ones who have been *Dien Bien Phued*? Too bad! For us, it has been a jolly little war."

"Fuck off."

She went through and made it to the kitchen with such determination that none of the parachute marines dared to interfere.

In the kitchen, she put down her rucksack and took a duffel bag out of it.

"Listen up," she said in Arabic. "I don't know what you have, but I want you to prepare food for my thirty surviving legionnaires. Couscous, merguez, chips, meat, Caesar salads. I don't care. Just cook it and put it in some thermal boxes. And in this duffel bag, I want you to put nuts, crisps and all kind of snacks you have, and even some bottles of wine, all right?"

"Where do you think you are?" a cook asked.

"Here is four months of legionnaire salary. We are paid in cash, you know. These poor devils died today with all the money on them. You can split it among you. Euros may be useful for you, now."

"If you ask it kindly," one of the cooks answered.

"By the way, the parachute marines in the hotel," Aisha said. "That's the elite of the European Army. Why are they here?

They are watching the kitchen?"

"Not at all," a cook laughed, "They are guarding the UN secretary-general and her staff."

"Are they in the hotel?" Aisha pretended to wonder. "Are they using the presidential suite?"

"No, only some regular business rooms on the second floor," a cook answered. "They have to stay in their rooms."

"Well, the UN boss must have enjoyed the European invasion this morning from the sea," Aisha tried.

"Barely," a cook answered. "She is blind. And her room is not facing the harbor anyway, she is in the south wing, facing west."

"*C'est quoi ce bordel?*" ('What the fuck is happening?')

It was a tall and imposing captain from the Parachute Marine Regiment.

"Ça va bien, Monsieur," a cook answered ('All is fine, sir.'). "She is buying food from us. For her legionnaires, she said."

"Buying? Legionnaires?" the officer asked.

"*Mon Capitaine*, Sergeant Barjaoui, from the 2nd Foreign Engineer Regiment," Aisha saluted.

"It was you on the phone, earlier this afternoon? I had no idea you were a *bougnoule* ['gook']."

Aisha strongly wanted to punch the captain in the face, but instead, she smiled and said: "Well, I am from the Foreign Legion, not the Roman Legion."

The captain laughed.

"So, you are buying food for your legionnaires, you said. Are you the one in charge?"

"All our officers have been either killed or wounded. So I guess I am in charge. We were given some military rations in a warehouse on the harbor. Many of our comrades died today. You know, legionnaires are paid in cash, and we were able to retrieve some money; we did not know whose it was. Instead of having legionnaires fighting for it, I thought I could buy food with it for the survivors."

"Well, as long as you are not looting."

"By the way, *mon capitaine*," Aisha asked, "Do you know where there are some bathrooms I may use in the hotel? You know, I am a lady, and I don't like urinating in the wild. I often get urinary tract inflammation when I do. So, I have been holding myself for some time, now."

"Ok, spare me the detail," the captain said. "There are bathrooms on the first floor, close to the conference rooms."

Aisha thanked the captain, took her rucksack with her, explaining she still had some explosives in it, and therefore she did not want to leave it in the kitchen.

She took the main stairs to the first floor, where she switched to the service stairs. She followed them to the second floor, where she looked at a fire evacuation map. By the size of the rooms drawn on the plan, she inferred that there could be only two business rooms in the south wing facing west. She walked up to the fourth floor and made it to the south wing.

There was no military.

She knocked at the door of one of the rooms above the two business rooms on the second floor.

"Room service," she said.

A Moroccan man opened the door.

"Here are some euros in cash, sir," she said in Arabic. "I would like to use your shower, but I would really appreciate if you go down to the bar and buy me a bottle of champagne."

Aisha had already put down her rucksack and was taking off her military jacket and her undershirt, showing her bra.

"What are you waiting for? Are you buying this bottle or not? We legionnaires are not allowed to buy alcohol at the bar, and I really need it. Don't tell anyone it is for me. That may cause you some trouble."

As soon as the man left the room with his wallet, Aisha locked the door and put her undershirt back on. She opened the window and looked around. It would be fine.

She opened her rucksack and took off her harness as well as some 5 mm wide cord. She had eighteen meters of it. It was used to build abseiling stations in mountaineering, and an alpinist would only cut two meters of it at the time. Now, she was planning to abseil down on it. It was not ideal, but it would hold.

She put the rope around one leg of the heavy bed and found the middle of the cord. She tied the two ends of it and threw the cord through the window. She would be able to abseil down seven meters on it, which should be enough to reach the second floor and check the two rooms. If the UN secretary-general was in one of them, EU soldiers would guard the room door, but probably not the window.

She put her harness on.

She passed the two cord strands into her belaying device and clipped it into her harness with a locker carabiner.

She went to the window and started abseiling down into the night.

Hira Dorjee-Sherpa was furious. She, the UN secretary-general, was *de facto* held hostage by the military force of a great power. She had done everything she could to avoid a conflict, and yet it had degenerated into a full-scale invasion of Morocco.

She had convinced the Moroccan king to have the crown prince fly to Switzerland to be heard as a witness by the French police on neutral territory. The Europeans had agreed to it.

Next, she had obtained that the Moroccan government would organize within six weeks a referendum in Western Sahara about its independence. Should Western Sahara become independent, it would break the Moroccan monopoly on phosphate production, thus offering a face-saving solution for everybody. The Moroccan government could invoke their generosity to offer independence to the Western Saharans, while the great powers would release the pressure on Morocco, seeing that a new source of phosphate would be independent.

It was a good plan, and it should have worked.

Instead, it had completely failed. Though the Europeans had, at first, agreed that the Moroccans had met the terms of the ultimatum, they changed their minds after the crown prince had been shot dead immediately after landing in Switzerland. Though the Swiss police had arrested the murderers, it was still unclear who had done it.

Next, there had been bombs falling over Casablanca. Her aide had rushed to her room to take her to the hotel's cellar. Hira Dorjee-Sherpa had suffered from blindness since her birth, something she had made a strength of, as it gave her more natural authority. However, being blind in times of war was frightening. She could hear the bombs, but had only a limited grasp of the situation.

Eventually, her aide told her that the Europeans were only bombing military installations and the poorer districts of the town. The bombing had lasted two hours and the UN staff had moved back to their conference rooms. Communication with the UN headquarters in New York had been cut off.

Later, she had heard the sounds of planes and her aid had told her that paratroopers were jumping over Casablanca. The UN staff had had no other choice than to rally in their conference room and wait. A moment later, a European officer with a heavy French accent had told them that the European President wished that the UN staff be kept safe. Each official of the UN delegation had been invited to return to their rooms.

They would be permitted to fly back to New York as soon as the situation was considered completely safe. The European military had wanted to search their rooms and luggage, but Hira had forbidden it expressly.

She had said she would rather be shot than permit a search of the rooms occupied by her staff, and had asked the officer how he would explain her death to the European President. The European military had not insisted, seeing the determination of the blind UN diplomat. Back in her room, she had realized she had forgotten her earGlasses, charging in the conference rooms.

The so-called earGlasses were electronic glasses she could connect to her earlobes, enabling her brain to 'see' 3D images, albeit in bad resolution. She did not wear them most of the time, but she now felt they could be useful to have, given the circumstances.

The European soldier guarding her room had first refused to fetch them, and when she had complained to an officer, the latter had said that they had looked for her glasses, but could not find them. Without them, she was blind.

Luckily, the telephone lines had been restored, but she was certain that the European intelligence was eavesdropping on them.

It was incredible that the Europeans would try such a venture.

She was outraged, she, who admired the European

civilization so much. The Europeans had been the first to understand the congregation dynamics in modern societies. They had understood that congregationism threatened liberal democracies. They had been the first to understand the need for integrationist factors to bring a whole society together, not only on a national level but on a continental level. It had been copied by Nepal and the South Asian Union, where she came from. In the SAU, like in the EU, there was Civil Service, forcing every young South Asian turning eighteen to do a public service mission in another South Asian country, or at least for the Indians, in another Indian province. It had successfully broken the caste dynamic in India, held male supremacism in check on the subcontinent, and fostered social peace. All these ideals now seemed worthless in the face of a realist EU president who wanted nothing else than to exhibit her force and strength to her nation.

Hira was outraged. How could a woman like EU President Bonavita behave like a real male-bitch? How could she even believe that she could detain the UN secretary-general? What the hell!

The European Union did have the veto right at the Security Council. The EU had inherited it from France, in 2054, when it became a federation.

As a result, the EU could do as they pleased, as long as they met little opposition from the other great powers, as was currently the case. The US president had proved disappointingly shy.

Hira Dorjee-Sherpa was now held hostage by French-speaking EU Soldiers here in Casablanca. Had it ever happened before that a UN secretary-general should be humiliated by a great power?

Yes, of course, it had. 1961, Bizerte, Tunisia. The France of General de Gaulle had humiliated Dag Hammarskjöld. President Bonavita was also French, before being European. What a pity that Khrushchev had not dropped a few nuclear bombs over Paris in 1956, during the Suez crisis. It could have calmed down those asshole frog-eaters.

Hira suddenly realized she had gone too far in her thoughts. She had to calm down. But how? She tried to take a deep breath and exhale slowly.

Suddenly, she heard a peculiar sound. What was it? It seemed to come from the window. Yes, someone was gently tapping on the window.

She went to the window. Someone was behind it. If only she could see.

Who would be out there? Could it be someone wanting to hurt her? If they were armed, they could shoot at her through the window anyway. She decided to open the window.

"Sorry, madame," she heard a feminine voice say.

"Who are you?" Hira asked.

"You'd rather not know," the voice answered. "I have to be quick. Can the European military search your stuff?"

"They have tried," Hira answered. "I have refused expressly. I have immunity, and I have invoked article 105 of the Charter of the United Nations, to which the European Union is a party."

"I have no idea what it means, but good," the voice answered. "Listen up, I will hide four orange boxes among your clothes in your suitcase."

"What are these orange boxes?" Hira asked.

"These are the black boxes belonging to drones of the EU Air Force, which were shot down this afternoon over Khouribga. A hundred kilometers from here, close to the phosphate mines."

"Khouribga?" Hira repeated.

"Legionnaires from the 2nd Foreign Parachute Regiment and from the 2nd Foreign Engineer Regiment landed there to secure the phosphate mines," the voice explained. "We were deployed there more than twenty-six hours before the expiry of the ultimatum. Whatever your peace effort, the dice were cast anyway."

"What are you saying?" Hira wondered.

"Bonavita had made her decision to invade Morocco anyway. I have also the briefing notes of my lieutenant. He was killed. But his notes were in his rucksack, safe in the hospital. Just say you have received them from a Moroccan soldier."

"These are grave accusations."

"There is something else," the voice went on. "Later today, some European drones came to provide air support, but they went crazy. They started bombing everything on the ground indiscriminately. Everything, legionnaires, Moroccan soldiers, and civilians alike. The only civilian casualties in Khouribga will have been those killed by these killer drones."

"I have always been against killer drones," Hira replied. "Robots should not be given the right to kill without human decision behind them."

"You are certainly right," the voice conceded. "Meanwhile, there is a risk the European government stop any investigation or even cover up the whole thing, if they manage to retrieve the black boxes. They are now well hidden in your suitcase. It will be a bit heavier, but not much. Please take them to New York".

The United Nations Secretary turned to the feminine voice and said gravely: "Be sure that I will."

"The civilians, Moroccans, and legionnaires fallen today would certainly appreciate an independent international investigation in that matter."

"I will see what I can do," Hira replied.

"I have to leave, now," the voice said.

"Wait," Hira said. "The 2nd Foreign Engineer Regiment, you said. You are part of it, aren't you? You served in Kirghizstan. I remember your voice. I gave you a *Dag Hammarskjöld* medal."

There came no answer. When Hira realized she was again alone in the room, she closed the window.

Mr. Kassari was waiting in front of his room with a bottle of champagne. It had been a hard day for him, being trapped in a hotel in Casablanca, not able to reach his wife in Rabat. But God was finally with him. A ravishing, athletic girl had requisitioned his shower, and he was certain he would enjoy a nice evening with her, perhaps even a night. But why had she locked the door, though?

Finally, the door opened. She was still drying her hair with a towel, but she had put her undershirt back on. That was unnecessary.

"Thank you for the bottle, sweetie," the girl said.

She laid the bottle on the desk, put her military jacket back on, grabbed her rucksack, and finally put the bottle into the rucksack and made it to the door.

"Where are you going?" Mr. Kassari asked. "Don't you want to stay here a bit longer?"

"I would love to, sweetie," the girl smiled. "But I am not sure your wife would. I have to go now."

When Aisha got back to the kitchen, the food was ready to be taken.

"You took some time," The captain of the parachute marines said.

"Well, I'm Moroccan," Aisha said calmly, "You know, and I happened to meet a man I know. I took advantage of it to use his shower. And I even negotiated to get some alcohol from the minibar."

"You are a very special sergeant, madame," the captain said.

"Do you need any help to carry the food to your jeep? Your Norwegian trooper is not very helpful."

"Yeah, I know," Aisha replied. "The poor devil ran earlier today in underpants while being chased by a drone. He escaped the drone but got completely sunburnt. He is still in shock, but he is the only man left I have from my squad. So, yes, I could use some help to carry the food to the jeep."

Two parachute marines helped her carry the food to the jeep. Once everything was loaded, Aisha thanked the marines, started the jeep and drove back to the warehouse. The legionnaires toasted her when she arrived with couscous, merguez, skewers, steaks, and chips but also snacks, bottles of wine, and even a bottle of champagne.

To her surprise, there were now more legionnaires. Preshti Ahma, the Indian girl who had been at Legionnaire School together with Aisha and Torbjørn, was among them.

"Our plane got shot off the coast," she said. "I was one of the few who could get out. We had to wait five hours before being rescued by the Navy. They finally brought us here."

Aisha gave her some warm merguez with couscous.

Later in the night, the colonel of the 2nd REP met with the legionnaires. He had been onboard one of the damaged transport planes and had jumped over Casablanca instead of Khouribga. With the rest of his group, he had been assisting an armored regiment landed in Casablanca to link up with the beachhead established in Rabat. He had returned to Casablanca as soon as the junction had been established.

He took Aisha aside and told her he had received reports about the seizing and the later evacuation of Khouribga. He believed Aisha should be promoted to the rank of lieutenant. She had displayed officer skills on multiple occasions: leading the initial charge, using the Moroccans' landlines to call the air force, negotiating a truce, organizing the evacuation of the wounded, and now providing excellent food to the remaining legionnaires.

Aisha looked at him with a weary smile. *If only he knew*, she thought.

10: A DIRTY LITTLE WAR (OCT 2097 –NOV 2097)

On the morning of Saturday 5 October 2097, Amina Dörflinger came out of her bathroom, wearing leggings and a sports bra. She had dark hair, blue eyes and a muscular but ripped body, the perfect climber's body. She looked around. Their Cambridge student flat was dusty and messy. Nobody had cleaned it in four weeks, and she was not planning to do it now either.

Noting the missing bike helmet in the hall, she inferred that Sanne had spent the night at some random dude's. Good for her. As long as she did not come back too late for their Saturday climbing session. Else she would end up sharing a rope with Samir and Emily, which was impractical, or do bouldering, which she had grown tired of: the risk of injury was too high.

The student flat was cold, and she decided to have a short morning warm up. She went to the kitchen and turned the kettle on. On the kitchen table lay the latest edition of *The Chained Palmiped*, a weekly satirical newspaper Sanne van der

Maas subscribed to. The headline read: '*A dirty little war.*'

Amina had no time for that kind of reading. Besides climbing for leisure and working as a climbing instructor, she had to dedicate her remaining time to what would be her bachelor's thesis. She wanted it to be so good a thesis that she would be given the opportunity to start a PhD immediately after, thus skipping a two-year-long master's. She was an A-student in her field, Earth science. Why would she waste two years of her life doing a master's? She did not want to be an extraction or construction geologist, she wanted to be a scientist. If she had wanted so much to study in Cambridge rather than in Switzerland, where she was from, it was just to skip the master's.

She went back to the student flat's living room and started doing circles with her arms. She was confident her bachelor's thesis topic was good enough to land her a PhD. It had a dull title, though: *Assessment and comparison of the eruption probabilities of Campi Flegrei and Yellowstone Caldera within the next two centuries*. It sounded boring, but was impactful for any serious Earth scientist.

She moved on, stretching her hands. The background? Human-induced global warming had put mankind in great peril. Of course, it had to be drafted differently. The new geological era Anthropocene had been marked by a rapid and unprecedented increase of greenhouse gases. She could quote *This dude et al.* This had resulted in the melting of glaciers and icecaps, and the thermal expansions of oceans (*This gal et al*). This reallocation of masses of water on the surface of the Earth had had an impact on the planet's rotation speed (*that guy et al*). Even if the change was only a few milliseconds a day, it was significant enough *(that guy et al* again and, of course, *Cooper et al*). This had in its turn an impact on the magmatic convection in the Earth's mantle and in the frequency of earthquakes and volcanic eruptions (*Cooper et al*). Of course, she could mention the 2096 earthquake in Nice, the 2094 earthquake in Bihar. The best would be to add a graph with the number of earthquakes of a certain magnitude over time. This could be put together with another graph showing the thermal expansions of oceans.

Amina was now warm enough and went to the fingerboard, hanging over the door between the kitchen and the living room. She jumped and caught it and started doing some pull-ups. A consensus was forming around the idea that global cooling was to occur in the following two centuries, due to an increase in volcanic eruptions. This was what had caused the Little Ice Age, or at least mainly contributed to it.

Thirty pull-ups. Not too bad. She went on doing more circles with her arms, and stretching them. But what about super-volcanoes? It was now certain that the Neanderthals had become extinct because of the eruption of a super-volcano under the bay of Naples, the *Campi Flegrei*. It had erupted 39,280 years before present time and had killed all life in Europe, including all the Homo sapiens individuals living there. If it had not been for the other humans living outside Europe and repopulating the area, there would be no European humanity today.

She jumped again on the fingerboards and started doing pull-ups with three fingers this time. And what about the Yellowstone Caldera, the super-volcano in the Yellowstone? If it erupted, mankind on Earth might become extinct pretty fast. Those who would not be killed instantly by the eruption would eventually starve to death, as a several-decades-long night, perhaps even century-long night, would follow, caused by the Sulphur dioxide that would hinder the sun's rays reaching the surface of the Earth.

Eighteen three-finger pull-ups. Not very good. She should now try with two fingers. No, her topic was the best one could have. She had got some data, thanks to her supervisor, Dr. Sheldon Cooper. She had had ideas about three different approaches.

Eight two-finger pull-ups only. How bad she was! Lucky, she was not competing anymore. She went to the kitchen, poured some boiled water in a cup and added a tea bag. When her tea was ready, she went to her room and cast a glance at the bronze medal in lead-climbing. She had come third at the 2096 Olympics in Riga. She had no regrets. Rather study Earth Science than compete in a stressful and wicked environment. She turned on her computer and opened her bachelor's thesis document. She could try and go through the methods until Sanne arrived.

Sanne van der Maas arrived at the flat a bit before 10:00 and knocked on Amina's door. She was a very tall but athletic grey-eyed brunette, wearing a dark blue evening dress.

"Sorry for being late," she said "I'll change my clothes, and then we can go to the climbing gym immediately."

"Was it good?" Amina asked, hinting at Sanne's one-night stand.

"Good, but not great," Sanne replied. "The guy talked too much. He was constantly criticizing the topic of my master's thesis."

Sanne went to her room to take off her evening dress and switch to sports clothes.

"Your stuff about space colonization?" Amina said through the wall.

"It's not a 'stuff about space colonization,'" Sanne corrected. "My master's thesis is about the prospects for liberal capitalism in an interstellar economy, it's not silly."

"It's very theoretical," Amina retorted. "Your bachelor's thesis was about survival economy with the example of the failed Martian colony. That was more impactful. Remember, a career as a scientist is all about impact. Oops, sorry, I forgot, economy is not a real science."

"Very funny," Sanne replied, now back in Amina's room with her climbing clothes on. "You've said it many, many times. And I know it's true. But I guarantee you my thesis will be impactful. Even if faster-than-light travel has made the prospect of interstellar travel and colonization possible, information flow cannot be instantaneous. With the warpedoes, it still takes a few months, or at best weeks, to communicate with a planet in another star system. Without instant information flow, no efficient market. Nobody has thought about it yet. I will be the first to write about it."

"OK. Let's go climbing." Amina said as she took her ready-packed rucksack.

"Wait, I need to take *The Chained Palmiped*," Sanne remembered, looking for the paper in the kitchen.

"*Quack, quack,*" Amina said as they took their biking helmets and went out.

The Cambridge climbing gym was only a fifteen-minute bike ride from their flat. It was located close to the university's Earth science department, a very logical choice according to Amina, as geologists were overrepresented among climbers.

At the climbing wall, they noted that Samir and Emily were already there. Amina and Sanne did a short warm up and went into lead climbing. Sanne was not in great shape: too much drinking the previous night, but that did not disturb Amina who flashed five new 7c routes (5.12d in the US system) in a row, after which she felt she had to take a break as well.

Samir and Emily, who had arrived earlier, were already having a coffee break at the gym's café. Sanne and Amina joined them after getting a cappuccino and a cup of tea.

"I borrowed your *Chained Palmiped*," Samir said to Sanne. "I wanted to get more information about Khouribga."

"I have not read it," Sanne said. "What is Khouribga?"

"A shithole in Morocco," Samir replied. "But there are some phosphate mines. The EU deployed a troop of legionnaires there."

"What happened?" Emily asked.

"First of all," Samir said, "it seems that the legionnaires had landed the day before the end of the ultimatum, which cast some doubt as to the sincere intent of the EU government. Second of all, there had been a bug with some of our killer drones. They started bombing and killing everybody there. Our troops, the Moroccans, the civilians. The UN has somehow managed to get a hand on the drones' black boxes and is leading an investigation. The UN had also got hold on some briefing notes from a dead European officer hinting that our president had planned to invade Morocco regardless of the outcome of the peace negotiations."

"Nice comeback for the UN secretary-general," Sanne commented, "From being held hostage by the EU army to leading an investigation against them."

"Besides admonishing the European Union, she now would like to push for a treaty to ban killer robots. Khouribga could give her an opportunity."

"Is it because of that, it's called a 'Dirty Little War', the headline?" Amina asked.

"Everything has been dirty," Emily replied. "We deployed soldiers in Morocco before the end of the ultimatum, we detained the UN secretary-general, but even worse, we mass-bombed the poorer districts of Casablanca and Rabat to have the middle-class rally around us."

"And we killed the Moroccan king," Samir added. "I received a message from my father. He was, of course, super-happy."

"We killed the king of Morocco?" Sanne asked. "When did it happen?"

"This morning," Emily said. "A Texan guillotine had been shipped from the USA despite the so-called embargo by EU forces. The Moroccan king was executed, guillotined with blade and laser. The marvel of technology. You can watch it on YouTube."

"But no worries," Samir went on sarcastically, "Western Sahara has become independent, and we are sending them more troops to help them become an autonomous state and extract the phosphate. So, it seems that this jolly little war, as they call it, will last forever."

Amina, who looked bored and had drunk all her tea, said, "All the more some good reasons not to waste your time reading or watching the news. You can't do anything about it, and it's depressing. Shall we go back to climbing?"

"What about Aisha?" Sanne asked. "Her family is from Casa. Are they all right? Was she deployed herself?"

"She's all right, but would not answer my calls," Samir

replied. "Her parents were both killed. She was in the regiment that was in Khouribga. The only words she wrote about it were '*it was not nice*'."

Aisha Barjaoui had been back at the 2nd Foreign Engineer Regiment's base in Saint-Christol, for about ten days. She had not been in the mood.

Her parents had been killed. Her Chinese ex-boyfriend in Casablanca had been killed. Lt. Hoffman had been killed. Sgt. Uwilingiyimana, whom she thought she had saved, had eventually died of his wounds at the hospital. Corporal Tran had been killed. Private First-Class Gonzales had been killed. Private Nguyen had been killed. Private First-Class Kowalski had been killed. Corporal Singh had been wounded, and so had Jean-Claude Rheinfeldt. Torbjørn Eriksen had been the only one in her squad to make it through, with nothing worse than severe sunburns.

While the paratroopers and engineers who had survived Khouribga, had been discreetly evacuated, the 58 engineers and 135 paratroopers who had been positioned in the phosphate mine ten kilometers south had, instead, all received the *Jean Monnet* medal for gallantly defending the phosphate mine against nobody. The same legionnaires who had refused to provide assistance to the wounded in Khouribga, had been called 'heroes'. This had outraged Aisha. In Kirghizstan, she and Tran had both been awarded the *Jean Monnet* medal for outflanking the enemy over an ice wall, but she now felt that the medal was worthless. She had thrown her own *Jean Monnet* medal in the garbage.

Like the other thirteen engineer survivors from Khouribga, she had been sent to consult a shrink. Aisha had not been in the mood but had complied nonetheless with the exercise. Had she had nightmares? She did not usually dream at all. Had she seen things that had upset her? They all had. Was she afraid of dying? She did not care. What did she care about? About those who had died and could have been saved. Did she wish she could have done more? Of course, she did. She had already proven herself to be an excellent leader, hadn't she? Why had she taken the lead? First at the airport, then under the drone attack and, later, during the evacuation? To save lives.

She had certainly given the right answers, because the next day, the regiment commander told her she was to be commissioned as a lieutenant. Wasn't she too young? She was only nineteen. The colonel admitted she was young, but there were those like Jean-Claude Rheinfeldt who would not even be sergeant at forty and those like her who showed great leadership skills already, at a young age.

Besides, he had only one officer left in the 2nd company, he needed more officers. What about captain Léger? Any news about him? *Capitaine* Léger had been honorably discharged. Too badly wounded. Couldn't she be happy and rejoice to be appointed to the rank of lieutenant at nineteen, instead?

She asked if she could then serve in the support company, the company that was building roads, installing cable cars and triggering preventive avalanches. The colonel promised it would be possible as long as she would first help him rebuild the 2nd company. Then they had a deal, Aisha said. The colonel pointed out that one never had a deal, in the army, one just followed orders. Of course, *mon colonel*.

Once again, Aisha was sent to Castelnaudary, this time to take an eight-week long course to become an officer. Torbjørn was also sent there, but to take another course and become a corporal. Torbjørn, corporal? Aisha wondered. They were really out of men in the regiment.

Meanwhile, she had the time to follow the news. Her father had been confirmed dead in the bombing of the Cité Djeema. Western Sahara was said to have been liberated by the European Union and had declared its independence.

The capitulation of Morocco had been followed by a short popular revolution, the outcome of which had been the abdication of the Moroccan king and the proclamation of a republic, the new constitution of which was a copy-and-paste of the Tunisian one.

The former Moroccan king had been put under arrest and accused of being responsible for Morocco's fate. He had been sentenced to death by a popular jury, and the sentence had been carried out quickly.

Officially, the European Union had opposed the execution

of the king, but had not hindered a Chinese cargo plane flying a Texan guillotine from the United States and delivering it to Rabat. Mohammed VIII had been executed under the most humiliating circumstances only two weeks after the invasion of Morocco.

According to *The Chained Palmiped*, the outcome of the ultimatum had been rigged from the beginning. Beside Lt. Hoffman's briefing notes retrieved by the UN, the satirical newspaper had received a recording from a briefing held in Saint-Christol on 17 September. In this recording, officers had gone through the plan of infiltrating Khouribga with three hundred legionnaires landing in gliders to secure phosphate mines. This, combined with other testimonies, proved that European troops had landed on Moroccan soil before the expiry of the ultimatum.

When the Moroccan crown prince had agreed to being questioned by the French police in Switzerland about the use of his private jet for cannabis smuggling, he had been murdered immediately after landing in Geneva. The Swiss police had somehow managed to arrest the two assassins, who had later been identified as European spies.

Everything pointed out that the European government had made up their minds to invade Morocco even before the outcome of the ultimatum was to be known.

Concerning the drone friendly-fire incident at Khouribga, the UN had somehow managed to retrieve the black boxes of the drones, and an international investigation had been decided by the General Assembly, even though the European Union had said to be unfavorable to such an investigation.

There had been investigations by the military police in Saint-Christol as to who had leaked the recording. Aisha, who had been at the meeting and was also a Moroccan citizen, remained under close scrutiny for a few weeks, and it was not pleasant. She was, however, proven innocent: her only recording device had been her smartphone, which had been confiscated at the time of the briefing. Aisha had indeed leaked information to the United Nations, but there was no way anyone could know. She had given the UN secretary-general Lt. Hoffman's briefing notes, but she had not leaked any recording to *The Chained Palmiped,* though. She wondered who had done it.

11: "EXACTORS"
VERSUS "APPROXIMATORS"
(DEC 2097)

On that last Friday of 2097, the weather was terrible in Edinburgh, Scotland. It was pouring rain, and a strong gale was blowing from the west. The thick cloud cover combined with the weak Scottish December sun gave an impression of imminent dusk, but it was only two in the afternoon. It was slightly better than a 27 December spent in Vaasa, Finland, Ralf Åhman tried to console himself.

He was now back with his children at his mother's apartment. He would always have their custody the week following Christmas. He would pick them up in Trondheim, Norway, where they lived with his ex-girlfriend and bring them to the Scottish Republic so that their grandmother could see them.

She was not in the flat, though. She was at the hospital. Although seventy-five and retired, his mother would still volunteer to work a couple of days a month at the hospital. Chalmers hospital had a constant lack of anesthetists. Friday 27 December 2097 was one of those days.

In the morning, Ralf had taken his two kids to the swimming pool. It had been an overall good session. Though Eleonore was only five, she was now able to crawl properly, but she would still have to work on her leg kick. Dag was now seven and a decent swimmer. Ralf had managed to have him swim a whole hour, but then he would only jump from the three-meter diving board. When his son had later tried to jump from the five-meter diving board, he had backed away and climbed down the stairs back to the pool.

Ralf did not like cooking. After the swimming pool, he had taken his kids to the nearest Burger King, and they had had some bugburgers, these burgers made of insect paste. The kids loved it. Ralf missed the beef burgers that used to be cheaper in the past.

Going to Burger King was always a sociologically interesting experiment, from Ralf's standpoint. As the director of the World's Agency for the Regulation of Space Exploration and Colonization, he was cut off from normal life and normal people. WARSEC employees were in no way representative of mankind. They were physically fit and highly intelligent. There in the Burger King, people had just been average Scots.

Scanning the other male customers, Ralf had been surprised

to see he had been the slimmest and fittest man in the restaurant. Sure, he had lost six kilos (13 pounds) since September. The Euro-Moroccan war had made him so angry that he had been hitting the gym every day, and sometimes twice a day. He had been using the punching ball intensively, pretending it was the EU President he was hitting. It had helped him release his aggression and do his work as a regular UN diplomat.

Burger King was also the place where he could get the confirmation that he and especially his ex-girlfriend Solveig had not been bad parents at all. While Dag and Eleonore had been alert, checking everything around them, at the table beside them, there had been an overweight couple with two kids who seemed completely autistic. Both kids, perhaps three and five, had had their heads sunk into their smartphone screens. They had barely been interacting with their parents and had seemed totally unable to look at a stranger.

How had it happened? Kids were recommended not to be given any smartphone before they turned four. After that, it was recommended to limit their access to it until they became teenagers. Otherwise it had a negative impact on the development of the brain. Public health authorities had handed over very clear instructions. The communication obviously still did not reach the average man.

"*Pappa, kan vi se en film?*" Dag asked in Norwegian ('Daddy, can we watch a movie?').

They had been physically active during the whole morning, sure they would be allowed to watch a movie, now they were back at their grandmother's home.

"What do you want to watch?" Ralf asked.

"*La meg velge,*" ('Let me choose,'), Dag said and took the remote control to go through all the movies available.

"Eleonore, what do you want to see?" Ralf asked his daughter.

"*Spiller ingen rolle… same som Dag*", the daughter replied ('Doesn't matter. The same as Dag.').

Ralf let his children browse through the list of movies available. Impossible to have them speak English in Scotland, they would stick to Norwegian. They spoke English only with their grandmother. Behind the living room's sofa, Ralf glanced at the pictures. One was a picture of his children with Solveig. One was a picture of him when he took his PhD in Cambridge. The wedding picture of his white mother and his black father, who had died of the Qatari Flu in 2073, when there were living in Sweden.

There was also the oldest picture of his parents together, taken in 2045, shortly after they had met when they were both 'slavants' in Haskovo, a godforsaken place in Bulgaria. They had been the first generation of *slavants*. *A European Dilemma* had been published in June 2037. Seven years later, one of its lead recommendations had been implemented by the European Union: The European Civil Service. Every European citizen turning eighteen would fulfil public interest missions for one year in another European country. In exchange for their service, they were provided with the opportunity to obtain their driving license for free.

His white Scottish mother and his black Finnish father had both been sent to Haskovo and had both been working with the integration of Romani people. Later they had moved to Finland. Ralf's mother had become a doctor, while his father had become a nurse. Ralf had been born in Finland, but Finnish had never been easy for his Scottish mother. They had eventually moved to Sweden. Swedish was so easy that everybody could learn it in a couple of months. After his father had died of the Qatari flu, they had moved to Scotland, but Ralf had then moved back to Sweden for his studies, before finishing them in the UK.

"*Kan vi se på* Armageddon? Dag asked. "*Det handler om rommet. Du jobber med det.*" ('Can we watch Armageddon? It's about space. You work with it.')

"Armageddon?" Ralf wondered. "From 1998? This is a very bad movie. Nothing is realistic in it. Don't you want to watch Alien? The first movie. At least, it's fun."

"*Vi har ikke lov til å se på Alien. Mamma vil ikke.*" Eleonore said. ('We are not allowed to watch *Alien*. Mommy does not want us to.')

"You are perhaps too young to watch it," Ralf admitted. "OK for Armageddon. But I let you watch it on your own, OK? I can't see a movie that bad another time."

Dag pressed a button on the remote control and the movie

started with the usual introduction message to sensitize viewers to the untenable population growth: *The story of this movie is set in 1998. Back then, the world population was about 5.9 billion. In 2097, the world population is about 10.5 billion.*

"*Hvordan kan verdens befolkning vokse så fort?*" Dag asked. ('How can the world population grow so fast?')

"Because the world can't use condoms," Ralf replied

"*Hva er kondom?*" the five-year old Eleonore asked ('What is a condom?').

"We can talk about it later," Ralf answered, "Like... in a couple of years. Now I will go to the kitchen and work a little bit."

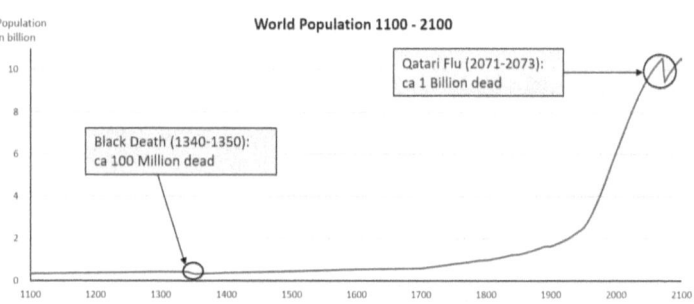

Figure 6: evolution of the world population between 1100-2100. At the end of the 21st Century, everything has been made to make the world aware of the untenable population growth, including displaying sensitization messages at the start of each movie.

Ralf went to the kitchen, set the kettle on and grabbed his tablet. Things were moving forward at WARSEC. The FAA was expected to certify the Space Bear by the end of January, and the Space Hound by the end of March. This was beyond all previous expectations. Production in the WARSEC Ventures lunar factory had just started, and Ryanair would have the first ten Space Bears delivered by the end of March. The orbital station was to open to commercial activities at the end of May, and Ryanair wanted to offer a cheap option to travel there. They would be competing with other airlines flying the Albaspace from V-Space.

The manufacturing of the first Forward class interstellar spaceship was to start on the lunar base at the end of January. If everything went according to plan, it would be put into orbit by the end of April. Then, of course, it would be followed by the integration of the compact fusion reactors and the final assembly, to be performed while anchored at the orbital station. The first interstellar ship would be fully completed by the end of June.

WARSEC was also to take over Orbit Control from the current national space agencies on the first of March. The transition was going according to plan. Even though Glover Johnson was on paternity leave to take care of his newborn daughter Rika, he had still been sending occasional emails.

One email had been to tell how great Finland was as a country to have a baby in: the healthcare authorities would just deal out a baby box to put the newborn child in, with all the necessary accessories. The Finnish healthcare system would also provide a clear a set of instructions as to how to handle a baby in order to raise it without killing it. And it was free! In fact, handling a baby in Finland was as easy as following the checklist for a nuclear strike. It was just about following designed procedures. That was awesome. Ralf, who had done his European military service in the submarines, could not help smiling at that email. Other UN diplomats may not have.

Other emails from Glover were related to the new WARSEC uniforms. In committed organizations, from hospitals to aircraft carriers, staff wore clothes of distinctive colors so that everybody knew each other's roles. Glover wanted to have the new color-coded uniforms implemented before WARSEC took over Orbit Control.

Ralf had decided to appoint Glover as the head of the Space Coordination Center, at the orbital station, and was looking forward to having him back from paternity leave. He had also promoted Tatjana Aydemir, the manufacturing director, to head of the Lunar Coordination Center, which meant she was also Head of Operations at WARSEC Ventures.

Browsing through his emails, Ralf was relieved to see that nothing unexpected had happened.

However, he was surprised to see an email from Michael Vahlroos, the CEO of Vahlroos Corporation, entitled *Merry Christmas and Happy New Year*.

Dear Ralf,

When we first met a bit more than three years ago, I remember you explaining to me the difference between idealism and realism. As 2097 ends, we can all frankly agree that realism beats idealism: Despite all the efforts deployed by the UN, the EU did invade Morocco to control the phosphate mines.

In a world characterized by the rarefaction of natural resources in a context of constant demographic growth, it was nothing but a logical and expected move.

With the Vienna Treaties and WARSEC, you naively believe that you can have all of mankind cooperate under your wing for outer space exploration and exploitation.

As the World Health Organization failed to tackle the Qatari Flu appropriately in the 2070s, your WARSEC will fail to properly tackle the next challenges put on mankind.

I think it's time for you to realize that an idealistic international UN agency such as WARSEC will lead us nowhere, or at least not far enough for this very real world.

I would, therefore, like you to reconsider the current Vienna treaties and become more open to the roles that can be played by private corporations such as Vahlroos Inc for resource extraction on celestial bodies.

Space mining should not be regulated by WARSEC and free access to it by private players should be reinforced as under the previous Moon and Space treaties. Private corporations should also be allowed to conduct interstellar exploration and exploitation missions on their own. Only then will there be enough resources for everybody to live on Earth in peace. Private corporations bring peace, while states and public authorities bring only war.

I would really like you to reconsider your entire approach.

I would also like to let you know that a Federal Court has ruled that the US Administration should question the validity of the Vienna treaties before the International Court of Justice. My lawyers and I are confident we will win as the Vienna treaties are in partial contradiction with the 1967 Outer Space Treaty and the 1979 Moon Treaty.

You are doing a great job at WARSEC. For you not to lose face, I can only recommend you steer your politics back to starboard, as port seems dangerously off course.

I wish you a merry Christmas and a happy new year, with a lot of good resolutions for 2098.

Best regards,

Michael Vahlroos
Vahlroos Corporation | CEO
Vahlroos Tower,
55bis Water St
New York, NY 10041
United States of America

Ralf read the mail twice. He was furious. He went to the kettle and made himself a cup of tea. He took a few sips before he went back to his tablet and started drafting an answer:

Dear Mr Vahlroos,

I thank you for your best wishes for the new year and wish you likewise. In geopolitics, idealists are indeed often opposed to realists, who seem to have the upper hand. In everyday life, I would rather choose to oppose 'approximators' to 'exactors'.

Approximators tend to use a great many approximations and unchecked data in their reasoning, leading their argumentation to be full of flaws. Approximators are a majority on this Earth, it seems. Sadly, approximators make most of the noise in the media. They are like a bunch of wild chihuahuas.

Exactors, on the contrary, will strive to gather all the data, check the sources, confront them and decide their opinion in a fully rational way. They are not driven by blind ideology, but by their desire to truly understand the world. They make less noise than the excited chihuahuas but may eventually succeed in calming them down.

I would like to remind you that WARSEC does not aim at stopping private initiative in space, but at regulating it. In fact, no public service organization has encouraged commercial space activities as much as we have. WARSEC Ventures associate closely with private corporations, but you refused to be involved, on ideological grounds. The orbital station will open to commercial activities in May, and you and Vahlroos Travel are one of the main stakeholders.

I would only recommend you take advantage of these last days of 2097 to decide what kind of person you want to be: an exactor or an approximator?

Best regards,

Ralf Åhman (PhD)
General Director
World's Agency for the Regulation of Space Exploration and Colonization
WARSEC Headquarters
FI- 65380 Vaasa
Finland – European Union

Ralf never used his PhD title in his signature. He was only a Swede, after all. But this time, it was time to remind Michael that he did not even have a doctorate. He read through his email one more time and tapped *send*. It always felt nice to return fire.

12: ICE AND SNOW
(JANUARY 2098)

Over the Christmas holidays, Aisha Barjaoui barely saw her boyfriend. Éric Legrand and the 27th Alpine Ranger Battalion, which had not taken part in the Moroccan invasion, was to be deployed in the mountainous ranges north of the Western Sahara. There was trouble.

The 'jolly little war' was officially over, but it seemed that never before had the EU Army been deployed overseas to the same extent as now. In her own engineer regiment, only her 2nd Company and the support company were left in Saint-Christol. The 1st Company had been sent to Morocco, while the 3rd Company had been deployed in the Caribbean and in European Guyana, where some tropical storms had caused some terrible damages at the end of the summer.

Because of the losses at Khouribga and despite the new recruits, the 2nd Company was only 90-men strong. Lt. Kowacz had been appointed acting CO and decided to organize it as a three-platoon company. With the new recruits coming, each platoon would progressively be given an extra assault squad, and eventually, they would be able to have a regular four platoon company. Aisha, as a newly commissioned lieutenant, had been put in charge of the second platoon.

The good part was that she now had her own little apartment in the base. There was more paperwork but she meant to endure it. Her plan was to stay in the 2nd Company until the summer only. Then, she would transfer to the support company and learn how to deploy field cable cars and drive earthmovers. She would take advantage of it to improve her mountaineering skills and be certified as a mountain guide. By the end of her contract in July 2100, she would be able to obtain a trade in the Alps and never ever again go to war. It was an ambitious plan.

As a lieutenant, she could decide what specific training program to impose on her platoon. There had been some snow falling in the southern Alps, and she would take her platoon to Oisan or Queyra to do some ski touring. It had been painstaking, but by the end of January, her platoon was the best on skis within the company, which was unfortunately not a feat to be so proud of, judging by the average levels of the remaining platoons.

Another advantage of being an officer was that she could decide that for some weekend exercises she would take only volunteers, as Lt. Hoffman used to do. That way, they could take the army equipment and vehicles and do some extra skiing, or even ice climbing.

On that last weekend of January 2098, Lt. Barjaoui suggested an ice climbing exercise in Queyra. The weather was horrible, and only Corporal Eriksen from 3rd Platoon volunteered. The Norwegian legionnaire also wanted to improve his mountaineering skills.

As they were driving to *Les Oules*, Aisha wished that Corporal Tran were still alive. She remembered their assault up the ice cliff in Kirghizstan. Éric had led the climb and Tran and she had only prusiked themselves up. Now would be the chance to do some actual ice climbing.

After parking the car, they put their harnesses on and took their rucksacks with ropes, slings, ice screws, carabiners, ice axes, and helmets. It was snowing, and the cloud ceiling was so low it was impossible to see the ice cliffs from the parking lot.

"Ça m'a l'air pommatoire, tout ça. ['It seems hard to find the way, over here.']" Torbjørn commented in his now excellent French. "I hope we won't get lost."

They walked their way up in the snow among the trees and eventually found their way to the start of the ice cliff. They took the two ropes out of their rucksacks and tied both of them to their harnesses. They put their climbing helmets on and went through the ice screws and slings.

The falling snow became rain.

"*Oh, putain!*" ['Fuck!'], Aisha sowre, "OK, we hurry to the top and come back to the car. It's only five pitches."

They put their crampons on, sitting on their rucksacks. They finally stood up on the ice, put on their bag pack and went for the cliff.

"*Sikring klar,*" *['Climb when ready']* Torbjørn said in Norwegian after checking the ropes were correctly set in his belaying device.

"*OK, je grimpe,*" Aisha replied in French ('Climbing').

She started to hack her way up, dragging herself on the ice axes while making long and decisive steps with her crampons.

She loved it. She was standing five meters (16 ft) above Torbjørn when she placed the first ice screw, clipped a quickdraw into it and then into the rope.

Easy peasy. She was in total control. The climb gave her a sense of total freedom. She did not mind the rain, nor the clouds. What a pity Éric was in Western Sahara and not with her! Why would they send Alpine rangers to the desert in the first place?

"*Bout de corde!*" she heard Torbjørn yell ('End of rope.').

It was time to install a belay station. As she was standing comfortably on her crampons, she used an ice screw to pierce two double V-holes in the ice. She cut some cords, and for each of the two V-holes, she passed a string through it and tied it with a double fisherman's knot. With one sling and three carabiners, she finished the belay station and tied her two ropes into the master locker carabiner, using a clove-hitch knot.

"*Vachée!*" she yelled back to Torbjørn ('On belay!').

She clipped her belaying device into the belay station, passed the two ropes into it and started belaying Torbjørn: "Climb when ready."

He had a good pace and took only ten minutes to do the fifty meters (165 ft) to the belay station. When he arrived, he had retrieved all the ice screws Aisha had placed.

"You do the next pitch?" Aisha asked.

"Sure, lieutenant," Torbjørn replied,

Torbjørn Eriksen went on immediately for the next pitch, placing ice screws as he climbed. Fifteen minutes later, Aisha heard: "*Relai, vaché!*" ('On belay!')

She unlocked the ropes from her belaying device. When she felt that the rope was tight, she retrieved the carabiners and slings used on her belay and started climbing.

They did a small break at the end of the second pitch.

"It's starting to rain a lot," Torbjørn noted. "That means it's plus degrees. The ice will be getting weaker."

"We are in the shadow," Aisha replied, "I don't think there is a risk."

"Still," Torbjørn said, "There was a section where I was a bit scared. The ice was breaking apart."

"If you want, I can lead the rest," Aisha said.

"I know: I'm a pussy and Donald's gonna come and grab me," Torbjørn admitted, "But I think we should abseil down."

"If you want to see a quitter, look at Norway," Aisha teased him. "OK, I go, you belay me."

Twenty meters (66 ft) above Torbjørn's belay station, Aisha regretted what she had said. She had put five ice screws, but only the first one seemed to hold. Now, the ice was just scrambling apart, and there was nowhere to put an additional screw.

"*Putain!*" she yelled, "*La glace est toute merdique.*" ('Fuck! The ice is completely shitty.')

It was impossible to go further up, but she could not retreat. She was four meters above the last ice screws. If she fell, she was certain the ice screw would not hold.

"*Putain! Putain! Putain! Bordel de merde!*" she swore. ('Fuck! Fuck! Fuck! Fucking shit!')

She started to feel her right leg shake.

She took a deep breath and exhaled.

She had to calm down. Her leg stopped shaking.

Three meters to her right, slightly above, there was a large tree, on the sides of the ice cascade. She would reach it and put a sling around it.

She could make it. She would make it.

"I go for a tree," she yelled to Torbjørn.

She hacked her right ice axe far to the right. It was a good grip. She held it and pulled her body toward it. She hacked her left ice axe just above it and matched hands on the ice axe properly set into the ice. She took the other ice axe with her right hand again, and tried to probe for another good spot to hack herself further to the right. It was only crumbling ice.

"*Merde! Merde! Merde!*" ('Shit! Shit! Shit!')

Then she heard a crack.

The ice, where her only holding ice axe was set, was cracking.

In despair, she cast her right hand up in an attempt to hack her right ice axe into a better spot further to the right.

It was not a better spot.

She fell.

"*Et merde!*" were the last words she said.

Fear struck her in the fall as she saw her last screw pop out of the ice. The second last ice screw also popped out, and so did the third. By then Aisha was so gripped by fear that she was not feeling anything. She was being bumped against the ice cliff, but it was painless. It was like being trapped in a washing machine, and she suddenly felt completely detached. She did not care.

She eventually felt a huge pain in her legs and then in her back and hip.

She took some time to regain some kind of awareness.

She was now hanging on the rope below, far below the belay where Torbjørn was. Somehow, the belay station and the first ice screw had held.

She must have had a concussion as she was not completely aware of the situation. It seemed she was now being hauled down. Someone was yelling. It took time for her to make out what was being said.

"Aisha," Torbjørn yelled, "When you see the first belay's Abalakov, clip yourself into it. Clip into the first belay."

She spotted the V-threads she had installed. She took two quickdraws and clipped them at one end on her harness, and at the other end into one of the V-threads.

She then untied the two climbing ropes from her harness.

"*Clear,*" she yelled. "Abseil down on it."

Meanwhile, she put a sling around the other Abalakov and clipped it as well into her harness.

She felt stiff in the back and had pain in the legs. She had fallen at least thirty-five meters (115 ft) before the ropes had stopped her! No wonder.

She looked beneath her. She was only fifty meters (165 ft) from the ground. Torbjørn would just haul her down and then abseil down. Then, easy to the car.

Something caught her attention. It was blood. Blood dripping down on the ice from her military pants.

Putain! ('Fuck!'). She was bleeding a lot. Looking at her legs, they did not seem right. Completely crooked. She tried to move them, but they remained lifeless.

Fuck! Fuck! Fuck! *Putain de bordel de merde!*

She took her Swiss army knife out of her pocket and tore apart her pants.

The horror! It seemed that she had hit one of her left knees with her right crampons in the fall. Her right leg was completely smashed. Bones were sticking out of it, and it seemed only flesh was holding the leg together.

"*Bordel!*" she yelled.

The right leg was bleeding most. She took a prusik loop, put it around her thigh, clipped it into a locking carabiner and twisted it until it was tight enough to stop the bleeding. She used the carabiner to make it hold. The other leg was also bleeding.

She did the same operation with her other prusik. Where was Torbjørn? He was taking time to repel! She remembered she had a radio in her rucksack. She took it out. 121.5 MHz was the emergency channel frequency.

"*Allo allo, Urgence en montagne. Lt Barjaoui 2*ème *REG,*" she called.

"*Allo, ici relaie 179.*"

"Climbing accident *aux Houles* under a military exercise. The victim has two legs broken with heavy bleeding. Giving first aid. Need immediate evacuation."

"Noted. We send you an ambulance by road. Expect maximum one hour. Helicopters can't fly in this weather."

"Copy that. Over and out," Aisha answered.

"*Et merde,*" she added for herself. ('And shit'!)

"What is it?"

It was Torbjørn. He had abseiled down to her level and was attaching himself to the belay station.

"I've got my legs pretty fucked" Aisha replied. "Still not

feeling much pain because of the stress, but it's nasty. No chopper to the rescue. Ambulance in one hour."

"Then we'd better move our asses," Torbjørn replied.

He called back the ropes. Then, he put a quick link in one of the Abalakov strings. Keeping the two ropes tied together, he attached one end to Aisha's harness, had the rope go through the quick link and passed it into his belaying device. He unclipped Aisha from the belay and started hauling her down. She screamed in pain as she bumped on some sections of the ice cliff, but finally reached the ground and untied the rope from her harness.

Torbjørn then put his belaying device through the two ropes, unclipped himself from the belay station and abseiled down.

At the foot of the cliff, he took off his and Aisha's crampons, left the ropes hanging and put Aisha on his shoulders to carry her down to the car.

"My ice axes," Aisha complained. "I have lost my private ice axes. They are expensive."

"I will come back to look for them," Torbjørn replied, somewhat irritated by Aisha's sense of priority.

"*Oh putain, ça fait mal!*" she yelled. ('Fuck, it hurts!')

As she had calmed down, she now felt the pain grow to some unbearable level throughout her body. She eventually passed out, while she was still on Torbjørn's back.

When Aisha finally regained her full consciousness, she realized she was lying in a bed in a hospital room. She was alone in her room. Her back was hurting, and so were her legs.

"*Putain*, it hurts," she moaned.

A male nurse came by.

"We tried to give you more morphine, but you kept throwing it up. We had to keep the dose lower."

"How bad is it?" she asked.

"Wait, I will call the doctor," the nurse said, and disappeared out of the room.

A moment later, the nurse came back with a short lady wearing a white blouse. She sat down beside her bed and smiled.

"Listen, Aisha," she said. "I have something difficult to tell you."

And then she knew. The doctor explained nonetheless. They had had to amputate her right leg, right above her knee. Then, she was told that her left leg had also been amputated, right below the knee. Were they serious? She was sure she had stopped the bleeding. She had. But the damage had been serious, and it had been a few hours before she could be operated on. There had been no operation room available at the Briançon hospital, and they had had to drive her here, to Gap. The doctor was really sorry.

When left alone, Aisha started to cry. Her parents had been killed. Her first serious lover in Morocco had been killed. Half of her squad had perished in Khouribga, not to mention

Rheinfeldt and Singh having been badly wounded. Lt Hoffman had been killed. Sgt. Uwil had died at the hospital. Morocco had been invaded for no really good reasons. The only joy she had left in life was mountaineering, and the dream of becoming a mountain guide. It was gone.

Was God so great? My ass! God, was a great asshole. He or She was an egoistic asshole who did not give a shit about mankind. Fuck, God! Fuck all these assholes who believed in God. How could she have been stupid enough to believe?

"God, you're a stupid asshole son of a bitch," she screamed when she was alone in her room. "If you disapprove of my loathing you, come and strike me with your lightning!"

She waited. Nothing happened.

Then what she thought was that God did not exist. At best. At worst, He or She was an asshole.

The following day, Aisha was transferred to the military hospital in Lyon, southeast France. There, an orderly informed her that her regiment's colonel had put in a request that she become a European citizen.

Oh great! That way she would not be evicted to Morocco! That was the least she could expect, after her service, she thought.

She would still have the opportunity to work in the Legion, the orderly added. The colonel could use her as an intelligence officer to her regiment. Aisha welcomed the offer and replied that she would think about it during the convalescence period.

When the orderly went away, Aisha was glad to recognize a familiar voice.

"Hi Aisha"

It was Karen Brown, who had been her platoon's medic until her service ended eighteen months earlier. Slightly taller than Aisha, Karen had short brown hair and deep brown eyes.

"Hi, Karen. Still at Med school?"

"Well, it's nine years long, and I started only one and a half years ago," she replied. "But I passed my first year. So... a climbing accident."

"Yes, I guess my mountaineering years are over. I am not even twenty."

"Don't say that, Aisha. We will have you learn how to use artificial legs, how to walk with them, run with them, climb with them and to ski on them."

"Do you believe in that?"

"Of course. There are even some specially designed legs to help you cheating when climbing. You could be a better climber than before."

"But not an Alpine ranger."

"Well, there have been some Alpine rangers with artificial legs. Though always with one artificial leg, not two, to be honest."

Over the following week-ends she received the visits of Torbjørn Eriksen, and even Jean-Claude Rheinfeldt, who came a few times.

Her boyfriend Éric was still in Western Sahara. She had informed him of the accident by email. It took a few weeks before she finally got a reply. She was devastated.

In his reply, Éric explained that he wanted to take a break from their relationship. He wanted to focus on his career and try to be selected for the human intelligence platoon, the elite outfit of the Mountain and Arctic Warfare Division.

"*Connard*!" ('Asshole!') she messaged back. She would certainly have been overwhelmed if it had not been for Karen's company.

During the last week of February, she received an unexpected visit. She was reading an article about the drone incident at Khouribga in *The Chained Palmiped* when she heard a familiar voice.

"Crazy story, huh?"

It was Captain Léger. His face was barely recognizable, it was so severely burnt.

"*Mon capitaine*!" she exclaimed.

"Only Antoine, Aisha. I'm not in the army any more. I thought I would check on you. You are reading about the investigation into the drone incident."

"Yes."

"Crazy. It was just an old piece of software someone had installed. It had not been properly logged, and no one remembered it."

"But what a vicious program," Aisha replied, "Designed to have a drone shoot at everything that moves when in doubt. Meaning, when the communication lines are scrambled, and the drone is feared to be lost."

"The program could only be activated when a drone was set in 'war mode', which it was in Khouribga. A pity everybody had forgotten about that program."

"Happy that the international investigation was properly made," said Aisha. "But still, those who coded that program were a bunch of assholes."

"Or just a bunch of developers waiting for their paycheck and not pondering over the consequences of their actions."

Aisha laid the newspaper on her bed and looked at her badly burnt ex-captain. She smiled and said: "How are you doing, sir? I mean... Antoine."

"Well, I'm alive," Antoine Léger replied." That's the most important. Then I can walk and even jog. My leg still hurts if I try to run. Of course, I am unemployed, and my face is so badly burned that I not only scare employers away but also any girl I try to talk to."

"Well, I'm still employed, it seems. But I can neither walk nor run," Aisha replied. "However, I also seem to scare guys away."

"Éric?"

"Over," she replied.

"Well, that's too bad." Antoine replied, "I came here because I think you ought to watch a movie. If you have time, I can connect my tablet to the TV.

Antoine switched on the TV. It was the closing ceremony of the Winter Olympic Games in Kathmandu.

"The Winter Olympics are boring," he commented. "Norwegians always get all the medals."

"Yeah, I know," Aisha replied. "When Torbjørn was here last weekend, he had his eyes glued on the TV."

He synchronized the TV with his tablet and played the movie. It was called *Reach for the Sky*. At the beginning of the movie, a text informed the viewers:

The story of this movie is set between 1928 and 1945. Back then, the world population was about 2 billion. In 2098, the world population is about 10.5 billion.

It was an old black and white movie about an English fighter pilot, Douglas Bader, who had lost his both legs in an aerobatic maneuver. As World War Two broke out, he somehow managed to be reinstated in the Royal Air Force, where he became an ace, before being shot down in France and captured by the Germans.

"If only I could become a pilot when I am out of the hospital, instead of doing some crappy paperwork in an office," Aisha commented when the movie was over.

"You could," Antoine answered. "That's why I showed you that movie."

"What do you mean?"

"You will be granted French and European citizenship by the middle of March, I have been told. That means you can apply to the Air Force Academy in Cranwell as soon as this spring. It's a competition exam. Academic tests scheduled at the end of May, physiological and physical tests scheduled in July."

"Academic test? I never finished high school."

"You don't have to have. I remember you told me you had good grades. Believe me, most fighter pilots are not as smart as you are. The question is more: will you pass the physical tests? It's not as tough as the Legion, but as far as I can see you have been lying in your bed for almost five weeks now."

"They told me I will start my re-education next week. I will be as good as Douglas Bader. I will be able to walk by the end of the first day."

"You will be better than Douglas Bader," Antoine Léger replied. "In the movie, they show him as a cool guy, and he was certainly a good leader. But he was also an asshole who supported apartheid in South Africa."

Aisha smiled.

"Then I will be better than Douglas Bader," she said.

13: THE FORWARD CLASS (APRIL 2098)

The first months of 2098 had gone beyond Ralf Åhman's most optimistic expectations. Both the Space Bear and the Space Hound had been certified by the FAA and the EASA, by the middle of February. The first exemplars of Space Bear had been delivered to Ryanair at the beginning of April and there were large pending orders from both the EU Air Force and the US Air Force. The US president wanted a Cargo Space Bear to transport her limos and motorcade support helicopters, while she would keep the Albaspace as her Air Force One.

As an aerospace shuttle, the Space Bear could not only reach the orbital station in eight hours but also reach anywhere on earth within maximum two hours.

WARSEC Ventures and its manufacturing on the moon were at last successful, and money would soon be cashed in. This would enable WARSEC to finance its expansion and the first interstellar missions.

Space Hound
(WARSEC Ventures)

Space Bear
(WARSEC Ventures)

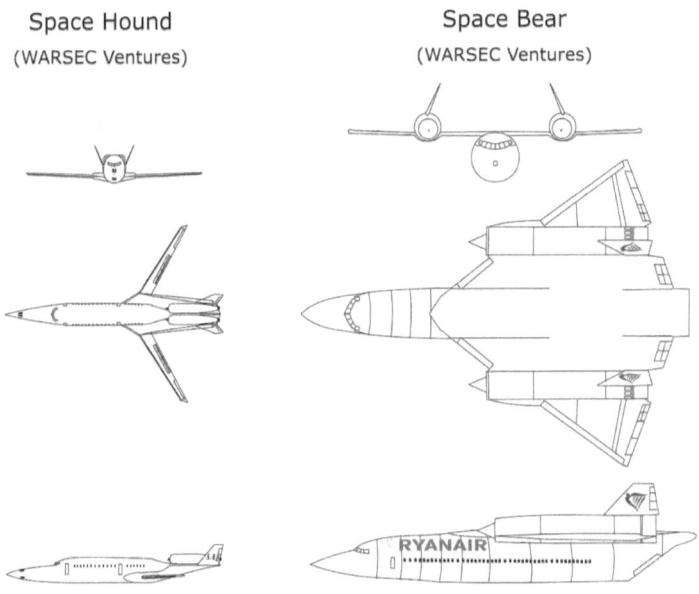

Figure 7: the Space Hound (originally a Boeing project) here with Scandinavian Airlines logo and the Space Bear (originally an Airbus Project) here with the Ryanair logo. Both logos are the propriety of the respective airline companies.

WARSEC had also successfully taken over Orbit Control as 1st of April 2098, and no incident had happened. The opening of the orbital station had been pulled forward to the Easter weekend, and this had become a major event, as not only premium airlines, but also Ryanair would be flying there for the occasion.

Meanwhile, the manufacturing of the *Forward*, the first interstellar ship, had been carried on without any significant delay. It was now planned to put it into the lunar orbit during the Easter weekend, under the gaze of VIPs from all around the world. It was a way to boost space tourism and, on that front, Ralf had a common understanding with Michael Vahlroos and his space tourism company, Vahlroos Travel.

Glover Johnson had been back from paternity leave since 7 April, and had been rather satisfied that everything had gone so smoothly while he was away. WARSEC personnel were already wearing the clothes with the agreed color codes.

On 15 April, both Ralf and Glover had been summoned before the 4th committee of the UN General Assembly in New York to answer questions regarding the opening of the orbital station. Once again, it could have been done over a video-conference, but diplomats liked shaking each other's hands, a bit like dogs like sniffing each other's buttocks, Ralf smiled ironically.

On 17 April, just before the Easter weekend, they found themselves boarding an Albaspace from NASA at New York JFK, together with the UN secretary-general, other diplomats, and a lot of VIPs. Everybody wanted to be in the orbital station for its commercial inauguration by UN secretary-general Hira Dorjee-Sherpa, she who, less than seven months earlier, had been badly treated by the European Union.

"*Passengers and crew. We will now initiate the gravity escape maneuver. You may want to put your noise-cancelling headset on. You will now be exposed to an unpleasant volume of noise and a force of up to 2.5-G for 20 minutes.*"

It was either the captain or the first officer who had talked over the intercom.

"I still don't like the scramjet and rocket part", Ralf said to Glover. "I hope it will be OK for the SG. It's her first time in space."

"She will do just fine," Glover replied, adjusting his headset and microphone. "It's safe and easy space travel, nowadays. We don't have to wear escape suits anymore."

"You are right. Only these colored fireproof jumpsuits."

Glover Johnson was wearing a flashy green jumpsuit, with the WARSEC insignia on his right shoulder, while Ralf, who was sitting next to him at the rear of the shuttle was wearing a purple suit with a UN insignia.

"From the moment we open the space station to civilians, tourists, and commercial activities, we have to be able to recognize each other, do we?" Glover replied.

He looked around. Only Glover wore green. Some of the passengers wore purple suits but most of them plain civilian clothes.

The Albaspace had taken off twenty minutes earlier and reached the altitude of 20,000 meters (65,000 ft), shooting through the sky at Mach 6, with its four CUBIC-R engines in ramjet configuration. The speed was now fast enough for the shuttle to ignite its scramjet, and it suddenly accelerated to Mach 14. The pilot was soon slowly steering the shuttle upward, and Ralf could feel how much heavier he had got. Why had he gained five kilos since Christmas? He glanced at Glover and envied the black ex-admiral, who was always fit and athletic and never seemed to gain a single gram of fat. Ralf, for his part, was always either gaining or losing weight. He seemed unable to just maintain.

"Everything is ready for the inauguration of the civilian rings of the orbital station?" Glover asked Ralf. "I have had my head in baby diapers since October, so I'm not completely updated."

"The station is ready," Ralf answered. "Both the Radisson and Sheraton have been fully operational since last week. It has already been used by some WARSEC Ventures workers and their families. This is only a formal inauguration. A short speech and a trip around the Moon for some VIPs to show them the *Forward*."

"What about the *Forward*? Ready to leave the moon?"

"She has been ready for one week already," Ralf replied. "The assembly time has been cut to 11 weeks. The next phase is to place her in orbit for the last few steps of the integration. It's been hard for Tatjana and her team to have wait for the official inauguration of the space station. They don't like this kind of politics."

"Well, few people always do what they like", Glover retorted.

Ralf smiled. He did not smile for long. An instant later the Space Bear switched the configuration of its CUBIC-R engines to rocket mode and roared vertically into the mesosphere. The Albaspace had no window, but he could see the sky darken on the TV screens. He switched his reader light on and grabbed his newspaper. It was *The Chained Palmiped*.

"Anything interesting in it?" Glover said in his microphone.

"Same old," Ralf replied. "Last year's invasion of Morocco. How President Bonavita had planned to invade Morocco whatever the outcome of the negotiations may be. How the European Military Intelligence Service quietly encouraged the prompt execution of the Moroccan king. And some lines about the killer drone incident at Khouribga."

"What about it?" Glover asked.

"Nothing new," Ralf answered. "The UN inquiry is formally over. At least the UN is now driving an international treaty to ban killer robots."

Ten minutes later the rocket engine shut off and all passengers welcomed this liberating silence. They were now in weightlessness.

"This part, I like," said Ralf, unstrapping himself from his seat. "I'll go to the front and check on the SG."

Ralf floated to the front of the cabin. The Albaspace shuttle was full of diplomats, politicians, business people, and tourists experiencing weightlessness for the first time. Most of them were smiling and laughing. Ralf managed to fly past them and reached Hira, who was sitting next to her husband, a short Nepalese working as Mountain guide and climbing instructor. Both were peering at their screens and smiling. She had her earGlasses on this time. The batteries seemed to be loaded.

"Madame secretary-general," Ralf said. "How do you like weightlessness?"

"Quite pleasant, Ralf," she answered.

"I'm glad your glasses are working this time, Hira," Ralf said. "We will orbit the Earth a dozen times before we reach the orbital station in seven hours and a dozen minutes."

"Eight hours from New York to the orbital station," she answered. "It's closer than Nepal."

Ralf floated back to his seat at the rear and sat back beside Glover. He was looking at his TV screen.

"What are you looking at?" Ralf asked.

"The Earth," Glover answered. "10.5 billion souls onboard and counting. Not enough resources for the human population to make it through the twenty-second century."

"Well," Ralf replied. "If mankind gets better at sharing resources, they may be OK."

"Our daughter, Rika," Glover went on. "She will soon be six months old. There is a decent chance she'll live until 2190, or even perhaps until 2200. How will the world be by then?"

"It should still be there," Ralf answered

"The Earth will be there for the next four billion years, indeed. But what about mankind? Scarce resources, potential risk for global cooling, or even super-volcanoes."

"You are reading too much Sheldon Cooper," Ralf replied.

"15 years ago, 2% of geologists thought he may be right. Now 40% believe him. A century ago, it took some time for scientists to believe in global warming."

"Well, if Dr. Cooper is right, the survival of mankind will depend on whether interstellar migration is possible".

"What if interstellar exploration is a failure?" Glover wondered. "What if there are no habitable planets within a reasonable range? Optimism cannot make habitable planets that don't exist. We can't cheat the random functions of the universe."

Ralf looked long at Glover. Being a father seemed to have changed him. Before he was mainly focused on safety, now he also seemed genuinely concerned about the future of mankind. Ralf had expected to enjoy the Easter weekend in the orbital station and did not want to be sunk in a pessimistic mood. He smiled at Glover and said: "Don't worry. We have Tintin Mutombo. He is a hell of a physicist. He believes that within fifty years we'll be able to build spacecraft that will warp 5,000 times the speed of light. That will increase our migration range. Statistically, we should at least find one habitable planet within

ASH GAWAIN

this range, shouldn't we, Glover?

"Unless we are on the wrong side of the statistics," Glover replied.

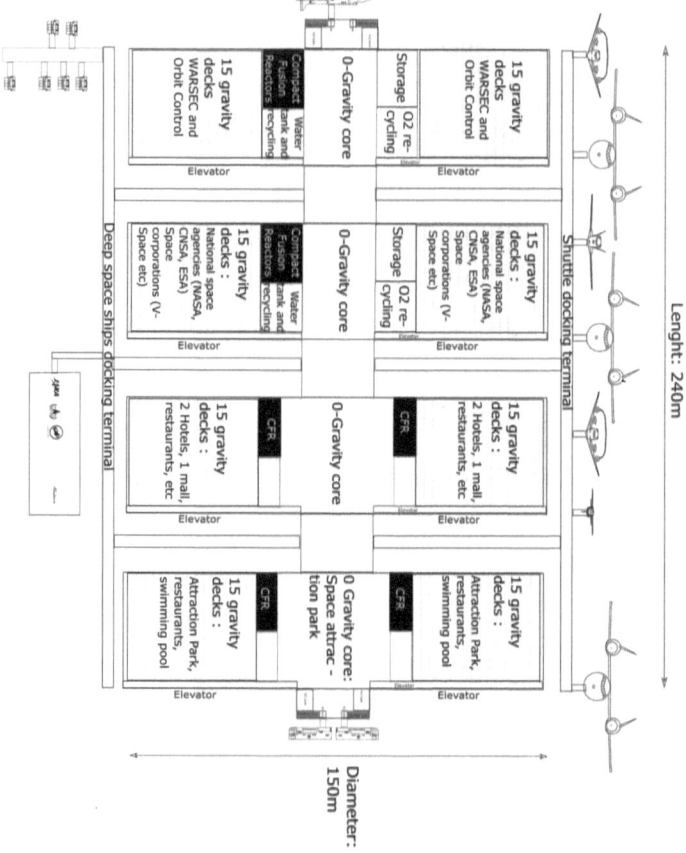

Figure 8: The orbital station in April 2098, with two extra gravitational rings dedicated to commercial activities.

The Albaspace docked at the orbital station a few hours later, and the passengers were led through a long, pipe-like corridor to the core of the station. They would just seize a handle attached to a slowly moving 'speedwalk' (or rather 'speedfloat') and be pulled in weightlessness to the core of the station. There, WARSEC personnel were redirected to the WARSEC habitable ring while other passengers were directed to the civilian rings were the hotels were located.

Ralf's children, Dag and Eleonore, accompanied by their mother Solveig and her latest boyfriend, were spending the Easter weekend in the station as tourists. They had come on a Ryanair flight via London. Ralf picked them up at the Radisson hotel and showed them around. While Solveig and her boyfriend would spend a romantic weekend, Ralf would take care of his kids. That was part of the deal.

The official inauguration of the commercial rings of the station was scheduled for Friday 18 April at 14:00 UTC. Before the UN secretary-general was to cut the red ribbon, she, together with Ralf and Glover, held a conference in the station's concert hall.

It was located on the outer deck (deck 15) of the outer civilian ring. It also encroached on decks 14, 13 and 12 because of its 12-meter (40 ft) height, opposed to the standard three-meter (10 ft) standard deck height. It was fifty meters (164 ft) long and thirty-six meters (118 ft) wide with an obvious concave floor and convex ceiling.

As Ralf was standing on the podium, he had a weird feeling, as if the auditors sitting furthest away were almost disappearing behind the convex ceiling. Had it been lower, the auditors on the last row would not have been able to see him. His children were sitting in the fifth row together with Tintin, the tall Congolese theoretical physicist. Close to them, he spotted Michael Vahlroos and Sophie Couillard.

Michael was casting evil glances at Tintin, but the latter kept smiling back at the CEO. Vahlroos Travel owned the hotels being leased to Radisson, Sheraton, and the Space Motel, the cheap hotel mainly targeting Ryanair customers. The space attraction park was also the propriety of Vahlroos Travel and they were planning to open a Space Casino and a Space Spa within the next six years. Both Michael and Sophie had naturally been invited to the inauguration.

Hira Dorjee-Sherpa first welcomed the audience and noted that this orbital station was a step toward international cooperation, not only between states but also between public service and private corporations. She thanked all private partners for being part of the space adventure. Without them, space exploration would not be possible.

There were some special acknowledgments to Airbus, Boeing, and Comac for their partnership with WARSEC Ventures. Ryanair was thanked for making travel to the station affordable to the less wealthy and, of course, Vahlroos Travel was shown warm gratitude for making the opening of the orbital station to commercial activities even possible. NASA was not forgotten for their EM-drive modules, into which aerospace shuttles and White Parrots could dock in order to travel faster between the Moon and the Earth.

The following day, an excursion to the Moon was organized onboard a few Space Bears, and a couple of Albaspaces made available by Vahlroos Travel. The participants would have the opportunity to see the new interstellar ship, the *Forward*, be put into the orbit of the moon and ferried to the Earth's orbit for the last step of her integration.

Hira then gave the floor to Glover Johnson, who introduced himself as the new head of the Space Coordination Center and the ex-Global Safety Director. That was why he wore a flashy green suit.

"As most of you know," Glover explained," in complex and committed organizations, members wore clearly distinctive colors so that their area of responsibility could be evidently identified. This is the case onboard navy ships, but also within hospitals and even retirement homes. Here in space, it is even more important that people with a clear area of responsibility and different set of skills wear distinctive colors. Green is the color of safety specialists. All personnel wearing flashy green are trained to organize a proper evacuation of the station if needed. Always follow their orders if any. Blue is for the medical team, also highly trained in terms of space safety. Orange is for our engineers. You can also rely on them for safety. Never block their way, as their intervention somewhere could be vital for the safety of all. Dark green is for space construction and mining. They are equally trained as engineers with extra safety skills on celestial bodies such as the Moon. Light blue is for scientists, while red is for the R&D department. They have some basic safety skills, but could not lead an evacuation. Finally, in purple, you have the WARSEC administration and the flight controllers of Orbit Control. The majority of them have no safety skills, but a whole set of other useful skills for all of us."

There was some laughter. A journalist rose her hand.

"What about the pilots?" she asked.

"Yes," Glover replied. "I forgot the pilots and navigators. They wear pink."

"According to some rumors," the journalist added, "Pink was chosen for pilots to discourage male supremacists from the air forces of this world to apply to WARSEC. What do you have to answer to that?"

"Those spreading these rumors are overthinking", Glover replied. "The colors were perhaps not the result of the random functions of the universe, but at least the result of a *randomize* function in a Microsoft Excel spreadsheet. If some male supremacist pilots are unhappy wearing pink, they should complain to Microsoft."

There was some new laughter in the concert hall.

"However," Glover added, "there had been some studies showing that pilots not caring about the colors they wear are more likely to follow security procedures than others. This matters to us. The Conquest of the West was perhaps the feat of cowboys. The Conquest of Space is the feat of nerds. Nerds are fine with wearing pink."

There was some more laughter, and Glover gave the word to Ralf Åhman, who introduced himself as the WARSEC director.

Ralf explained that the current WARSEC budget was only 20% of that of NASA. Half of it came from the contributions of member states, the rest from the tax levied on space activities, such as the fees on satellite and orbital flights, as well as the corporation tax on space profits. In short, boosting commercial activities in space was necessary for WARSEC to finance interstellar exploration.

They also generated income through WARSEC Ventures and the sales of aerospace shuttles to private airlines.

"And to air forces around the world," a journalist added. "Do you think it is right for a UN agency to earn money on sales made to the US Air Force and the EU Air Force?"

Ralf had long expected this question, and had been struggling with his conscience quite a lot, but it was not his role to show his doubts in public. He decided to answer like a true diplomat:

"The Space Bear will be used by air forces only as a transport aircraft. The US president will use a couple of them to transport her motorcade when traveling abroad."

His answer did not satisfy the journalist, who retorted: "The US Air Force and the EU Air Force have together ordered more than five hundred Space Bears. You talked a lot about Ryanair, but you will generate most of your income over the next six years on sales made to armed forces. According to my calculations, next year, the WARSEC budget will already be 80% of that of NASA, and you do not have as expensive a research program as they do."

Ralf knew their budget would increase significantly, and that was even the point of WARSEC Ventures. He looked at the inquisitive journalist and replied: "We have to finance interstellar exploration. 80% of the NASA budget for five years will allow us to send exploration missions to Alpha Centauri and other star systems nearby."

"Even it means earning your money on the armies of this world?" the same journalist insisted.

Ralf took a deep breath and answered as a politician would: "We are not responsible for what armed forces do with the aerospace shuttles they acquire, but I would like to remind you that most of the time, military transport is what is first deployed in the event of natural catastrophes, which have been on the rise lately. Military transport is primarily meant to save lives."

Another journalist raised her hand and asked: "What about the manufacturing of your aerospace shuttles on the Moon?

The ILO treaty does not apply to international territory, and robots are therefore not taxed in your lunar assembly lines. Don't you think you are doing social dumping?"

Ralf looked at Michael Vahlroos, who was smiling.

The WARSEC director was now used to this kind of politics and calmly replied: "No, I don't. Currently, we are not driving any unfair competition in a contracting market but are expanding the total market size of aerospace shuttles. Mr. Vahlroos sitting here will confirm that the V-Space has been benefiting from the market growth due to the inauguration of this station, and the sales of their Albaspace are also soaring. I came here in an Albaspace from New York, and I want to congratulate V-Space for manufacturing a shuttle more comfortable than the Space Bear or the Space Hound."

"You're welcome, WARSEC," Michael shouted, showing his fingers in a V.

There was some laughter in the room.

"Talking about Michael Vahlroos", the journalist went on, "The US government has now formally asked the International Court of Justice to examine the legality of the Vienna Treaties. They believe it is a breach of the former Moon Treaty, which stated that no international organization could own resources on the Moon."

"The Moon Treaty dated from 1979 and was, frankly, inadequate to the current situation," Ralf replied. "I am looking forward to the ruling of the International Court of Justice, but

I do not expect any surprise on that front."

"What outcome do you expect?"

"I don't want to spoil anything," Ralf replied. "Besides, the international judges at the ICJ are paid well enough to give a ruling without needing me to whisper the answers. Please ask them when the judgement comes."

There was some more laughter in the room, and the guests were invited to proceed into the lifts to reach the 0-G core. Hira was to cut a red ribbon in front of the attraction park.

As they were floating to the entrance of the 0-G attraction park, Michael, who was holding a bottle of champagne, stalked the WARSEC director for a while and said: "Ralf Åhman, you're good. You're so damned good that one could even believe you believe in your bullshit."

In front of the attraction park, Hira cut a red ribbon to great applause. To everybody's astonishment, Michael opened the bottle of champagne, and drops of bubbling wine were propelled away in weightlessness.

"Now you can just float towards them if you want to drink it," Michael said, and there was some cheering.

To Ralf's dismay, both Dag and Eleonore managed to swallow some drops of champagne. He was happy Solveig failed to see it.

Ralf took his kids to the Attraction Park and Tintin Mutombo, in his red jumpsuit, went with them. Tintin was like a kid anyway. Who would imagine this tall, light-skinned Congolese had won the 2095 Nobel Prize in Physics? They played some 0-G Quidditch with specially designed broomsticks, but their team was beaten by some Boeing engineers, who were also behaving like grown-up kids.

The following morning, the UN secretary-general, Glover, Ralf, and his kids boarded one of the first Space Bears to actually belong to WARSEC.

With them were the three main architects behind warp propulsion. Tintin, of course, but also his former supervisor at Moscow University, Anatoli Govorov, a tall, hefty Russian with short brown hair and blue eyes, who had shared the 2095 Nobel Prize in Physics for the *Unified Gravity Theory* with Tintin. Alice Fù, a slim, dark-haired Afro-Asian lady of medium height and recipient of the 2095 Novel Prize in Chemistry, had been the inventor of the green matter. This exotic matter had negative-energy attributes on the quantum scale and could be used by a spaceship to warp spacetime and travel faster than light. All three scientists wore red jumpsuits.

Unlike the Albaspace, the Space Bear had windows, and it was nice to be able to see the Earth and the Moon from the window. Both Dag and Eleonore were peering through the window with wide-open eyes.

As he sat down close to them, Anatoli took a little brown dog out of his jumpsuit. Glover, who sat in the row behind next to Tintin and Alice, was irritated at the sight of the canine.

"Couldn't you have left that space bitch at home?" he asked Anatoli.

"First of all, she is called Calypso," the Russian physicist replied. "Second of all, as the first warp-speed traveler, she is entitled to follow me wherever I want."

"I don't know who decided this rule," Glover grumbled.

"Hush, this is sensitive," Tintin remarked. "Anatoli has just been permanently dumped by his girlfriend for a New Zealander biologist."

"A biologist!" Anatoli lamented. "Why did she have to leave me for a biologist? From New-Zealand, moreover. A geologist or a geophysicist could have been OK. But biologists are killers. They spend their time killing animals."

"Look", Eleonore said pointing at the dog. "Calypso is pooping".

Though Eleonore had just turned six and Dag was about to turn eight, they could speak quite good English when they wanted to.

"0-gravity pooping", Anatoli commented. "It can be really tricky. The poop can be expelled pretty far and pretty fast. Better be ready".

He grabbed a plastic bag from his pocket, opened it and swiftly captured the floating shit as it was propelled from the kokoni dog's bottom.

"Yuh," Dag said, grimacing.

"There are journalists onboard, not to mention the secretary-general", Ralf said with a distaste. "It will be in the next issue of *The Chained Palmiped*".

A moment later, the pilot informed that the Space Bear was docked into one of the modular EM-drives. The modular EM-drive consisted of two compact fusion reactors powering an electromagnetic drive, the whole thing the size of a truck container. Space shuttles could dock their noses into one of them and use them to be pushed backward, propelled by the drive's electromagnetic waves. This was more efficient and faster than using chemical propulsion.

The Space Bear orbited several times around the Earth while accelerating. After ninety minutes of orbiting at full speed around the Earth, they were finally catapulted toward the Moon.

During the long journey, Anatoli irritated Ralf by telling his two kids how big an issue farting in the orbital station was. Both Dag and Eleonore had indeed noted that everybody was farting all the time in both the station and the aerospace shuttles. This was due to pressure, Anatoli explained. In order to speed up the time for astronauts to put on a space sorties suit, the orbital station's pressure had been decreased to 70% of a normal atmosphere. Of course, the oxygen concentration had been increased so that passengers felt as if they were at 2,000 meters (6,500 ft) altitude rather than 3,000 meters (10,000).

This pressure difference caused human beings to fart. That was physics, Anatoli insisted, and it made both Dag and Eleonore laugh a lot.

Anatoli explained it was such an issue that it had required a great deal of engineering to efficiently purify the station's atmosphere from methane and get rid of the stench. He also explained that all the microphones deployed in space had built-in sound filters to cancel out the noise of farting people. That made the two kids laugh even more, and Ralf wondered how Anatoli could have won a Nobel Prize in Physics.

That was true, though, that they had deployed fart-cancelling microphones. This was Public Relations. If people on Earth knew how bad it was, they would not dream that much of coming to space.

Five hours later, they were approaching the Moon orbit. Looking through the window, Ralf saw that there were three other Space Bears, two of which belonged to Ryanair, and two Albaspaces belonging to Vahlroos Travel. They were all going too fast to insert into the Moon's orbit, but that was not the purpose. They would just use the Moon's gravity to fly back directly to the Earth. It was only a twelve-hour excursion.

As they were getting closer to the Moon base, the pilot connected the radio communication on the intercom.

"You are now listening to the Moon base communication," she explained. "They are about to fire the *Forward* into orbit."

"*Thirty seconds to launch*," a remote voice said.

"The launch pad is on the left," the pilot informed. "About ten o'clock, around the lunar equator... It is too far away to see with the naked eye. However, we will see when the boosters on the side of the forward are ignited."

"*10...9...8*," a remote voice counted down. "*5... 4... 3... 2... 1... ignition*"

Suddenly, the passengers could see a tiny object take off from the surface of the Moon. As they were closing in, they could now all make out the *Forward*, with attached boosters on the side to put her into orbit.

"We are only five kilometers away," the pilot explained. "But we won't come any closer. "The boosters are supposed to detach shortly and land automatically back on the lunar launch pad to be re-used."

A moment later they saw how the boosters detached themselves from the spacecraft and how the *Forward* stabilized onto the lunar orbit. The *Orion*, from NASA, was there to dock onto the *Forward* in order to ferry her to the Earth orbit. This would take eighteen hours.

"It looks like a huge cylinder," Eleonore said, commenting on the shape of the *Forward*.

"Yes," Anatoli replied. "A thick cylinder. It requires less energy to warp. 75 meters [246 ft] long and 32 meters [104 ft] wide. Three decks with artificial gravity."

"It must now be ferried to the Earth's orbit," Tintin explained.

"It will take eighteen hours."

"When it is docked at the orbital station," Anatoli continued. "We will add the compact fusion reactors and most of the avionics as well as the furniture. It will be ready for launch at the end of June."

"In sci-fi movies, spaceships don't look like this one," Dag noted. "They are never boring cylinders."

Tintin smiled and said: "Dag, this is because sci-fi is more about fiction than science. The *Forward* is more about science than fiction."

Six hours later, they were back at the orbital station. As they docked into the station, Tintin was informed that his mother had tried to reach him. Fearing the worst, he rushed to the crew room he shared with Anatoli in the WARSEC gravity room. Using the satellite phone connection, he called his mother back. His mother told him his grandfather had died. Anatoli joined him later in the room, and Tintin told him. The kokoni dog perhaps felt Tintin's sadness as she climbed onto his lap.

Tintin's grandfather had been a white Frenchman who had become a Congolese citizen. In his youth, he had been nicknamed 'Captain Haddock', one of the main characters in *The Adventures of Tintin*, because of his black beard and hair. Even though the second album of that comic series had been an insult to the Congolese nation, back in the early 1930s, the Congolese had since then turned this offense into a pride and it was not uncommon to see references to the Belgian comic series in the streets of Kinshasa. Tintin himself had inherited his name from this legacy, Tintin meaning 'funny' in Congolese. He had been vastly attached to his grandfather.

"I shouldn't be sad," Tintin said eventually. "He had a good life. It's just that I will miss him."

Anatoli grabbed a bottle of vodka.

"Finnish vodka," he said. "Koskenkorva. I drank half of it when Liisa dumped me. We should drink the other half."

"And be in underclothes." Tintin laughed nervously. "How do they say it in Finnish?"

The WARSEC headquarters had been located in Vaasa, in Finland, for a year and all the WARSEC personnel tried to learn a few Finnish words.

"*Kalsarikännit,*" Anatoli replied. "Or something like that. We should ask Ralf or Mikko."

"OK, let's drink," Tintin said, and he grabbed the bottle of vodka.

The next morning, at least in UTC time, both Tintin and Anatoli were woken up by a knock on their door. Calypso started to bark.

Anatoli, wearing only his underpants, opened the door. It was Thierry, in his orange suit, as well as Mikko and Valeriya in their red suits.

Thierry Diakité was a well-built, black, robot engineer in his late twenties. Before joining WARSEC, he had worked together with Tintin at V-Space, in Bobo-Dioulasso, Burkina Faso, where he was from. Mikko Andersson was a brown-haired Swede with Asian-shaped grey eyes and Valeriya Limonov, a short but stout Russian brunette. Both were also in their late twenties and both physicists specialized with the optimization of the warp fields.

They all three had been on the Moon with Tatjana Aydemir, the new head of the Lunar Coordination Center, to supervise the putting into orbit of the *Forward*. They had now returned to the orbital station, hitch-hiking a ride onboard NASA's *Orion*.

"It smells like animals in here," Valeriya noted.

"We have a space bitch with us," Anatoli explained, as Calypso was jumping with happiness at meeting Valeriya, Mikko, and Thierry again.

"Hangover," Tintin explained. "My grandfather died yesterday. He was 104 years old, though, but still. We finished Anatoli's bottle."

"Sorry to hear that," Thierry said. "When is the funeral?"

"On Thursday. I will take the shuttle back to Earth on Tuesday," Tintin said before changing the subject: "We saw the *Forward* be put into orbit. Did everything go fine?"

"Everything went smoothly," Thierry said. "The *Forward* is now docked into the orbital station, and the nuclear reactors have been successfully inserted. We are now installing the missing avionics and all the furniture. In three weeks, they will ferry it back to the Moon to start the nuclear reactors and then here again to load the green matter and do the finishing."

The following Tuesday, Tintin boarded an Albaspace operated by Vahlroos Travel and bound for Bobo-Dioulasso, in Burkina Faso. From there, he would take a set of connecting flights to Kinshasa, in Congo.

As the Albaspace departed from the orbital station, Tintin looked one last time at the *Forward* and smiled. A chapter of his life had closed, but another one had opened. The *Forward* was the first spaceship of a whole class, and half a dozen were planned. Interstellar exploration was to begin soon.

14: GEOLOGICAL PHILOSOPHY (JULY 2098)

Sanne van der Maas had made it! Not only had she received her master's in Economics with an A in her thesis, but she had also had her first scientific article published and, moreover, been accepted for a PhD at Cambridge University.

She had been hoping for it all along and had been fairly confident in her chance of success, but still. The subject she had picked for her thesis had had an obvious return on investment. The prospects of fully liberalized capitalism in an interstellar economy? They were simply not good.

First of all, the impossibility of instant communication would make any market imperfect, and any limited regulation ineffective. Second of all, the capital intensity required to succeed in an interstellar enterprise was such that it was bound to lead at best to oligopolistic, and at worst to monopolistic economic situations, which were the very ones the free market strove to avoid.

In conclusion, interstellar exploration and colonization by private corporations would automatically lead to a situation similar to the conquest of the Wild West, with a concentration of wealth around two or three corporations called to be the new Rockefellers and Carnegies. This would be both inefficient, in terms of market economy, and damaging to the future of society as a whole.

Her thesis had not impressed Amina. Her geologist flatmate had just shrugged:

"You economists, do you really need to do those advanced mathematics just to state the obvious? Why don't you try real science, instead? Geology is a good branch."

Her thesis had impressed all the faculty at Cambridge, however. Not only had it landed her a PhD in economics, but she had also been asked to write a paper summarizing her findings. It had been accepted and published. And it had been impactful. This was what mattered most, in science: writing impactful articles. Without it, no funding. Without funding, no research.

Of course, her article had stirred some bickering among economists, and the ones from Chicago University were the first to return fire. They were joined by Michael Vahlroos, the CEO of Vahlroos Corporation.

According to him, Sanne's article was just another proof that Cambridge was nothing but a leftist university when it came to the economy. Had not this asshole Maynard Keynes also professed at Cambridge? Her thesis was allegedly biased by the fact that she had been the only survivor of the Martian colony. Just because the Martian Show Corporation had been a mighty failure, that did not mean that all private corporations were incompetent and evil.

But it did not take long for her opponents to find the incontrovertible reason her thesis was wrong: she was a woman. Women knew nothing about mathematics. Ergo, her thesis should be discarded.

Her Cambridge friends Samir and Emily had been outraged. Samir had volunteered to fly to Chicago and New York to punch all her critics. Sanne had been touched, but had declined his offer.

Ralf Åhman, the director of WARSEC, had sent her a few words of encouragement. WARSEC was funding her PhD after all. According to him, she was a so-called *exactor* and should not let herself be disturbed by so-called *approximators*.

She was not the only one among the Cambridge Four to have done well during the first term of 2018. Samir had passed his first year in robotics with mostly Bs, while Emily was now starting a specialization as an oncology nurse.

Nonetheless, as usual, it had been Amina who had outperformed. Less than two years after obtaining a bronze medal in lead-climbing at the Riga Olympics, she had written an outstanding bachelor thesis and published *the* 2098 scientific article that shocked the world: The probability of the largest super-volcano Yellowstone Caldera, in Wyoming, USA, to erupt before 2200 was 7,4%. The probability for the super-volcano Campi Flegrei, under the bay of Naples, to erupt by 2200 was 19.1%. Her article had also landed her a place studying for a PhD in Cambridge, still under the supervision of Dr. Sheldon Cooper.

Starting a PhD in Cambridge was not all good, Sanne reflected. The pay was barely more than what she made when she was working half-time as a waitress at *the Honourable Schoolboy*. She also had to assist with teaching and had been made assistant of a summer course, which deprived her of a summer holiday. Amina was also stuck in Cambridge.

On Saturday 12 July 2098, it was pouring with rain in Cambridge. As Samir and Emily had just come back from a short holiday in the Alps, the Cambridge Four decided to go to the indoor climbing gym, located by Parker's Piece.

"When is the Football World Cup final?" Sanne asked as she was belaying Amina.

"Tomorrow, I think," Emily answered as she was belaying Samir.

"Who is playing?"

Emily focused a short moment on her belaying, before saying: "Sweden against South Korea. Shall we watch it?"

"Perhaps I should," Sanne replied. "I'm not much into

football, but it's the first World Cup since I landed on Earth."

"I'm not much into football either," Emily admitted. "But this is women's football, and it's more interesting than male football. Men play too much as individuals. Not enough teamwork. Nothing elegant. A good thing that the men's World Cup is in August this year, when nobody watches."

"*Scheisse!*" ('Shit!!')

It was Amina who had yelled. She had just fallen from a ceiling section and was now hanging on the rope from the last clipped quickdraw. Sanne lowered her down to the ground and teased her: "Amina, you have softened a bit. You should have spent less time on your paper and more at the gym."

"You're jealous again," Amina replied. "You complain about Chicago economists harassing you, but I have religious people on my back. I'm tired. Shall we have a coffee break?"

"I'll join you when Samir is back down," Emily said.

A moment later the Cambridge four were drinking coffee on the sofas in the climbing hall.

"Which are the most handsome men?" Sanne tried. "Climbers or footballers?"

"Climbers for sure," Amina replied. "Footballers' legs are too thick."

"For men, I kind of agree," Samir replied, laughing. "For women, it's harder to say. Lady footballers are fast and powerful, while lady climbers are agile and flexible. I would say that in bed, it reaches a high standard in any case."

Sanne turned to Emily and said: "And you let him say things like that, Emily?"

"As long as he is looking at athletic women only, I don't mind," Emily replied, flexing her biceps.

"Hey, look," Amina said suddenly. "A new climber with artificial legs. Looking at her arms, I'd guess she is better than all three of you."

"I know her," Samir said. "You have seen her as well, on the Liskamm."

It was Aisha.

Aisha Barjaoui had had a busy 2098 spring. After Captain Léger had found her in her hospital room, she had decided that she would apply for the EU Air Force. Pepped by the movie *Reach for the Sky*, she had started an intensive rehabilitation program and had been able to walk with her prostheses by the end of March. She had trained not only physically, but also academically. In high school, back in Casablanca, she had been an A-student. Unfortunately, she had never graduated, because of a necessary abortion in Ireland, which had led her to the Foreign Legion. This had, however, certainly saved her life. All the people she knew in Casablanca had been killed in the bombing.

This had motivated her all the more to become a fighter pilot. She wanted to take revenge on drones. Her studies had paid off. After writing the competitive exams, she had been selected to pass the final selection tests in Cranwell, in the United Commonwealth of South Britain, where the European Air Academy was located.

After the selection process, she had realized that Cambridge was not far, and had decided to drop by to look for Samir and Sanne. They had not replied to her last-minute messages, and she had guessed this was because they were busy climbing, hence her checking the climbing gym.

"What happened to your legs, Aisha?" Samir asked. "You had not mentioned anything."

"A stupid accident," Aisha replied. "Fell while ice climbing. The screws would not hold."

"Ouch, bad luck," Emily said.

"It was not bad luck," Aisha corrected. "Only my own stupidity. Ice climbing when it's raining equals ice climbing when it's plus degrees. Never a good idea."

Samir invited Aisha to join them in the sofa corner, and went to the bar to get her a cappuccino. When Samir was back, Aisha explained the reason for her stay in the UK. She had done well at the physical tests but was not certain she would be selected at the Air Academy. After all, it was a competitive exam, and it depended on how better or worse the other candidates were than she was. Of course, the conversation drifted to Khouribga.

Amina, who was not really interested in politics, just

commented: "The war in Morocco was all about the phosphate. It's the demography, stupid. It's always been the demography, stupid. Nearly 11 billion people on Earth unable to correctly share natural resources. So, you get this kind of war, for resources which are not even environment-friendly."

"A hundred years ago, countries were fighting for oil," Sanne remarked. "And it was not environment-friendly either."

Amina took a sip from her cup of tea and said: "Sure, but this conflict is just a perfect illustration that mankind is screwed."

"What do you mean?" Emily asked.

"We are unable to share resources and cooperate. The demography always increases unchecked. The pressure on the environment has been such that we are most likely experiencing the sixth mass extinction since life has existed on Earth."

"Is that so?" Aisha asked, faking to be interested.

"Sixty percent of all animal species existing 150 years ago are now extinct, "Amina went on. "Pandas, Bonobos, they are the extinct animals everybody talks about, but they are only the top of the food chain. At the bottom of it, far more species have become extinct. Besides, the melting of the ice caps and the thermal expansion of the oceans has an impact on the frequency of volcanic eruptions. My supervisor says it will cause global cooling. I say it's gonna trigger an eruption from a super-volcano."

"Super-volcanoes?" Aisha asked.

"Huge volcanoes with a volcanic explosivity index above

seven," Amina replied. "65 million years ago, dinosaurs died out when a meteorite crashed on Earth and triggered a chain of super-volcanic eruptions. 39,000 years ago, Neanderthal man died out when a super-volcano in Naples erupted. Such an eruption has a decent chance to occur within the next hundred years."

"You are really optimistic," Emily said.

Sanne laughed and said: "You should try sharing a flat with her. It's pure geological philosophy. For a geologist, what is mankind? Nothing. Mankind has existed for 350,000 years and will be extinct in less than 200 years, while velociraptors survived for dozens of millions of years."

"OK, that's perhaps geological philosophy," Amina admitted, "but I'm realistic. And if you know that mankind has a reasonable probability to become extinct within a century, then you can lead a relaxing life as long as you commit to never having children. You don't want to have children that may live through the extinction of our species."

"But I want children!" Emily exclaimed. "OK. Not now, but in, like, ten years. What else is the purpose of life?"

"To have fun," Amina answered.

Sanne deeply disagreed and knew how to contradict her: "Come on, Amina. What are you writing your PhD about?"

"About the terraforming of an Earth-like planet with the presence of liquid water, but the absence of life and oxygen," Amina replied.

"So, you are working with space colonization?" Aisha wondered.

"She is," Sanne replied. "And space colonization is about the future of mankind. So, don't pretend, you don't care, Amina."

"I don't," Amina assured her. "I really don't give a damn about the future of mankind. I'm faking it to be left in peace by fellow scientists like I sometimes fake an orgasm to be left in peace by a bad lover. Nothing wrong with it."

"You are faking to care about mankind just to get a PhD?" Emily wondered.

"Of course," Amina replied. "In science, you go where the money is. If I could pick, I would prefer to work with the various snowball Earth theories. Much more exciting. But there is no money. Now, some people are ready to spend money on space colonization and terraforming. So I go into it."

"You're so cynical, I cannot even conceive it," Sanne reacted.

"You should," Amina replied. "I guarantee you, a hundred years ago, geologists faked to deny the human cause of global warming, just to get more funding from oil corporations, and the geology extraction businesses as a whole. The only thing a geologist will ever want is to have fun on fieldwork. The rest does not matter."

After this, to Sanne's taste, irritating discussion, they resumed their climbing, with Aisha this time. Despite her legs, she turned out to be an outstanding climber. Sanne invited her to crash in her and Amina's flat.

In the evening, they were joined by Samir and Emily to watch the so-called little final of the Women's Football World Cup, played in Armenia. It was the USA against Burkina Faso. Sanne had a little flag of Burkina.

As they turned the TV on, they saw the WARSEC channel was broadcasting live the first warp test of the *Forward*.

"Perhaps we could check that out before we watch football?" Sanne asked.

The others did not mind. The broadcast seemed interesting.

"It seems that Alice is the commander for the test. With Mikko and Valeriya."

Aisha remembered that Sanne had been born on Mars. She had met the WARSEC people subsequently to her rescue. She remembered the Afro-Chinese astronaut Alice Fù from the first testing of the then-called *Alcubierre* drive, back in September 2094. Back then, she had watched it with Deng Hoang, Alice's ex-boyfriend, who was then a Chinese expat in Casablanca.

As Aisha was watching, she envied Alice. As far as she was concerned, she would perhaps become a fighter pilot, but she would probably never qualify to be a spaceship commander. She had not graduated high school and was far from having a PhD like anybody else involved in the testing of the *Forward*.

"We have watched the test broadcast for almost two hours and we now know that the *Forward* can warp. We should perhaps watch the football match, just to know the result,"

Emily suggested.

They switched the channel. The match was over. Burkina Faso had won the bronze medal over the USA with 3 goals to 1.

"OK. Tomorrow, we'll try to watch the final more seriously," Sanne said.

15: REASONS AND POLITICS (SEPT 2098)

The commissioning of the *UNSS Forward* occurred on Wednesday 17 September 2098, four years after the successful testing of the Alcubierre metric. After her first maiden warp travel in July, the starship had been extensively tested and was now considered ready for space travel beyond the range of Mars.

Only a few journalists and representatives of some of the UN member states attended the commissioning ceremony onboard the orbital station. It was mostly a question of room and practicality as the whole took place in weightlessness. There was simply not enough space for more than three dozen people in the 0-G pipe corridor leading to the rear hatch of the ship.

Ralf Åhman and Glover Johnson were the only attendants from WARSEC, together with Alice Fù, the ship commander. The Afro-Chinese astronaut, inventor of the green matter and recipient of the 2095 Nobel Prize in Chemistry, had been the commander of the *Alcubierre* for her first test, back in 2094. She had now been in charge of the testing of the *UNSS Forward* and had swapped her red jumpsuit for a pink one, the color of pilots and ship captains.

The commissioning ceremony was chaired by the UN secretary-general. Hira Dorjee-Sherpa cut a ribbon in front of the hatch. She explained to a journalist that the name stood for *United Nations Space Ship Forward*, and then gave the space to the ship commander. Alice Fù would show them around.

Like the *Alcubierre*, it was a long cylinder. Unlike the *Alcubierre*, which had some windows in the rear hatch, there was no window at all. It was like being in a military submarine.

From the entry hatch, Alice led the guests through a long transparent crawl pipe, going through the cargo bay.

"As you can see through the pipe corridor," Alice said, "the cargo bay is quite large, about 11,800 cubic meters [400,000 cubic feet]. There is enough room for an AF5 Dachshund S and a couple of White Parrots."

The AF5 Dachshund S was a twenty-seven-meter-long aerospace shuttle developed by Airbus Space, and able to carry up to six passengers and crew. The SX-White Parrot was a fifteen-meter-long, double-decker, space-only vehicle developed by NASA. White Parrots had been used intensively for the construction of the orbital station, and were put into orbit using the space elevators.

Alice added: "During our exploration journeys, we will only have two White Parrots and, of course, a great many scientific satellites and probes. This is also where we store the warpedoes 65."

"What are warpedoes?" a diplomat asked.

Alice explained: "They are torpedo-looking devices able to warp 65 times the speed of light. This is how we can send messages back to Earth from a remote star system. Radio waves go only as fast as the speed of light, and we cannot wait decades for an answer."

From the transparent pipe corridor, they floated their way through a second airlock and into the 0-G core.

"So, under us, you have this cylinder in the middle of the 0-G core. This is connected to the cargo bay and is an extension of it. Straight in front of us, you have the secondary flight deck, still in the 0-G core. From it, you can handle a set of twelve periscopes to check what is happening around the ship, should there be a failure of the cameras and sensors."

"What is in front of the secondary flight deck?" a journalist asked.

"Past it, you have the nuclear fusion reactors," Alice replied, "As well as the water and oxygen recycling units. The water tank is just under the flight deck. Around the compact fusion reactors, you have the green matter generator. As I am sure you already know, it enables us to create a negative energy field around the ship, thus enabling it to warp spacetime, that is to say to travel faster than the speed of light."

"What about the habitable sections?" the journalist asked.

"They are revolving on magnetic rails around us," Alice explained. "The habitable section is split among three circular gravity decks revolving around us. Since the *Forward* class is only 32 meters (105 ft) in diameter, the gravity decks cannot simulate Earth gravity. The inner deck, or deck 1, simulates 40% of Earth gravity, deck 2, 50% and deck 3, the outer deck, 60%."

"How do we get into the gravity decks?" the journalist asked.

"Well, they revolve quite fast," Alice admitted, "Six rotations per minute. You have to float to the core's ceiling, over there, and when a ladder handle goes, by, you grab it. Gravity will then pull you to the decks."

Alice showed them how to follow her into deck 1. The UN secretary-general, who was blind, had trouble grabbing the ladder, despite her earGlasses. Ralf Åhman helped her out.

The inner gravity deck, or deck 1, was where the primary flight deck was located, as well as the operation and briefing rooms, a living room and a kitchen. On deck 2 were two living rooms and another kitchen, as well as a gym and some cabins. Deck 3 consisted almost entirely of cabins. Further toward the front, there was a section of the gravity ring where all the decks were merged into one. It was planned to try and have a greenhouse in that section to provide the crew with fresh vegetables and fruits.

After the short visit, all attendants were back in the

WARSEC gravity ring of the orbital station, where they were served glasses of champagne. Diplomats could not have been expected to drink champagne in weightlessness from a closed mug with a straw!

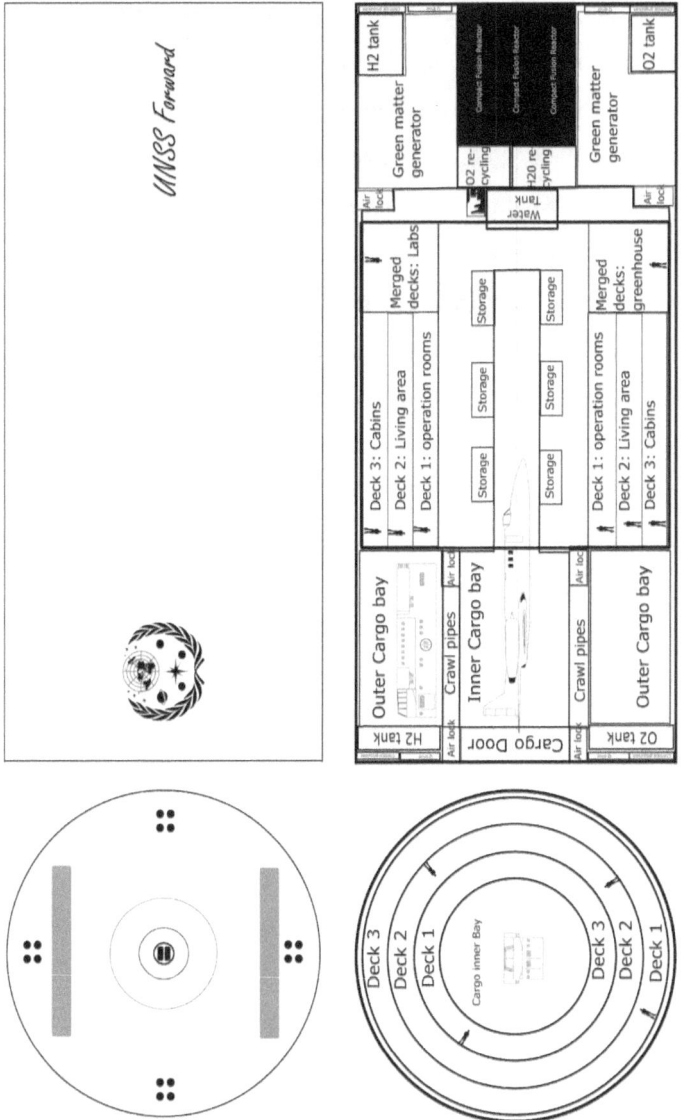

Figure 9: the Forward starship with its three circular gravity decks.

The only noteworthy event before the commissioning had been that the name *Fram* had been painted just beside the name *UNSS Forward* on the fuselage. It turned out it had been painted by one of WARSEC's chief science officers, Synøve Solberg,

"It's Norwegian for *Forward*," Synøve explained to Hira Dorjee-Sherpa, as they were drinking champagne in the windowless WARSEC cafeteria. "When Jules Verne sent Captain Hatteras to the North Pole onboard the *Forward* in his 1866 book, it was only in his dreams. When Fridtjof Nansen made his attempt to reach the North Pole in 1893, it was onboard the *Fram*, and it was for real."

"Is it OK to just amend the name of a spaceship?" The UN secretary-general wondered.

"I don't see it as an amendment, but as a relevant subtitle," Glover Johnson replied. "In the failed 1895 North Pole expedition onboard the *Fram*, all souls onboard returned safely to Norway. In Jules Verne's book, Captain Hatteras clearly does not have the leadership attributes of a Nansen or a Shackleton: he makes it to the pole, but abandons three-quarter of his crew to their death. Leaving the two names, *Fram* and *Forward,* side by side on the fuselage could be a good reminder for the crew."

The next moment, the secretary-general was solicited by a journalist and Ralf took advantage of it to ask Glover about his wife and soon to be one-year-old daughter.

"Rika has just started kindergarten," Glover answered. "Laura will move permanently to Finland. She has just obtained a job as a second officer at Viking Line, a Finnish passenger boat company. Not as good as being the captain of a Maersk cargo ship, but it will be easier. However, if I am to spend more time in space, I will have to bring the baby. Otherwise, Laura will kill me."

"We will have to reduce your time in space for the time being," Ralf said. "Shuttle travel to space is not advised for children under five. If you start coming here with the space elevator in Guyana, it will take forever. And it would be ironic, just at the time when direct liaison between Vaasa and the orbital station has been made possible."

After the commissioning ceremony, the secretary-general summoned Ralf and Glover to a short meeting. Ralf led them to a small, windowless conference room and they sat around a square white table.

"Gentlemen," Hira said, "Next Monday begins the 153rd session of the General Assembly. On top of having to listen for ten minutes to each of the member states' representatives, I will most likely be pressured to have a first interstellar journey completed before the next century."

"That gives us some time," Glover said. "The twenty-second century starts only on 1 January 2101."

"Very true indeed," Hira said. "Diplomats know that. But I will be pressured by heads of states who are not that intelligent. For them, the twenty-second century starts on 1 January 2100, that is to say in one year and three and a half months."

Ralf Åhman turned to his head of the Space Coordination Center and asked: "Glover, Alpha Centauri is the closest star. When would an exploratory mission have to depart to be back by the end of December 2099?"

Glover looked reluctantly at both Ralf and Hira and said: "I don't like the idea of rushing into an interstellar mission under the pressure of some national governments."

"Yes," Ralf acquiesced. "But these government still contribute up to a third of our budget, even if our own resources have been increasing lately."

"Alfa Centaury is 4.37 light years away," Glover answered. "At warp 10.3, the *Forward* will take 155 Earth days to get there, five months and four days. The return journey will be ten months and eight days. Then it depends on the exploration time there. However, be sure that I will not authorize any exploratory mission without any ready-commissioned back-up starship, and the *Alcubierre* does not count."

"The *Fridtjof Nansen* is in her final integration phase now," Hira remarked.

"True," Ralf said. "Her maiden warp test is expected to occur at the beginning of November. She could be commissioned by mid-January 2099."

"She could," Glover said, "But it's risky. Anyway, if we schedule an interstellar departure in the second half of January and want the *Forward* to be back by the end of December 2099, our exploratory team will have barely more than a month at their disposal in the Alpha Centauri system. Synøve will hate it."

"What is there to explore in the Alpha Centauri system anyway?" Ralf asked. "We can just deploy a lot of probes and satellites and collect the information with a four-year delay. The main purpose of an Alpha Centauri exploration is not to do science but to exhibit for the world that mankind can now go interstellar."

"I know another Norwegian woman who will hate you," Glover said to Ralf.

"Well, we are not there yet," Hira said. "We will see what the General Assembly decide. But it could be wise to start thinking about it."

In the first week of October, Glover was changing Rika's diapers in his office, at the Vaasa Center in Finland, when he heard that the UN General Assembly had asked for a first interstellar journey to be completed before the 31 December 2099.

He was in a particularly bad mood. Not only did they want to force their schedule on an interstellar exploration, but they also wanted to have a say on the composition of the crew. Each country wanted to have one of their nationals onboard, and there would be only 27 scientists and crew, WARSEC had decided.

After he had changed the diaper, he brought Rika with

him into Ralf Åhman's office nearby. Glover made it clear to him that he would have full authority on the composition of the exploratory team, though he would do his best to have it internationally represented.

Ralf agreed. They would announce the composition of the crew when the *UNSS Forward* was back from its first four-week mission in the outer solar system.

On Ralf's initiative and with the blessing of the secretary-general and the approval of NASA and US President Fang, the *UNSS Forward* had embarked on a peculiar mission: to attempt to retrieve both probes Voyager 1 and Voyager 2.

These two probes had been launched by NASA in the 1970s to travel across the solar system and reach deep space. Both probes were carrying a Golden Record with information about the human race and a recorded message by the then UN secretary-general Kurt Waldheim. In the 2010s, they had finally reached the outer limits of our solar system and gone 'exostellar'.

Their batteries had died out and they were both drifting through deep space at only approximately inferred locations.

There were two reasons why everybody was so eager to retrieve these probes. First of all, humanity had grown up and was no longer expecting any salvation from higher intelligence from space. The so-called 'New Age' era had been over for quite some time.

However, one had become more cautious about the idea of having unnecessary information about mankind being captured by a higher intelligence that might be hostile, however improbable it may be.

The second and main reason was more symbolic. Kurt Waldheim, who was the UN secretary-general in the 1970s, had happened to hide his past as a former Nazi during World War Two. For both Ralf and Hira, it was not acceptable that the first recorded human message received by extraterrestrial intelligence should be voiced by a Nazi.

Anatoli Govorov was leading the mission, together with Mikko Andersson and Valeriya Limonov. Eamon Windsor who, to Glover's amusement, had been the last king of England, was the ship's chief medical officer. Both Tintin Mutombo and Thierry Diakité accompanied them to help determine the possible trajectories needed to retrieve the probes.

The mission turned out to be a success. However, Glover was informed by Dr. Windsor that Anatoli sometimes drank more than was reasonable. Too bad for him. He would not be on the mission to Alpha Centauri, he would pick Alice Fù as the commander.

Glover also received concerns from the crew who complained of having to eat dry food. A section of the ship had been designed to contain a greenhouse, but there had been no real progress on that front.

Glover passed the information to Ralf, who was summoned

to New York at the end of November 2098 to present for the General Assembly the plan of the first interstellar journey.

Ralf took Eamon Windsor with him to New York. A thin man of medium height with South Asian origins, Dr. Windsor was a psychiatrist, and his input was welcome regarding the psychological impacts such a journey may have on the crew. They first held a presentation for the 4th Committee of the United Nations General Assembly, which was in charge of both colonization matters and outer space affairs.

They then met with the secretary-general in her spacious, but not huge, office, on the 38th floor of the UN building. Her earGlasses were charging and it was a blind Hira who welcomed them.

"Sometimes, I guess working at the UN is like working in a lunatic asylum," Hira said, as she invited them to sit in the sofa corner of her office.

"The comparison is slightly far-fetched, if I dare say so," Dr. Windsor retorted as he sat down. "As a psychiatrist, I promise you there is a huge difference. Lunatics have no rationality. Nationals representatives at the UN have at least a kind of rationality."

Hira sat down on the coach opposite Ralf and Eamon and said: "I apologize, Doctor. It was just a figure of speech, perhaps not respectful of psychiatrists and their patients, I may admit. But still. I just had a meeting with the representative for the

Israeli-Palestinian Republic, and he seriously asked me to find two habitable planets so that all the Salafi could emigrate to one and the Haredim to the others."

"I know this representative," Ralf said. "He is a kind of a weirdo, though. He just has the job because he is the nephew of the current Israeli-Palestinian prime minister."

The secretary-general changed the subject and first complimented WARSEC on successfully salvaging the probes Voyager 1 and 2. She added, joking: "We shall now send new probes with my voice recorded in them. I also want to compliment you on the planning of the expedition to Alpha Centauri. I know our scientists won't like it, but WARSEC is first about diplomacy and then about science."

"Perhaps it's not so bad, though, to have only an eleven and-a-half-month-long mission for the first interstellar journey," Eamon noted. "We don't know for sure how people will react for so long in a confined environment on a mission that cannot be aborted. Even Synøve Solberg, the chief scientist for the mission, rallied to this viewpoint."

"Good".

"The only issue is the absence of fresh food," Ralf pointed out. "According to Eamon here, access to fresh food could play a vital role in the *esprit de corps* onboard a spaceship for a longer mission."

"I understand what you mean," Hira said. "Diplomats always eat good food. If they did not, there would be war all the time."

All three laughed.

"Seriously," Eamon added. "In the long term, good meals are essential to keep one's spirits up and to avoid smaller conflicts growing unchecked. For a one-year mission, it will be OK with dry food. Previous missions to Mars made it that way. But for a longer mission, we would need to be able to grow our own food onboard. Like they did in the Martian colony."

"Then you should check with the Western Asian Union," Hira suggested. "They are used to growing food in the most barren places."

16: THE WESTERN ASIAN UNION (NOVEMBER 2098)

On a Sunday morning in late November 2098, Rebecka Levi was standing at the intersection of Yekhezkel Street and Me'a She'arim Street, in old Jerusalem. She was a tall, thin lady with long, curly black hair. With her modern cream suit, white hat, and sunglasses she clearly contrasted with the other passersby, who wore clothes which would make a layman think they had gotten stuck in time and were trapped in the 1920s. A duffel bag was lying at her foot. At last the little electric car arrived. Shida was at the steering wheel, and Emir was sitting next to her.

"Come on, in, Reb," Emir shouted.

Rebecka opened the right back door and jumped into the car.

"Go! Go! Go!" Emir laughed. "That rabbi just cast an evil eye at me!"

Shida pressed on the gas pedal, and they were on their way.

"How has your weekend been?" she asked Rebecka.

"Same old, same old," the latter replied.

"Your family is still pissed off at you?" Emir wondered.

"Father still spends his days reading the Torah, Mother cleaning the house and cooking. She was having her period and therefore was kept in a separate apartment. Women and men still live in a more or less segregated manner. I don't mind, though. Those male supremacists are so intellectually retarded that the less time I spend with them, the better. Yesterday, they were still discussing how to pull down the Great Mosque to rebuild the Old Temple."

Emir burst into a hearted laughter and said: "Some things never change."

Shida tried to console Rebecka:

"You complain about your father. My grandfather is far worse, back in Iran. He still wants to kill all Jews and call them responsible for everything bad that has happened on Earth. Even though there has been peace in the Middle East for fifty years, now."

"You're welcome, Middle East," Emir said.

"Come on!" Shida challenged him. "If we listen to you, the Kurds are to be thanked for all good things that have happened here. You defeated the Islamic State at the beginning of this century. You liberated Jerusalem from the crusades. What more have you done?"

Sitting next to Shida, who was driving, Emir shrugged and

said: "It's not my fault if Salah ad-Din was Kurd. He did set Jerusalem free from the crusaders, in 1087."

"With an Arab army," Rebecka corrected. "Anyway, did you lot have to insist on having some commemoration of the crusade? All the next year will be a mess in Jerusalem."

"Well," Emir objected. "Next year, it will be a thousand years since the fall of Jerusalem to the Christians. They massacred the Muslim population. Of course it requires a commemoration!"

"I could skip Middle Age nerds invading our city," Rebecka said.

"It seems that, after all, Kurdish is the new Jewish," Shida concluded.

All three laughed cheerfully.

Twenty minutes later, Shida parked the car in front of the Agricultural and Irrigation Agency (AIA) of the Western Asian Union, where the three of them worked as agronomists. Shida Zakaria was a Shia from Iran. Emir Mazîn was a Sunni Sufi from the Kurdish part of Turkey and Rebecka Levi was a Jew from the Israeli-Palestinian Republic. Of course, if they referred to each other as Shia, Sunni or Jew, it was only in an ethnic way of speaking. They all three were rather atheists, which was still not mainstream in Western Asia, the area which westerners used to refer to as the Middle East.

The Western Asian Union. It was how the trouble had stopped in this part of the world, Rebecka thought. And, of course, what anthropologists called 'joking relationships'. The UN envoy who had been leading the peace process in Western Asia in the 2040s had encouraged the locals to gently make fun of each other's origins rather than kill each other. It was this custom that accounted for Emir's humor.

The first half of the century had been uneasy in the region, partly because of the six-century-old rivalry between Turkey and Iran but also because of Saudi Arabia, which was trying to emerge as the third power of the region. Not to mention various despicable doctrines being spread in all directions among different religions, but with one common denominator: male supremacism. Indeed, Muslim, Jewish, and Christian fundamentalism were nothing more than various branches of male supremacism, with one clear goal: the denial of female autonomy. However, in a real world with real physical constraints and a true need of cooperation, doctrines favoring the subjugation of half of their population were bound to collapse.

In the end, the oil peak, combined with the decreasing availability of water, and demographic factors, forced all the players in the region to play with each other rather than against each other. *It was the demography, stupid. It had always been the demography, stupid*, Rebecka thought.

It was only necessary to look at the history of Israel, which was to become the Israeli-Palestinian State. When Theodore Herzl had written his book about Zionism, he had assumed that Jews migrating to the so-called Holy Land would just live peacefully with Arabs. Herzl should have worked as a screenwriter for Walt Disney movies, instead.

When the UN had looked into the problem, back in 1947, the then so-called minority report advocated a Single-State solution where all would be welcome to live, regardless of their faith. It had been backed by Iran, the only Muslim country asked at the time.

The majority report advocated a split of the English protectorate between Israel, the Gaza Strip and the West Bank instead. It had been vastly criticized by economists at the time, as the area was simply assessed as not economically viable without a customs union anyway. Lack of shared economic prosperity equaled war. These economists had been so right.

All attempts to create an independent Palestinian State had failed. Between 1949 and 1967, Gaza and the West Bank had been occupied by Egypt and Jordan respectively, before passing under Israeli occupation. The Two-State solution had been abandoned in the late 2020s and Israel had subsequently been, luckily, for a very short while, what was to be called – Rebecka was not afraid to use the bad word – an apartheid state.

Ironically, it had been a hundred years after the South African apartheid had been officially proclaimed that the Israeli apartheid ended. *It was the demography, stupid!*

In the Jewish Israeli society, Orthodox Jews paid fewer taxes and did not have to do either their military service, or their civil service, but would expect full protection from their non-Haredim fellow citizens. As Orthodox Jews had been averaging seven to eight children per woman, while secular Jewish ladies had been limiting themselves to two children, secular and atheist Jews had had to stand for the increasing burden of their religious counterparts.

Then had happened what had been bound to happen. Secular and atheist Jews had teamed up with secular and atheist Muslims and Christians to abolish the apartheid and decrease the privileges of the Haredim, while silencing the demands of the Salafi. The Israeli-Palestinian Republic was then proclaimed a hundred years after the birth of Israel. The One-State solution had prevailed.

Could it have ended in a different way? Most likely not, Rebecka reflected. Even if a Two-State solution had been successfully implemented against all the odds, a customs union between Israel and Palestine would have still been needed to secure peace in the long term. It would most likely have resulted in a Federal Israeli-Palestinian Republic, anyway. In the long run, an Israeli-Palestinian Republic had been the only possible outcome of the Israeli-Palestinian conflict, regardless of the chosen geopolitical paths.

Meanwhile, Turkey, Iraq, Syria, and Iran had found out they had to increase their cooperation in terms of water supply and redistribution of oil resources if they wanted to avoid famine for their populations. The Western Asian Water and Oil

Community (WAWOC) had been founded in 2037. In 2056, it had become the Western Asian Union (WAU), when its member states had decided to increase the shared competencies of this inter-state community. It had later been joined by Lebanon, Jordan, Egypt, the Israeli-Palestinian Republic, and the former monarchies of the Persian Gulf, with the notable exception of Saudi Arabia.

The Western Asian Service (WAS), based on the European Service, had been established in 2067 to force the youth of each country to serve as *slavants* in another county, and thus forge an integrated population.

Saudi Arabia had been the last to join the WAU in 2075, but many Western Asians still had a lot of prejudices against Saudis, who were said to be lazy, male supremacist zealots. As the head of the Agricultural Research Department of the AIA, Rebecka tried not to have any opinion on that matter.

Since 2079, Jerusalem had been the capital of the WAU (which was pronounced Waòo!) as a sign of the reconciliation of the region. At 35, Rebecka had been working for ten years at the research department of the Agricultural and Irrigation Agency, and she had been very active on several projects to grow forests to hold in check desert progression caused by global warming.

This morning, as she was scanning through her emails (her parents would forbid her even to peek at her smartphone during Shabbat), her eye was caught by a peculiar memo sent by Ralf Åhman, the Director of WARSEC. What did he want?

She opened the email and read through it. He wanted to start farming in space. Not only onboard the orbital station, but also onboard the interstellar spaceships, so that the space explorers could grow fresh vegetables during their journey. He was crazy. It would require putting tons of earth into orbit. She answered to his email that she was not interested in impossible projects.

An hour later, she received another email from that Ralf Åhman. He did not think that was impossible, nor stupid. Did she know Pyramiden, on Svalbard? It used to be a Russian coal mining settlement on the Arctic island of Spitzbergen. During the Cold War, the Soviets had kept quite an impressive civilian presence up there. It was to ensure that the NATO member state Norway, which was administrating this demilitarized international territory, would not be tempted to bring any military force into the archipelago. To the point: neither food, nor grass ever grew there, on Svalbard. There was tundra in summer and snow in winter. Yet, the Russians had brought tons of earth from Ukraine to grow grass, to make this godforsaken place feel like home. It had not been easy, but they had done it.

But it was certainly stupid, Rebecka thought. A moment later, her phone rang. It was Ralf.

"Good morning, Rebecka," he said. "My name is Ralf Åhman, I am the WARSEC director, and I have just sent you an email".

"Hello…" she answered. "I'm reading it. Are you serious about starting large-scale farming in space?"

"We have two Space Elevators which can carry earth into Space. They have already put tons of material into orbit. I am more than serious."

"They have researchers at NASA," she replied.

"They do," he admitted. "However, we do not want only to grow a few tomatoes in a flower pot. Farming in space is hopefully only the first step. If we find a habitable planet with liquid water, we will colonize it. If there is no oxygen on it, we will have to force a Great Oxygenation Event, if you see what I mean."

"A Great Oxygenation Event?" Rebecka wondered. "You mean you want to grow trees and plants on barren soil in an atmosphere consisting mostly of carbon dioxide?"

"Quite a challenge, I admit," Ralf replied.

Rebecka remained silent. Ralf added: "But should you accept this job. You won't be on your own. You will of course work with geophysicists and planetologists."

Rebecka burst into laughter, while Ralf remained silent on the other end of the line. She finally restrained herself and said: "I will work with other people. It suddenly makes things much easier. It still remains a challenging project."

Ralf went on: "Given your current status, we would, of course, hire you in a senior position."

Rebecka took a short while before she replied: "Let me

think about it. I will tell you by the end of the week. Just please keep in mind that I have a three-month notice on my current contract."

"That's good enough," Ralf said. "We don't plan to colonize any planet in the next three months."

Both laughed before Rebecka hung up.

While they were in a nearby restaurant for lunch, Rebecka told Emir and Shida about Ralf's call.

"You are serious?" Emir asked. "I hope you say no. If you leave, Rachid will be the new head of the department, and he is a pain in the butt."

"I've not made my decision yet," Rebecka answered. "But why would I stay in Jerusalem? I barely talk to my parents, and my childhood friends, or rather acquaintances, are all religious pricks."

"Not to mention that next year, Jerusalem will be a traffic jam inferno due to the commemorations of the first crusade," Shida pointed out.

The following morning, Rebecka called Ralf Åhman to tell him she accepted his offer. She would quit her current position as soon as her new employment contract was signed.

17: INTERSTELLAR DEPARTURE (DEC 2098 – JAN 2099)

December 2098 went by pretty fast as far as Ralf was concerned. He spent the first three weeks in the orbital station as Alice Fù and the selected crew for the Alpha Centauri journey executed a twenty-day exercise. Part of their program was the evacuation of the *UNSS Forward* and the necessary maneuver to transform what could be its remnants in a space life-raft. The key to survival was to at least secure one nuclear reactor. As long as there was power, there was hope.

On his return to Earth, Ralf just had the time to pick up his kids at his ex-girlfriend's, in Trondheim, and take them to Scotland to spend Christmas with his mother. He spent New Year's Eve with his cousins in Jyväskylä, Finland. They reproached him for not visiting them more often as he was now living and working in Vaasa, which was only 300 km (190 miles).away.

The next starship of the *Forward* class, the *UNSS Fridtjof Nansen,* was commissioned on 9 January 2099. This time, there were no representatives from any UN member states and hardly any journalists attending. The secretary-general herself had been held up in New York, and Glover Johnson had to take care of Rika, who was now one year and four months old.

The departure to Alpha Centauri was scheduled for Saturday 17 January 2019 at 13:00 UTC, so that viewers in most countries could follow it on the WARSEC webcast.

The crew of the *UNSS Forward* had already gathered in the orbital station on Tuesday 13 January to finish the preparations.

Glover was there for the occasion, and he had brought his daughter with him. He had first taken a flight to European Guyana, during which other passengers had cast evil eyes at him and his constantly crying baby. There, he had transited to the European Space Elevator.

In 2099, the Earth had two space elevators. One, on Tarawa Island, in the Pacific, operated by the Chinese and Japanese Space agencies, and one in Kourou, European Guyana, operated by NASA and the European Space Agency. The space elevators were 50,000 km-long cables made of nanocarbon fibers, anchored on Earth not far from the Equator, and attached to captured asteroids. As the gravity mass of the resulting system was beyond the geostationary orbit, the space elevator looked to the observer on Earth like a cable shooting vertically through the sky.

Since nanocarbon fibers conducted electricity, space elevators could use the power to climb the cable. Glover had taken one of the special 'baby lifts', which were extra safe, and in which it was not required to have an atmosphere escape suit. From the space elevator's undocking station, he had taken a White Parrot to the orbital station. The whole trip had taken two days.

It was a pity that children under five years old were assessed to be too young to endure 2.5 G. Otherwise, he would have boarded an Albaspace, and the whole trip would have taken less than eight hours.

On Thursday 15 January 2099, Glover and Ralf attended the last briefing given by Alice to her crew in one of the conference rooms of the WARSEC ring. Ralf glanced at the crew. It was a truly international team.

Beside Alice Fù, who was Afro-Chinese, the pilot and navigation team consisted of Mikko Andersson from Sweden, Valeriya Limonov from Russia, Rajesh Kapoor from India and Nari Kim from North Korea.

The medical team consisted of course of Eamon Windsor, the Psychiatrist from the UK, and two medics and space rescuers, both from the USA; Jason Jackson and Scott Washington.

The Safety team was led by John Wick, a giant black Irishman. Under him were the two safety specialists Fred White, an Asian-Australian, and Romeo McMillan, a Canadian.

The engineering team was under the leadership of the Iranian Chief Engineer Officer Iman Nassirbakli. The two nuclear engineers were Lucile Gillier, from France, and Naema Faqir, from Pakistan. The robot specialists were Vilmantas Kalvelis, from Lithuania, and Nina Jokinen, from Finland. Federica Campana, from Italy, was a system engineer together with Nadia Al Amoudi from Syria. Finally, the last in the engineering team were the two structure engineers, Pedro Simoes, from Brazil, and Iyabo Stanley, from Nigeria.

The scientific team was led by Synøve Solberg, from Norway. Among the scientists, there was a geophysicist, Heidi Schmidt from Germany, a planetologist, Laura Rodriguez, from Argentina, and a geologist, Chen Wang, from China. There were also three astrophysicists: Gregory Wilson, from the USA, Dan Singh, from India, and Oliwia Bukowski, from Poland.

Of course, the USA, China, and India were slightly more represented than other nations, but demographically speaking, it only made sense. In all, there were 27 crew, 14 of whom were women.

Alice Fù was the captain, and Iman Nassirbakli was her XO, or executive officer. This was the rule. The captain-XO duo should consist of both a pilot-navigator and an engineer.

The windowless briefing room was located in the WARSEC gravity ring and, like all the gravity rooms, had a somewhat disorienting concave floor and convex ceiling. Alice Fù was standing in front of a canvas screen on which a projected picture was displaying a map of the Alpha Centauri system.

Alice was briefing the team one last time, mostly for the sakes of the invited journalists:

"We depart on 17 January and arrive at the outer border of the Alpha Centauri system on 21 June. Upon arrival, we locate the two Warpedoes 65 which WARSEC will have sent us with the latest news from Earth. We send one back to them to inform them of our successful arrival. Then we start our exploration."

"The system consists of two stars, Alpha Centauri A and Alpha Centauri B, as well as a faint red dwarf, Proxima Centauri. We will first deploy our telescope and study the system carefully for about ten days. So far, we know there is at least one planet orbiting the nearby red dwarf, but there may be more that have been missed by our instruments on Earth.

"Depending on the results we then do a milk-run-delivery. We deploy communication satellites around each planet and send at least one probe to each of them. We also send probes to each of the three stars. The data will be collected by the communication satellites we will leave over there.

"In one year, a new Warpedo 65 will be sent there, to collect the gathered data and bring it back to Earth. We have to abort our exploratory mission on 28 July at the very latest, in order to be back on Earth on 30 December, just before the 21C celebrations.

"Before we leave the Alpha Centauri system, we send the

other Warpedo 65 to inform the Earth of our departure from that system."

Dr. Eamon Windsor then took the floor.

"We will be locked for more than eleven months in a cylinder with no way of getting back to Earth. There will be long periods of boredom. In such circumstances, it is unavoidable that there will be sexual relationships between members of the crew. We have been provided with enough condoms, and we have all been tested for sexual diseases. We are all clear to go, so to say.

"However, it is important that sexual intercourse between some of you do not affect the work of the crew. Therefore, some basic rules have been issued, and you are forced to respect them if you do not want to be evicted from WARSEC upon your return.

"Sexual relationships between a supervisor and his or her direct report are prohibited. Sexual relationships between two members of the same sub-team are also prohibited, unless first approved by the supervisor and myself. Valeriya and Mikko, you are already approved to pursue your relationship."

There was some laughter in the room.

Ralf Åhman and Glover Johnson both knew it could be a real problem, though. Sexual relationship regulation onboard exploration spaceships had therefore been discussed seriously by all senior executives within WARSEC. Poor sex and relationship management could lead to the rise of conflicts, setting the whole crew in peril.

As a psychiatrist and medical doctor, Eamon Windsor's mission was to keep a functional crew no matter what.

Later that evening, they had a farewell dinner at the orbital station's Radisson hotel, where the food was much better than in the WARSEC cafeteria. The following morning, on Friday 16 January, the crew boarded the *UNSS Forward* and proceeded with two warp journeys to Mars to ensure everything was ready. The *Forward* spent the night in orbit of the Moon.

On Saturday morning, Alice asked each member of the crew one last time if they were absolutely sure they wanted to embark on an eleven-month journey with no way to bail out. Each of them confirmed.

At 12:32 UTC on 17 January, the *UNSS Forward* was almost clear to go. They had to wait for the green light from the WARSEC Orbit Control.

In the orbital station's concave-floored control room, Ralf saw that Tintin, Thierry, and Anatoli were also there. On a large TV screen, an image of the *Forward* filmed by the NASA spaceship *Orion* was broadcasted. Glover, who was carrying his daughter Rika, joined them shortly after. Ralf glanced at the clock. It was 12.38 UTC.

"UNSS Forward *to Orbit Control*," Alice's voice said. *"All departure checklists completed. We are clear to go."*

Glover took the microphone.

"Orbit Control to *UNSS Forward*. Departure time still set for 13:00 UTC."

"*Copy that.*"

Tintin grabbed the microphone: "Orbit Control to *UNSS Forward*. Canned food and dry food for almost a whole year. No alcohol. Are you sure you want to go?"

There was some laughter in the control room, and they could hear over the wireless that they were also laughing onboard the *UNSS Forward*.

"*Tintin, Anatoli*," Valeriya said over the wireless. "*You take care of Apollo. Don't forget, he needs quite some exercise.*"

Anatoli grabbed the microphone: "First, my girlfriend dumps me with a kokoni dog, and now you dump me with a husky dog. I should switch profession and open a canine shelter."

There was some more laughter.

"At least I can eat a bugburger tonight," Anatoli continued.

"*So can we*," Mikko's voice answered. "*We have some deep-frozen burgers. Though we will save them for later, I guess.*"

"*Orbit Control to UNSS forward*," a voice interrupted. "*Departure in five minutes.*"

"*Copy that*," Mikko answered. "*Anatoli, we have to stop talking shit and focus on our warp ignition checklist. Goodbye.*"

"Goodbye, man."

Five minutes later, Orbit Control gave the green light.

"*Orbit control to* UNSS Forward. *You have warp departure clearance. Go when ready.*"

"*Copy that,*" Alice's voice answered. "*We have warp departure clearance. We go when ready.*"

"*Departure in 10 seconds,*" Alice's voice went on. "*5…4…3… 2…1-*"

Her voice was cut.

On the large TV screen, the cylindrical starship disappeared in a flash of green.

18: TERRAFORMING AND COLONIZATION (SPRING 2099)

It was cold and dark on that evening in Cambridge, when Sanne van der Maas parked her bike in front of *The Honourable Schoolboy*. She took off her gloves and put them in her pocket, locked the three locks on her flashy green bike (bringing it from Mars, where she had been born, had been the best decision she had ever made), took off her helmet, and went into the pub. It was Saturday 28 February 2099.

Amina was sitting at a table, working on her laptop. Sanne went to her.

"Still working on a Saturday night?" she asked as she took off her jacket and put it on one of the empty chairs.

"Just trying to finish something," Amina replied, keeping her eyes on her screen. "I've already ordered a bottle of wine. No beer for you. Beer makes one fat. We climbers can't afford that. How's your PhD doing?"

"It has not improved since yesterday," Sanne replied as she sat down opposite Amina. '*Study of the Economic feasibility of interstellar colonization under the WARSEC's supervision*'. At first I thought it was a great subject. After all, it got me the funding from WARSEC. But I'm still missing too much data."

"Like what?" Amina said, still typing on her computer.

Sanne looked for her smartphone in her jacket pocket and said: "Like all of it: What kind of planet will be colonized? Will there be a breathable atmosphere or not? What kind of terraforming will be needed? How far away will that planet be? How long will it take to get there? I've spent now ten months taking advanced courses in economic modelling, but my thesis is going nowhere."

"What does your supervisor say?" Amina said as she eventually pressed Ctrl+S and closed the lid of her laptop.

"I can barely get hold of him," Sanne replied. "He does not seem to be much interested in my subject. He likes the WARSEC funding, though."

Amina smiled.

A waitress filled their glasses with red wine and left the bottle on the table. They each ordered a bugburger with salad.

Amina raised her glass to Sanne and said: "*Cheers*, Sanne. Your problem is that you think too much. The goal of your PhD is not to find a universal economic way of colonizing a planet. That they ask a PhD in the first place to look into it means that they have not even taken the time to think seriously about it."

"What shall I do, then?" Sanne asked.

"Limit your subject," Amina replied bluntly. "For instance, concerning the distance, don't pick a hypothetical planet which is between ten and fifteen light years away. Just state that the colonized planet is within twelve and eighteen-month travel reach. Currently, starships travel at warp 10. However, you have read about the new purple matter being developed: in a few years, starships will be able to travel at warp 30 or even warp 50. That will increase the range of planets reachable within an 18-month journey. Think in terms of travel time rather than distance, then your research will hold up for longer."

"Good point," Sanne acknowledged. "What about the terraforming?"

Amina took a few sips of her red wine, smiled, and said: "Pick the same as me. A planet of a size similar to that of the Earth, with the presence of liquid water, but no life and no oxygen in the atmosphere."

"Why should I pick that configuration?" Sanne said.

"Because it is the easiest."

"What about a hypothetical planet with life and oxygen on it?"

"It would not make sense," Amina replied without any hesitation. "First of all, the probability of finding this kind of planet within a reasonable range is close to zero. Second of all, no reasonable person on Earth would give their OK to colonize such a planet."

"Why not?"

Amina shut her eyes a short while and said: "Think, Sanne, think! Life on a planet implies diseases. In the *War of the Worlds* by H. G. Wells, Martians invading the earth eventually die of diseases. If mankind starts colonizing a planet with life on it, it will certainly be hit by unknown diseases. In the worst-case scenario, they could even bring these diseases back to Earth, and it could lead to the end of mankind."

Sanne pointed her finger at Amina and said: "You see. In the end, you do seem to care about the future of the mankind."

"Not at all," Amina replied seriously. "I'm just promoting my own thesis, and it is about terraforming an Earth-like planet with a carbon dioxide-rich atmosphere and liquid water. I thought we could cooperate and even co-write a few articles."

Sanne's face was lit up with a broad smile. She could not help teasing her flatmate: "Are you drunk, Amina? You, an earth-scientist, are ready to team up with an economist for your research?"

"As a matter of fact, I have drunk a glass of wine already," Amina replied, pouring more wine in her glass. "But I'm serious. I've been making progress on my model. From a geological standpoint, the only issues are the emission of carbon dioxide from volcanic eruptions and the speed of oxidation of metal in the planet's crust."

"What is the oxidation of metal in the planet's crust?"

"You know," Amina replied, "On Earth, there is 200

times more oxygen trapped in the lithosphere than in the atmosphere. Iron ores, present everywhere in rocks and in the Earth's crust, will eventually rust. When terraforming, you just need to produce an excess of oxygen, since you know part of it is absorbed. Not a big deal, as long the population is kept low."

"How low?"

"It's my preliminary assessment that a terraformed planet should not harbor more than two and a half billion people, max three billion."

"You previously mentioned there was a high risk of a super-volcanic eruption on Earth within a hundred years," Sanne said. "In short, you mean we have to find, terraform and colonize three planets this century if we want to save all of mankind. We will never do it."

Amina grimaced, took a few sips of wine, and finally said: "Sanne, once again, you think too much! Of course we won't make it! Indeed, it's likely mankind will become extinct within a hundred years! I have never said anything otherwise. I don't care, I will most likely be dead before it happens. What I care about is my PhD and the articles I want to publish. You should do the same. Now listen to me."

"I'm listening."

Amina went on: "For my PhD, what I am missing is what can realistically be transported to a planet in terms of terraforming equipment. On the planet, oxygen can be first obtained by hydrolyzing water. With what power? Will it be relying on wind and hydraulic power, or can you bring some compact fusion reactors? Of course, to force a Great Oxygenation Event, you need to grow plants and bring microorganisms, most of all fungi. I need to know what is feasible."

"And you need my help as an economist?"

"Yes," Amina replied. "I'm already forced to cooperate with biologists. If I can put up with them, I can put up with an economist. The Great Oxygenation Event on Earth took three billion years. Some believe that, with existing plants, it could be reproduced in less than a thousand years. I would like to check what is the fastest timeframe that could be realistically be reached with available resources."

"Then you can count on my help," Sanne replied.

"Great. We will also be working with a certain Rebecka Levi, based in Finland. She is taking over as the head of the agricultural department at WARSEC, though I am not sure quite what that means."

They were brought plates with bug burgers and salads.

"*Bon appétit*! I did not see you at the climbing gym today."

It was Samir, who was still working part-time as a cook in the pub restaurant.

"Too much work," Amina replied. "How is Emily?"

"She is at a meeting with some supporters of the Democratic party. The EU elections are approaching, and she is determined not to have Bonavita re-elected."

"I don't like that Bonavita bitch," Amina said. "But I'm Swiss, and I can't vote in the EU. Even if I could, I would not, since I don't care."

Sanne rolled her eyes: "Oh, Amina. I've been sharing a flat with you, climbing with you, and now I'm gonna work with you. How am I gonna survive?"

The rest of spring 2099 went on in Cambridge without anything spectacular happening. Now in his second year of his bachelor's in robotics, Samir was getting more Cs and fewer Bs. However, he had calculated he had the highest grades in his class per hour actually spent studying. He would have gladly studied more, but he also had to work six evenings a week as a cook at the *Honourable Schoolboy*. Not to mention that both Amina and Sanne wanted him to help them with some programming issues. He had indeed become a good-enough programmer, and the two scientist could not do without him.

Meanwhile, Emily had become an active supporter of the Democrats and was campaigning for Guido Niedling against sitting European president Eugenie Bonavita. The elections were scheduled for the last Sunday of May 2099.

On some occasions, the Cambridge Four would meet Aisha Barjaoui, who was now a cadet in the EU Air Force in Cranwell, 130 km (80 miles) north of Cambridge.

Aisha had not been particularly pleased with her first five months at the Air Force Academy. They had trained to parachute and her artificial legs would pop out every time on landing. It was really painful. They had also trained to evac a crashed helicopter in a swimming pool. She dreaded all the pool exercises. She had never been a good swimmer, despite Deng's coaching in his villa, back then in Casablanca. Besides, swimming without legs was exhausting.

In terms of pilot lessons, the first half year had been mostly theory, and she had spent just twenty hours in the simulator.

The spring of 2099 had been more exciting, though. She had obtained her Private Pilot License and had accumulated sixty hours on a single-engine propeller plane. She was now training to qualify to fly the Airbus 910V. The A910V was a small twin-engine vertical take-off and landing propeller plane used by the air force as the main training aircraft.

On Sunday 31 May, in the evening, they all met in Sanne and Amina's student flat. The results of the EU presidential elections were to be announced, and Aisha did not want to be in Cranwell, where almost all the air cadets supported Bonavita anyway. Emily had brought a bottle of champagne.

"If Guido Niedling is elected, we open the bottle," she said.

"According to the latest polls, it's tight," Sanne announced.

They were all sitting on the couch in in front of the TV in the small living room, except Amina who was sitting at the little table nearby, working at her laptop on her thesis. She raised an eye at her friends and commented in a bored voice: "How weird. The first interstellar journey is happening as we speak and no one talks about it. Instead, we are commenting on a presidential election."

"That interstellar journey will not kill anyone," Samir retorted. "But President Bonavita could if she is re-elected."

"Nobody can follow the interstellar journey in real time anyway," Sanne added. "It's not interesting. They should arrive in the Alpha Centauri system around the end of June, but we will not know it before the end of July."

"June 21st," Aisha said. "They will arrive on June 21st. We should get news of their arrival on 17 July."

Emily, who was holding the bottle of champagne in her hand, interrupted them: "We have the results in five seconds… three… two…one."

The cork popped.

Guido Niedling had been elected EU president with 51.3% of the votes. He would be sworn in on 15 September.

On 21 June 2099, late in the evening, Aisha was flying an A910V above the North Sea. She was flying northeast and was somewhere between Cranwell and the Danish coast. The sky was cloudless, and the stars were shining. Beside her sat an instructor.

She had obtained her Private Pilot License in early April and could fly single-engine propeller planes on her own, but she still had a few more flying hours to do before being qualified for the twin-engine tiltrotor Airbus A910V.

Despite the computer-assisted flight control system, however, the small four-seater was not easy to fly. Aisha had found it hard to learn how to land the aircraft vertically but even flying level was challenging. The A910V tiltrotor aircraft demanded much more concentration from the pilot than a regular twin-engine airplane. After accumulating twenty-two flying hours on the A910V, though, Aisha felt she now had full command of the aircraft.

The instructor sitting beside her asked her to turn south.

She looked to her right.

"Three o'clock, low on the horizon, that's Jupiter," she said to her instructor. "Two o'clock, higher, that's Saturnus."

"Not bad, Barjaoui," the instructor replied. "You fly completely steady and level and can marvel at the stars at the same time."

"It's today the *UNSS Forward* arrives at Alpha Centauri," Aisha added. "Though we can't know if they have arrived safely."

"And where will Alpha Centauri be?" the instructor asked.

"You can't see it from here. We would need to go to the southern hemisphere."

"What a pity we don't fly an AF5 Dachshund," the instructor replied. "We could get there in just a couple of hours. You've got the best grades among the cadets, Barjaoui. If you keep up like that, you will be selected to fly an AF5 Dachshund."

Aisha smiled.

The Airbus A910V was a nice little aircraft once one had learnt to fly it, but it really was way too slow.

19: DOCTOR'S LOG
(JULY 2099)

Albaspace neo
(V-Space)

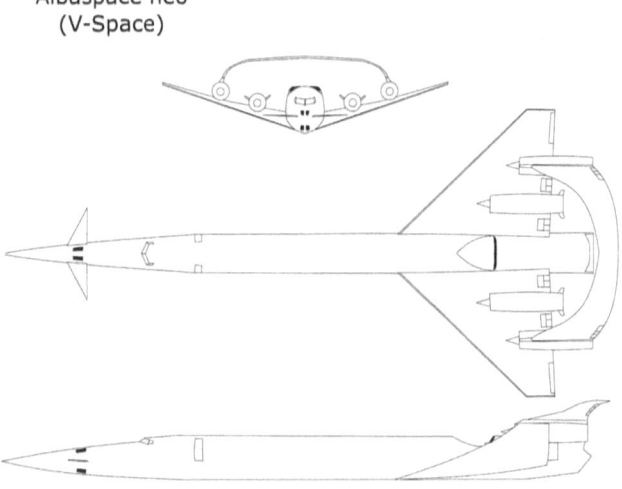

Figure 10: The Albaspace Neo developed by V-Space has the same design as the Albaspace, but is equipped with an EM-drive and has VTOL capabilities. Like the Albaspace, it has no windows, but the cabin is equipped with a multitude of video screens.

As she stepped out of the Albaspace Neo in her light pink space suit, Sophie Couillard was happy: she was walking on the Moon! She was the first of all the Vahlroos personnel to set foot on the Earth's satellite.

"Welcome to the Moon," a voice crackled in the wireless.

It was Tatjana Aydemir, the director of WARSEC's Lunar Coordination Centre. She happened to be on rotation just that week.

"If you wish, we invite you and your test crew to eat dry food in our lunar habs," Tatjana added.

Sophie gladly accepted. A moment later and she and her test crew were picked up by a WARSEC lunar minibus, which drove them into a long tunnel gallery. Neither the minibus nor the tunnel was pressurized and they had to keep their lunar suits on.

The tunnel had been dug by specially adapted tunnel boring machines. The lunar habitation modules were located in this tunnel gallery in order to be protected from both solar radiation and asteroid impacts.

Sophie's crew had met some Boeing test pilots they knew and joined them in hut 7. The minibus drove on to hut 3 where Tatjana Aydemir was staying.

After having gone through the air lock, Sophie removed her lunar suit and was greeted by Tatjana Aydemir, the head of the Lunar Coordination Center. The short, dark-haired WARSEC chief engineer was wearing an orange inner suit.

"Congratulation on the Albaspace Neo," she said to Sophie, looking at her with her piercing blue eyes. "It's impressive."

"Thank you," Sophie replied, "Congratulation to you too."

"For what?" Tatjana asked.

"For all… this, your promotion, the lunar base and WARSEC Ventures. You now have three Forward class star ships manufactured."

"Thank you," Tatjana replied. "I'm only a small part of a well-oiled machine."

She was too modest, Sophie thought. If only she realized how great she was. Women were too often self-deprecating. Tatjana was the one who had made WARSEC Ventures possible. Now, three starships had been manufactured, one of which was currently in the Alpha Centauri system. Of course, she had had help, from Thierry Diakité, for instance. But at least she had been able to hire him, while she, Sophie, had only been able to lose him, because of Michael Vahlroos's stubbornness.

Not only was Tatjana a good leader and manager, but she was also happily married and had two children. If only she knew how lucky she was, Sophie thought.

When Sophie had changed to her inner suit, Tatjana offered her a glass of water and said: "The Albaspace Neo is impressive and you are the architects behind it."

Sophie took a few sips from the glass, smiled, and said:

"Thanks for the compliment. It is equipped with a compact fusion reactor and an Electromagnetic-drive. Takes only five hours to the orbital station and only eleven hours from anywhere on Earth to the lunar base. Of course, vertical take-off and landing capabilities."

Tatjana invited Sophie to sit down in the sofa corner of the windowless lunar habitation and asked: "When will it be certified?"

"We hope by September," Sophie replied.

"I wish you all the best with that," Tatjana said as she sat on the opposite sofa. "If you are successful, it will take another ten years before we launch our own Space Bear Neo, knowing WARSEC. I'm pretty sure you will be able to convince WARSEC to acquire a couple of your Albaspace Neos. Our engineers would love to have only an eleven-hour journey between Vaasa and the Moon."

Sophie drank from her glass of water and said: "We would be happy to sell you a couple of Albaspace Neos. But for us the most important thing will be to boost tourism on the Moon, before we really promote our Albaspace Neo. Ideally, Vahlroos Travel would like to build a lesser lunar resort, as well as a minor lunar orbital station. Some wealthy nerds would pay a fortune just to land on the Moon on board a replica of the lunar module that took Buzz Aldrin and Neil Armstrong there."

"You mean, you would have a hotel on a small lunar orbital station. And from there, tourists will fly an L.E.M. to land on the moon?"

"With a trained pilot, of course."

"That sounds like a great idea," Tatjana said. "You should talk to Ralf about it."

"I don't know if it's my prerogative," Sophie hesitated. "I'm only the GM of V-Space, and I have only a seat on the board of directors of Vahlroos Travel. Michael always has the final word."

"Michael is not the best person to talk to Ralf," Tatjana objected. "WARSEC would also benefit from a smaller orbital station around the moon. We have construction workers currently doing nothing but some simulations back down in Vaasa."

"If you say so."

"Ralf is currently at the orbital station. We are all waiting for the warpedoes sent by the *Forward* from Alpha Centauri: they should arrive anytime. My rotation on the Moon is ending. Just give me a ride to the orbital station onboard your Albaspace, and I will make the proper introduction."

Sophie was starting to like Tatjana already. She was unsophisticated and would find common ground in understanding in the most natural way. Later that day, the Albaspace Neo took off from the Moon base and set course to the orbital station.

In the aerospace shuttle, Tatjana was wearing her WARSEC

orange suit. After the take-off, she went to the cockpit, to ask questions to the pilots. Was it easy to steer a shuttle powered by EM-drive? Was it not counter-intuitive, as compared to chemical propulsion? No, the computer assistance made it so easy that even a US Air Force pilot could fly it. The test pilots were all from the US Navy.

The flight to the orbital station was still six and a half house long, and Tatjana took advantage of it to draft a business proposal. She showed it to Sophie.

When WARSEC eventually colonized planets in remote interstellar systems, they would need to be able to quickly deploy lesser orbital stations and assemble lunar bases. There were currently a few projects in the pipeline, but they were moving slowly because of the lack of resources.

If V-Space was willing to co-finance the project, they could become the owner of the second test 'deployable moon base', as well as co-owner of the small lunar orbital station. Should WARSEC also deploy such a module around Mars, V-Space could become co-owner of that orbital station as well.

Mars? But it would still take between two and three months for an Albaspace Neo to fly there! Sure; however, WARSEC was planning to lease some modified Forward class ships shortly, to promote space tourism *within* the solar system. Vahlroos Travel would certainly be interested in acquiring a Forward class ship and organize tourist trips to Mars.

Sophie pondered one moment over Tatjana's proposition.

It would boost Vahlroos Travel's growth much faster than she could imagine in any of their most optimistic scenarios. She was curious to see what the WARSEC director would think of it.

Tatjana and Sophie met Ralf Åhman in his windowless office in the WARSEC ring, shortly after their Albaspace Neo shuttle had docked into the orbital station.

To Sophie's surprise, he was very positive about Tatjana's proposal. In fact, Ralf was looking for a private partner as well, and had been thinking of Vahlroos Travel himself. However, his currently chilly relationship with Michael Vahlroos had discouraged him from even asking. Sophie informed him she needed to look more carefully into it, but assured him she was definitely interested.

She contacted her business analysts in Burkina Faso. Most of them were on holiday, but there was a summer intern working. His name was Johan Staël von Trollstein, and he was studying business at the London School of Economics. He was an A-student and needed less than four hours to give her a preliminary answer: According to his calculations, V-Space needed only to sell an additional fifty Albaspace Neos to break even. This breaking even did not include the additional income they would get from leasing their space installation to Vahlroos Travel. Not to mention the extra income from the sales of LEM replicas.

Later that evening, she met the CEO of Singapore Airlines in the lounge of the orbital station's Sheraton hotel. He had been disappointed by the Space Bear and the Space Hound, which were not meeting the required level of comfort for his customers. He wanted to invest in forty comfortable aerospace shuttles, and was now thinking of the Albaspace, he told Sophie. Wouldn't he rather try the Albaspace Neo instead? It was faster and could land and take off vertically. Thanks to its EM-drive, it required much less hydrogen and oxygen to be propelled in space, meaning savings in the long run.

The CEO of Singapore Airlines pondered one moment. The acquisition cost of an Albaspace Neo was twice that of a regular Albaspace, which was already the most expensive aerospace shuttle on the market. It was because the EM-drive was powered by a compact fusion reactor, and these were not cheap. As Sophie had said, though, the extra cost would be amortized over twenty years, due to the lower consumption of hydrogen and oxygen. The CEO was still uncertain.

Sophie looked at him and smiled. He could hitch a ride with her if he wanted. She could take him to the Moon, and then up in the stars again and back down to Earth.

He certainly misunderstood, because he tried to follow Sophie to her room. She was saved by some cheering in the orbital station's intercom:

"*Ladies and Gentlemen, please be the first to be informed that the* UNSS Forward *safely reached the Alpha Centauri system on*

22 June. We have just received their warpedo. More information about the first leg of their journey will follow tomorrow."

Everybody went back to the lounge to drink, and Sophie took advantage of it to disappear into her room alone. It was 19 July 2099.

Sophie was back in Bobo-Dioulasso on Wednesday 22 July. She was happy, in a way, that the V-Space headquarters and main factory were located in Burkina Faso. She was doing so much better without Michael. Not only had the most recent tests of the Albaspace Neo gone beyond expectations, but she had obtained three letters of intent, one from Singapore Airlines, one from Qatar Airways, and one from the Chinese Air Force, totaling sixty Albaspace Neos.

She was obviously a good sales representative. She had also struck a deal with WARSEC for the development of lighter orbital stations. The only real condition from WARSEC was that Vahlroos Travel had to pay taxes on the resulting additional profit on space activities, and there was nothing weird about that.

Of course, Michael had at first been highly critical about it. Everything that was not his idea was wrong. She had spent five hours in video conferences trying to persuade him that she was making the right call. In vain. She would resume her efforts the following week.

In the meantime, it was the weekend.

July was the rainy season in Burkina. She did not mind. She was vaccinated against malaria and had a good spray against mosquitoes. She took her mountain bike and went out for a long ride, having fun in the mud. She had got to love Burkina, its green trees, its red earth, its peaceful and merry inhabitants.

She was delightfully exhausted and covered with mud when she came back to her bungalow. She was happy.

She took off her muddy clothes, threw them in the laundry basket and went in the shower. When she came out, she put her towel around her waist (her neighbor, a Saudi expat would often peek through her window) and went to her room.

There was a naked man on her bed.

It was Michael.

That was the collateral damage of the Albaspace. It took only forty-two minutes to travel from New York to Bobo-Dioulasso, and the CEO of the Vahlroos Corporation now had his private Albaspace.

"What are you doing here, completely naked, without even a mosquito net?" she asked him. "Are you suicidal? Are you even vaccinated against malaria?"

"Don't worry about me," Michael said as he stood up. "I came here to apologize."

He went to Sophie and tried to hug her.

"Sorry, Mike, I have my period," she lied.

"Your periods? Oh, sorry."

Sophie noted satisfactorily how his reproductive organ

downgraded itself to a mere urinary device. She would be left in peace.

"Let me get dressed," Sophie added. "And you should do the same. Mosquitoes are real bitches here. It's not nice when they suck you."

A moment later, they sat on the couch in Sophie's living room, each holding a cold bottle of Sobebra, the locally brewed beer.

"I really love it," Sophie said. "Definitely the best beer in the world."

"I agree it has a lovely and charming taste."

"Not as expensive as your Château Petrus wine, but better," Sophie went on. "So, what is wrong with my deal? It's economically sound."

Michael took a sip from his beer and said: "In the plane, on the way here, I realized you were right after all. This will give Vahlroos Travel the opportunity to expand their activities on the Moon while boosting the sales of the Albaspace Neo."

"Not to mention an option to open a tourist center on Mars," Sophie added. "WARSEC wants to encourage tourism within the whole solar system and is ready to lease warp-ships to private corporations. They will be modified so that you cannot warp beyond the outer limit of the solar system, but still, that means that tourism to Mars or any other planet becomes possible. You know, Ralf Åhman is a good and intelligent man. I don't think you should keep seeing him as your archenemy."

Michael shrugged: "Come on, Sof, you know he is not my archenemy. However, I think he has softened his position thanks to my bringing the case of the Vienna Treaty to the International Court of Justice."

Sophie calmly took a sip from her bottle of beer before she replied: "You are wrong. They just want money to finance interstellar exploration. They can only increase their revenue by encouraging commercial space activities. There is nothing convoluted in that."

"Sophie, Sophie, Sophie, sometimes it seems that you are so naïve," Michael said, and took the remote control to switch the TV on.

That was typical Michael. When he was losing an argument, he would just bury his head in the sand, or rather bury his brain into a TV program.

This time, it was interesting, though. It was about the interstellar mission to Alpha Centauri. The *UNSS Forward* had arrived in the Alpha Centauri's comet belt on 22 June, early morning, after a journey of 156 days. The journey had proven a few hours longer than intended. On 24 June, they had made contact with the warpedoes previously sent from Earth, and sent one back with messages and all sort of data.

The spaceship's Chief Medical Officer, Dr. Eamon Windsor, had recorded a series of humorous videocasts, which were now being released by the WARSEC press department. It was a brilliant PR coup, Sophie thought.

Dr. Eamon Windsor was not just any psychiatrist. He had also been the last king of England. When his mother, the queen, had died after a long-term illness in July 2096, he had been made king, King Eamon. It had caused a lot of stir. His crime: he was not white. His father had happened to be of Pakistani origin, and even the fact that that he had died during the 2073 Qatari flu, like so many other healthcare personnel, while working to save and protect English lives, had not seemed to soften right-extremists in the UK.

King Eamon had then surprised everybody, committing to staying on the throne until the UK became either a constitutional monarchy with a written constitution, or a republic. The South British government had been left with no other choice than to organize a referendum, and the English and Welsh citizens had voted for a republic.

Eamon Windsor had subsequently applied to WARSEC and been accepted as a medical officer. He was now on the first interstellar mission, and it was, of course, good PR for WARSEC to have a popular ex-King onboard.

Michael decided to go to the WARSEC online channel to check the videocasts. He picked the teaser.

Dr. Eamon Windsor was sitting in front of a camera.

"Doctor's log. Earth date: 2099-01-17. We have today departed from the Earth's orbit. Twenty-seven men and women trapped in

a cylindrical spaceship. It seems that couples are already forming. I have to ensure it will not impact the teamwork."

"Doctor's log. Earth date: 20 99-01-31. The first two weeks have been exhausting. The captain, Alice Fù, has insisted on having a fire drill every second day. Many onboard believe that the departure was rushed for no other purpose than to please some politicians. As a former head of state, myself, I choose to believe their suspicions are unfounded."

"Doctor's log. Earth date: 20 99-02-13. This Friday 13 February is our lucky day. The captain has decided to reduce the frequency of fire drills to only once a week. Finally. Safety is still in focus, though. She might come to you and ask: A nuclear reactor is about to explode, what do you do? Or, we are coming out of warp, and a comet is coming straight at us, what do you do? You'd better answer correctly, or you will be forced to watch some old Ridley Scott movies."

"Doctor's log. Earth date: 20 99-03-13. This Friday 13 March has been my unlucky day. I happened to watch a Ridley Scott movie called Prometheus, *followed by another one named* Alien: Covenant. *I should have stayed in bed instead. Do not watch these two films. They depict space exploration as executed by morons. Luckily, the recruitment at WARSEC is slightly more serious. I have so far not spotted any morons onboard."*

"Doctor's log. Earth date: 20 99-03-20. One of our fellow scientists, the geologist of the team, decided to test the beornine and go into hibernation. Beornine is a substance that has been

retrieved from hibernating bears. It allows you to sleep for a longer period and keep your muscles while burning your fat. You basically need one kilo of fat per week spent in hibernation. Unlike in sci-fi movies, though, you continue to age. So, there is no real good reason to want to use beornine. The only explanation is therefore that our good geologist got bored with the movies available on this cylindrical ship. I put the blame on Ridley Scott."

"Doctor's log. Earth date: 20 99-04-17. It's wonderful how astronauts never need to clean anything in sci-fi movies. The truth is less glamorous. Engineers are responsible for keeping the core clean. Pilots have to keep the flight deck and operation rooms clean. The rest of us have to keep the kitchens and common areas clean. Not to mention our own cabins. I have to change the sheets of my bed, and the captain inspects it to be sure it is done every week. I should have remained king of England and Wales in Buckingham Palace. Back then I had working servants and non-working robots to help me."

"Doctor's log. Earth date: 20 99-05-08. This week we had the first serious breakup onboard with impact on the team spirit. There had been a violent argument as to who would keep a dog. The incident has now been resolved and life onboard that ship continues normally."

"Doctor's log. Earth date: 20 99-05-31. Today is the election for the EU president. I guess we will not know the results before the end of July, when we depart Alpha Centauri after receiving the second wave of warpedoes from Earth. I just realized I forgot to vote. *Was not thinking about it back in January. I don't even know who the candidate against sitting President Bonavita is."*

"*Doctor's log. Earth date: 20 99-06-22. We just arrived in the comet belt around the Alpha Centauri system. There was quite some tension before we came out of warp in the comet belt. The probability of hitting a comet upon arrival was less than having a car crash on Earth. We were all very scared, though: some people sometimes win the lottery. Now we have to make some observations to spot the warpedoes Earth sent us and plan our next trip."*

"*Doctor's log. Earth date: 20 99-06-24. It took us some time to spot the warpedoes sent by WARSEC with news dated from 22 May. We were quite disappointed to see that we did not miss any good movies. What is wrong on Earth? Anyway, now starts our full exploration. Next update will be sent by the end of July."*

"Well, that means we will not know before the end of August", Sophie concluded.

20: TWO STARS AND A DWARF (AUG 2099)

In that last weekend of August, the leaves had started to turn orange in the archipelago off the city of Vaasa, on the Finnish West Coast. Thierry Diakité was jogging along the coast line. Husky Apollo was trotting beside him, his tongue hanging out. Kokoni Calypso had to be carried. It was a hot, sunny Saturday, and Thierry could see the Swedish coast far to the northeast.

After a small turn, he finally spotted the camping car, a few hundred meters away, just by the sea. He put Calypso on the ground and started to sprint toward it.

The camping car's number plate read "SPACE BITCH". Besides it, Anatoli Govorov and Tintin Mutombo were sitting in fishing chairs, holding fishing rods, both wearing long shorts, polo shirts, and sandals. Thierry was sweaty and panting when he joined them. Apollo had outrun him and jumped into the sea, splashing around.

"Apollo!" Anatoli screamed, "We are trying to fish, here."

"Apollo, *kom, kom hit,*" Thierry said ('Come here').

Apollo had a Swedish owner, and understood Swedish better than English. The Husky came out of the sea holding a fish in his jaws.

"He's a better fisherman than you two," Thierry said.

"Where is Calypso?" Anatoli asked.

"Your kokoni bitch is a real bitch," Thierry replied. "She kept just sitting down and refused to run. I had to carry her most of my jog. But she is coming now."

The little brown kokoni was now at the camp, jumping on a water bottle. She was thirsty. Thierry took the bottle and poured some into the dog's bowl.

"*Isä! Haluan juuri tuollaisen koiran!*" ('Daddy! That's exactly a dog like this one I want.')

It was a small blond Finnish boy pointing out Calypso to his father.

"What is its race?" the father asked in English.

"It's a kokoni," Anatoli replied. "It's an ancient Greek dog breed."

The Russian physicist looked at the boy and went on in very approximate Finnish.

"*Moi pojka. Se on kokoni. Pieni koira on iso paska. On väsynyt kun iso paska murmeli. Et halua kokonin.*" ('Hi, boy. This is Kokoni. Small dog is big shit. Is tired like a big shit marmotte. You not want kokoni.').

The boy laughed, and his father took him away.

"I love Finnish men," Tintin said. "They barely talk, they are quiet, and not unnecessarily sociable. That's the dream, to live in Finland. And now we are having a perfect Finnish holiday: doing nothing by the water."

"Do you like it?" Thierry said as he went to grab a can of beer.

"I hate it," Tintin replied.

"It sucks," Anatoli admitted. "But we had to try at least one typical Finnish holiday. Besides, Mikko put me in charge of Apollo. I cannot just travel around."

"We are only sixty kilometers from WARSEC's HQ," Thierry noted. "I could consider spending the night back in Vaasa."

"Wrong suggestion," Tintin replied. "Anatoli is leasing that camping car. He has committed for two years. We have to use it."

"I was not picked for the Alpha Centauri mission," Anatoli defended himself, "Why not lease a camping car?"

"Because you are only thirty-four," Tintin replied. "Your mid-life crisis shouldn't be starting for at least six years."

"Let's say, I am moving into social sciences," Anatoli replied. "I try to find out what it is like to be an average middle-class, middle-aged Scandinavian. It's a sociological project. And, you see, it's not that bad."

"Nobody would ever guess you two shared a Nobel Prize in Physics," Thierry commented. "Let's look at the bright side: we have a good internet connection. Orbit Control retrieved the warpedo sent by the Alpha Centauri mission a few days ago. They will release some of its content on the intranet today. We can check it, this evening."

The three space-people turned out to be unable to catch any fish in the afternoon, and they decided to grill some bugburgers instead. Anatoli lit a fire and installed a grill on the side of it. The sun was now low on the horizon, and about to disappear behind the Swedish coast. The air turned chilly, and they put fleeces on. Suddenly, they heard some people singing and playing the guitar. The sound was coming from a group of teenagers around another fire, a few hundred meters away.

"Oh no," Anatoli complained. "The worst species ever, which will never become extinct. The guitar player by the beach. They are gonna pollute our ears all night long."

"You can't escape them if you go to the sea," Tintin commented.

"Still, we are in Finland," Anatoli objected. "We could at least have had a hard rock group playing!"

They put some peppers, mushrooms, and bug burgers on the grill, while Thierry checked his computer, sitting on a fishing chair.

"OK, I have it all now," he said. "It seems that Eamon has done another of his 'Doctor's logs.'"

Tintin sat down on his chair, while Anatoli put his chair just by the fire to monitor the barbecue.

Thierry clicked on play, and they heard Eamon's voice.

"Doctor's log. Earth date: 20 99-06-26. Nothing worth studying around Alpha Centauri A and Alpha Centauri B. Two stars, of spectral type G2 V and K1 V, with only two asteroid belts orbiting around them. Boring for me, as a psychiatrist. Boring also for our scientific team. We hastily deployed some satellites in the asteroid belts and directed some probes into the two stars. A few tours in a White Parrot were not impressive. Our solar system is much better. However, we spotted a planet around Proxima Centauri. Proxima Centauri is a red dwarf, 0.3 light years away from the Alpha Centauri AB system. We just went into warp, heading for it."

"Doctor's log. Earth date: 20 99-07-07. Yesterday, we came out of warp in the vicinity of Proxima Centauri. We went on a tour onboard a White Parrot today. Scientists are thrilled to be the first humans to approach a red dwarf. I'm not. It barely emits any light. It's dark and gloomy.

"Doctor's log. Earth date: 20 99-07-08. We are now orbiting the planet around Proxima Centauri. We are the first humans to reach an exoplanet. Scientists onboard are all thrilled as to how many articles they will manage to get published in Science. *The rest of the crew is not. It's a dark planet. The red dwarf emits such dark light that one barely sees the planet with one's own eyes. You need infrared vision."*

"Doctor's log. Earth date: 20 99-07-10. Today we have

deployed satellites around the planet. The only thrilling part was when we could see the sun. Our sun, from the solar system, shining 4.2 light years away. If people were one day to colonize this planet, they would need more than one shrink to keep the suicide rate in check."

"Doctor's log. Earth date: 20 99-07-13. We now have some information about this dark and shitty planet. There is a magnetic field. The planet's revolution around Proxima Centauri is 24 days long. However, the planet's rotation is also 24 days. That means that it always keeps the same side oriented toward the red dwarf, while the other face is always in the dark. Probable presence of liquid water on the red-star oriented side, but not on the other side. Unbelievable it took so long for the scientists to conclude this planet was not colonizable."

"Doctor's log. Earth date: 20 99-07-25. All attempts to land a working probe on the planet have failed. The first probe exploded upon atmosphere entry. The two other probes had parachute malfunctions. Today, one probe finally landed, but we lost the signal shortly after. The engineers blame it on being rushed by the scientists. The geologist of the crew is angry he will not be able to publish any articles that could make it to Science, but only to regular geological journals. One year lost for him, he said. One year lost for all of us, I say.

"Doctor's log. Earth date: 20 99-07-28. We warp away back to Earth today. The scientific team is not happy about this, but there is political pressure on Earth for us to be back before the

31 December 2099. It seems, however, that the rest of the crew is happy to go back to Earth. We have indeed been the first humans on an interstellar mission but, for most of us, it has felt like a wasted year in our lives."

When the podcast was over, Anatoli finally said:

"Well, perhaps I am not so unhappy not to have been selected for that mission."

"Dr. Windsor is funny," Thierry said, "But the reports by Alice Fù are more interesting."

"Alice's reports are certainly good," Tintin admitted, "But you couldn't broadcast them. They are too serious. Not funny enough."

"As a spaceship commander, she has done really good work, and she raises real questions," Thierry went on. "For instance, when you come out of warp, the risk of collision in the comet belts has not been properly addressed. Once you are in the comet belt, it takes an incredibly long time to calculate the coordinates to warp into the exact wanted location within the star system. There is room for improvement. Then, there is the problem with the crew. It seems that Mikko's and Valeriya's breakup almost led to an incident. The main reason behind the failed probe landing, actually."

"Poor Apollo," Anatoli said, looking at the husky dog, "His dad and his mum are now separated, and he does not know about it."

Both Apollo and Calypso were looking at the bug burgers being grilled. Anatoli took one, split it into several pieces and gave them to the two dogs. He then gave the other burgers, peppers and mushrooms to Thierry and Tintin, who put them between pieces of bread on their plates.

"Mmm, that's good," Thierry said. "Happy not to be onboard the *UNSS Forward*."

Which caused Tintin to add: "Then, there is the problem of not being able to grow fresh food in the spaceship. They have only a few tomatoes, and it seems to have impacted the morale of the crew."

"Rebecka Levi is working on it," Thierry pointed out. "For the next exploration wave, there will be fresh food onboard the ships."

"That's the very least they can do to improve life quality onboard," Anatoli said. "For a three-year mission, you want to eat something other than lyophilized food every day. How is it going with the Ambassador class, by the way?"

"Slowly, but surely," Thierry answered. "Within one year, we should have completed the first Ambassador class shipyard on the moon. If WARSEC keeps earning money from the sales of aerospace shuttles, the first Ambassador class ship will be ready in two years."

"Any insider information about her name?" Anatoli asked.

"She will be called the *UNSS Eleonore Roosevelt*," Thierry replied.

"Eleonore Roosevelt?" Tintin wondered.

"All the Ambassador class ships will have the name of UN diplomats," Thierry explained, "and Eleonore Roosevelt is Ralf's favorite US ambassador to the UN."

"I still believe WARSEC is making a mistake," Tintin said. "We rush into manufacturing colonization ships the size of an aircraft carrier and which can travel at warp 10 because we can. We should, instead, wait for the new purple matter and build an interstellar ship able to reach warp 100 or even warp 200."

"You are not being realistic," Thierry said, "WARSEC is more about politics than science anyway. You want to ask the UN General Assembly to wait another ten years before launching true interstellar missions? The Assembly represents governments elected for four or five years."

The sun had now disappeared behind the horizon, and all three felt a chill despite their fleeces, as night was falling. Finnish evenings always cooled so fast. They could still hear the teenagers singing and playing the guitar further away.

"I know politics steer WARSEC," Tintin admitted. "It's a pity."

21: 21C
(DEC 2099)

In Cambridge, Amina Dörflinger had been satisfied with her year 2099 overall. Her cooperation with both her economist roommate, Sanne van der Maas, and WARSEC's agronomist Rebecka Levi had proved fruitful. She had built a satisfactory model to realistically simulate an artificial oxygenation event on a planet with the presence of liquid water and a carbon dioxide-rich atmosphere.

According to astrophysicists, the odds of finding such a planet within an acceptable range (i.e. less than 500 light years from Earth), were quite decent, hence her funding.

When Earth had been formed, four and a half billion years ago, there had been, at the beginning, only tiny concentrations of oxygen in the early atmosphere, consisting mainly of methane, nitrogen, and carbon dioxide. The first living organisms had been energy efficient enough to survive on these quantities, though. They fed on carbon dioxide, through photosynthesis, throwing out oxygen as a waste product. The Great Oxygenation Event on Earth had probably taken three billion years for the atmospheric dioxygen to reach an acceptable concentration, for more advanced animals to thrive in.

If mankind was to colonize a habitable planet, one did not want to wait three billion years before one could walk on its surface without a spacesuit. Hence the purpose of Amina's PhD.

There had been two reasons why the so-called Great Oxygenation Event had taken so long on Earth. The first reason had been that the first eukaryote cells producing oxygen were far from being efficient. With today's rate of photosynthesis, it was believed that a Great Oxygenation Event on Earth could happen in just one thousand years. The second reason had been that most of the first oxygen molecules produced were absorbed in the soil in the form of iron oxides.

On a non-geological timescale, the oxidation of a planet's iron ores was not an issue. One had to simply ensure the production of a large excess of oxygen by keeping the colony population below three billion inhabitants at its maximum.

Sanne's model was simulating how fast an oxygenation event could occur on a given planet, with a given set of parameters, while optimizing the use of available terraforming resources. The speed of oxygenation was also a function of the volcanic activity. The more volcanic a planet was, the more release of carbon dioxide there was, and the longer an oxygenation process would take. However, it could be offset by the percentage of the ocean surface. Underwater volcanic eruptions would have their CO_2 emissions trapped in the sea before leaking into the atmosphere.

The WARSEC plans for oxygenizing a planet were to attempt a combined approach. They would release photosynthetic microorganisms in large quantities in the oceans. The more seas, the better. They would deploy oxygenation modules, hydrolyzing water and releasing oxygen and hydrogen into the atmosphere. Most importantly, they would grow oxygenation forests on all available grounds. The trees would be grown under tents, specially designed to be able to provide them with the required amount of oxygen. The forests would be tended with the help of robots.

Assuming a reasonably steady supply of photosynthetic microorganisms and seeds from Earth, as well as at least 2,000 initial settlers, to be reinforced in subsequent waves, Amina's model was showing that it would require between five and thirty years to reach an oxygen concentration of 10%, which was half the concentration on Earth, but enough for any trained mountaineers to breathe normally.

Amina's supervisor had not been impressed, though. Dr. Sheldon Cooper, author of *Feedback from the Earth* had been very disappointed that Amina had suddenly shifted interest from calculating the probability of a super-volcanic eruption on Earth, which would condemn mankind to its extinction, to the science-fiction project of terraforming another planet.

Amina had argued that there was more funding in terraforming research than apocalyptic scenario planning. Though Dr. Cooper had admitted it was good for his department, he could not really get used to cooperating with biologists.

Biologists just whined about extinct pandas and bonobos, and focused on protecting dying species. That was unrealistic! All species were meant to become extinct anyway, including mankind. If only these idealist scientists could keep their ideas down-to-earth and better comprehend the geological timescale. What was life compared to rocks? Nothing! Biologists had better get serious and show more respect to geologists.

This childish conflict between Amina's supervisor and the biology department meant that she was stuck in her writing of three scientific papers. Dr. Cooper did not want to have the name of Rebecka Levi as second author, not to mention the names of two Cambridge biologists he did not like.

To Amina's consolation, the situation was even more absurd for her flatmate, Sanne, who was doing her PhD on the '*Study of the Economic feasibility of interstellar colonization under WARSEC's supervision*'. She had followed Amina's advice and limited her subject to the colonization of an Earth-sized planet to be force-oxygenized.

She had obtained quite some data from WARSEC, thanks to her connection with Ralf Åhman, and had come up with some quite realistic scenarios for the colonization of a planet. During the oxygenation phase, the whole colonization would happen under close supervision by WARSEC. Private corporations could be associated, but only within a regulated consortium. The first settlers could be the stakeholders of that large consortium, as they would initially not be paid in money, but in various credit units, to be used for different purposes (food, housing, etc.). For the duration of the initial phase, the economy had to be very strictly regulated, according to Sanne. Only when the oxygen concentration had reached an acceptable level, and the colony population had reached a critical mass, while warp communication had been made faster, would it be possible to consider a gradual liberalization of that economy.

The WARSEC director had been really impressed by Sanne's first three drafts. Her supervisor had not. According to him, she was completely biased, a leftist, and should not even have graduated her master's, for which she had written an unacceptable thesis.

It was only then, having heard him say this, that Sanne realized her supervisor had in fact been an adept of the Chicago school. A *Chicagoan* in Cambridge! She should have checked earlier.

According to him, it was inconceivable to propose that only planned economy would ensure successful colonization. She was trapped in her vision of space economy as a 'survival economy', similar to 'war economy', in which, it was true, public authority had a leading role to play. According to her supervisor, space conquest had to be approached as a 'frontier economy'. When Cortez had conquered South America, had he resorted to the so-called planned economy? Of course not! When the Americans had conquered the Wild West, or the Russians the Far East, had they resorted to a planned economy? Of course not! Her supervisor would show mathematic models demonstrating why the space conquest was more in phase with a frontier economy than a survival economy.

On two occasions, Sanne had shown him that his model was flawed because of wrong assumptions related to the speed of information. She had been told in response that she knew nothing about mathematics because she was a woman. She had tried to point out that the so-called frontier economy had been a wild economy with very inefficient markets anyway, as she had shown in her master's thesis. Her supervisor had just replied that she knew nothing about history.

As Christmas was approaching, both Amina and Sanne were having a difficult time, not at all because of their scientific progress, but because of their respective supervisors.

They had little time left for climbing, and on the few occasions they met Emily and Samir at the gym, the latter boasted he would never do a PhD. He had now started the last year of his bachelor's in robotics and was quite satisfied that robots were more logical than PhD supervisors. Robotics was not magic to him anymore, it was pure logic.

So-called 'deep learning' was nothing than recursion loops and database optimization, and the concept of deep learning was vastly exaggerated. A baby could be shown a dog and be told 'dog': it would learn instantly a dog was a dog. A robot had to be shown tons of images of dogs before being able to recognize one and, even then, it could never do it with 100% accuracy. If people only knew the calculation efforts that were needed for a machine to tell that a dog was a dog, compared to that of a baby's brain, they would just stop writing sci-fi movies about artificial intelligence taking over the world.

Robots were nothing but algorithms, recursion loops, and probability calculations, and each interaction needed quite some calculation power, which in its turn required energy. They were dependent on sensors, which all needed high maintenance. The least technical trouble and the debugging effort could be enormous. In fact, the average manpower required to heal a sick or wounded human being was just less than that to fix a broken robot.

Human beings were still, in 2099, simply better than robots, and Samir had sincerely no idea when robots might realistically be able to take over from mankind. His best guess was: never. Of course, the drone incident at Khouribga had been the proof that robots ought to be better regulated, as bugs or bad update procedures could have dreadful consequences.

The so-called 'transhumanists' of the start of the century had been nothing other than a continuation of the New Age movement that came from that same west coast of the USA. These engineers, who used to believe that they would be able to transfer their minds into machines, had been nothing else than a bunch of weirdos afraid of dying, like Chinese emperors trying immortality potions before them. At least, so Samir's teacher had explained.

When the Christmas holiday finally arrived, Samir took a train to Paris. He hated his father, but his siblings had insisted on seeing him. Emily accompanied him. Samir's sister Soraya was bringing her Swedish boyfriend, and they would be quite a majority to hold their male supremacist father in check. Fat Ali would hate them. Samir liked the thought of it.

As Amina was also visiting her mother in Switzerland, Sanne was quite happy that Aisha spend the Christmas holiday in Cambridge. Aisha had now flown another fifty-five hours on the A910V, obtaining certification for instrument flight, while doing her debut on a training jet aircraft. During the fall of 2099, Aisha had also enrolled in a correspondence class to pass her commercial pilot license, which she had obtained just before the holiday.

Christmas in Cambridge was generally rather depressing, but the Christmas week that year had not been completely uneventful.

The new EU president, Guido Niedling, had decided that the *Church of Quantology* should be considered as a dangerous cult and be forbidden throughout the EU. The EU headquarters of that cult was located in Cambridge, just in front of the *Honourable Schoolboy*. There had been some confrontation between Quantologists and the English riot police. Aisha and Sanne did not really mind, except that they could not access their favorite pub.

Finally, Amina, Samir, and Emily were all back in Cambridge for New Year's Eve, which had been called 21C by the media, as the year 2100 was about to begin.

They spent New Year Eve's in Sanne's and Amina's flat.

There was a ring on the bell and Aisha opened. It was Robin, Axel, and Joe from the climbing center.

"Good that you came," Amina said. "I was hoping to climb on somebody tonight."

There was some laughter.

Their New Year's Eve dinner consisted of a raclette with cheese and charcuterie Amina had brought back from Switzerland. With it, they had Valais wine.

"That's why we exercise so much," Robin said, "to indulge ourselves in fatty food once in a while."

"No climbing tomorrow morning," Samir said. "The rope will not hold if you fall."

"No worries," Axel replied. "He can slow down his fall by farting."

Joe, who was the nerdiest of the invited climbers, changed the subject: "The *UNSS Forward* has just returned from its interstellar mission. Amina, Sanne, you are the smart people here, anything to say?"

Amina drank her full glass of white wine and said: "They went, they saw, they did not like it, they went somewhere else, they did not like it either, they lost expensive equipment, they ran out of condoms and came back, to be put in quarantine. What do you want me to say?"

Robin laughed and added: "At least they have alcohol in their quarantine. I saw it in the news this morning. Even though they have to wait in quarantine for a few weeks, WARSEC send them fresh foods."

Axel put some melted Swiss raclette cheese on his bread and said: "Samir, you know Eamon, the doctor of the *Forward*, from your time as a slavant. You are not jealous of him?"

"Sincerely not," Samir replied, "After hearing his description of the journey, I'm happy I spent this year with my feet on Earth."

"It was a stupid mission from the beginning," Sanne pointed out as she was laying melted cheese and ham on her piece of bread. "They knew it was nothing but exhibition. Now, the protocol dictates that we have to say 'waaooh! Mankind has completed their first interstellar journey'... But I am not impressed."

"Of course, not," Aisha agreed. "Nobody is impressed. It's time-related."

"What do you mean?" Emily asked.

"In our society," Aisha answered, "people are only impressed by the things they can see and live in real time. The first warping of Alcubierre, that was impressive. We all remembered what we were doing back then. I was sitting by the pool at a friend's place. What were you doing?"

"Watching it from the TV at the pub in front of the climbing center," Robin replied

"I had just been released from custody by the French police," Samir said. "My asshole father was so absorbed by the show that he did not yell at me spending the night at the police station."

"I was working as an orderly at an old man's place," Amina answered. "We had just climbed the Matterhorn. I fell asleep in front of the show."

"But you remember where you were," Aisha said. "The point is that people are only impressed by what can be shared or broadcasted live. I have served in the Legion. We did some good stuff in Kirghizstan. It was impressive to me. But to nobody but the people who were there. We did some bad stuff in Morocco and were punished by even worse. Khouribga. Nobody has ever been truly shocked by what happened there. There was no live transmission and an effective censorship. The investigation afterward never disclosed any image of it.

There was a silence around the table.

Aisha went on: "This journey to Alpha Centauri and Proxima Centauri was never live broadcasted. Interstellar exploration will never be live broadcasted. It's a question of physics. Radio waves will never go faster than light."

Joe burst into laughter and said: "Except in *Star Wars Episode 28*, where they have a real-time holographic conversation, though they are on different planets!"

"Exactly," Aisha admitted. "Interstellar exploration is, and will be, boring. But it does not make it less impressive."

"Cheers to Aisha," Sanne said. "You should become a pilot in WARSEC."

They all raised their glasses.

"Why not? But first I want to be a fighter pilot and shoot drones."

Later that night, Aisha went out for a walk. Samir and Emily had gone home at two in the morning. *Couples never have the energy to stay late at night*, she thought. Sanne was hooking up with Robin, and Amina with Axel, while Joe, the nerdiest of the climbers, had gone home.

She decided to follow the river Cam to Sheep's Green. She had not drunk much. She was not in the Legion anymore. She was training to be a pilot, and wanted to avoid taking on bad habits. The fourth term would be very competitive. Out of the 150 cadets, only twelve would be selected to become fighter pilots. The others would have to satisfy themselves with being transport pilots, helicopter pilots, or, even worse, glider pilots. She was aiming to become a fighter pilot. She wanted to be able to shoot through the clouds onboard an AF5 Dachshund.

Speaking of the devil, the clouds were dissipating to the south, and she even caught a glimpse of the Moon, further to the east. Above the horizon, she recognized the Great Dog constellation and spotted Sirius. That star was a bit more than eight light years away, she remembered. Some people would probably embark on an interstellar journey to explore that system quite soon, in a couple of years maximum. They were lucky. Amina, who was writing a PhD about terraforming, did not seem to realize she was one of the perfect candidates to be part of the next exploration wave.

Aisha would happily volunteer for that kind of mission, but she knew no one would accept her, and the ghost pain she constantly felt in her amputated legs was always there to remind her.

He smartphone biped. She had received a message. It was from her ex-captain Léger:

Bonne année, Aisha. J'ai été pris en tant que safety officer au WARSEC. ['Happy new year, Aisha. I have been accepted as a safety officer at WARSEC']/ *Antoine. PS: Will be better than guiding fat tourists to the top of Mont Blanc.*

22: Reaching For The Stars (Spring 2100)

In Cranwell, discipline among the air force cadets was the responsibility of the most senior among them. The majority were warrant officers, while the others, coming from other branches of the forces, had kept their original ranks. The most senior cadet was a captain from the marine paratroopers. Aisha Barjaoui, as a former lieutenant in the Foreign Legion, was the second highest ranked cadet.

As such, she had been tasked to ensure that her barrack was kept tidy. She hated it. She had always hated clearing up and, at the beginning, had failed to keep her room exemplarily clean. As the only female senior officer, she was the only occupant of her two-bed room, and it had not incited her to lead by example. Lower ranked cadets in her barrack had used it as an excuse not to keep their dormitories that tidy. Some female cadets had also complained to her that most of their male counterparts expected them to do most of the cleaning.

As a result, the female cadets had gone on strike, and all the barracks had been denied permissions a few weekends in a row.

Aisha had tried to defuse the crisis by being more exemplary, showing how she was cleaning her own room, and asking every cadet in her barrack to do so. Some of the male cadets had refused, though. There were led by a certain Nicolas de Villiers. Aisha had had no other choice than ask the base wing commander to discipline these refractory cadets.

Since then, Nicolas de Villiers and his henchmen had been extremely resentful toward Aisha, insinuating she had been accepted at the academy only because she was a quadruple minority: she was an Arab, a Muslim, a cripple, and a woman.

First, she had tried to react to these allegations. It only caused the rumors to spread more within the academy. She had tried to complain to her superiors, but she could see most of the senior officers were rather mocking her behind her back.

The cadet captain would only say: "What do you want me to say? You are a Muslim, an Arab, a woman and a cripple. That's not a rumor, that's a fact."

In the end, Aisha just gave up. She accepted that she would have to live with it. The whole training was only three years long. She now understood why Captain Léger had left the regular EU Army for the Foreign Legion, a few years back. Douchebags were overrepresented in the regular armed forces.

She focused instead on studying and training and socialized

as little as possible with the rest of the cadets. This had not been a major issue during the first three terms of the training. Now, she feared it may negatively impact her chance of becoming a fighter pilot. With the exception of the evacuation and parachute training, where she had done rather poorly, she had been majoring all the courses despite all the mocking and laughing. As a result, both the tall Nicolas de Villiers and his shorter wingman François Wauquiez, who had white hair despite his young age, saw her as a threat. Both of them also aimed at becoming fighter pilots.

During this fourth term, the whole class would take three seven-week-long specialization modules in three branches: the helicopter branch, the transport branch, and the fighter branch. The cadets would be graded for each of the modules, and be given an overall rank. Depending on their final rank, they would be given the possibility to choose their specialization for the last year. The top twelve cadets usually chose the fighter branch, while those with the lowest grades would become glider pilots.

For this term, the class had been split into three groups of fifty cadets, which would take each of the three specialization modules one after another. During the first seven weeks, Aisha's group was sent to the helicopter module. She would certainly have enjoyed it more if the weather had been better. However, she accumulated sixty flying hours, including eight hours in a combat helicopter. For this module, she was ranked second in her group, behind François Wauquiez.

The next module was perhaps the least thrilling as it was the one for transport aircraft. However, in most of the flights, they would go over the cloud ceiling and see the sun. Aisha soon learnt to like it. As part of the transportation module, Aisha first flew two dozen hours on the Airbus 920V, which was a twin-engine vertical take-off and landing aircraft. It was slightly more tedious to fly than its little sister, the training A910V. She then accumulated twenty hours onboard the Airbus 800M, which was a large four-engine turbo-propeller transport aircraft.

She also got to fly the Airbus 590C on a simulator. The A590C was a gigantic four-engine cargo jet, sister of the A590, which was the largest passenger plane in the world. They would only fly it on the simulator, because of a cost reduction program, but Aisha thought it was a fantastic aircraft anyway. When they saw how happy she was in the simulator, Wauquiez and de Villiers hinted that she should join the transport branch.

Perhaps they were right, since she majored the module with grades far above the second-best cadet of her group. However, she wanted to become a fighter pilot. This was personal. She wanted to pilot an Airbus Fighter 5, also known as AF5 Dachshund. She wanted to use its twin 25-mm Gatling guns and shoot down drones.

When they started the fighter module, they were not handed AF5 aircraft immediately. Their skills were first tested on the AF1 Chihuahua. The Airbus Fighter 1 was a single-engine twin-seated training jet. It had been nicknamed Chihuahua by an air force general who claimed that it was way too noisy for such a small, harmless thing. The AF1 was indeed subsonic and would not stand a chance in aerial combat against enemy aircraft. However, it was quite maneuverable, and Aisha really enjoyed it.

After the first twenty flying hours, they started practicing aerial combat, and especially dog fighting. Their instructor was Major Kenneth O'Malley. He recognized Aisha Barjaoui from Khouribga, where he had bailed out after himself gunning down five drones.

"For about 100 years, aerial combat was mainly about firing missiles and eluding them," he said. "However, missiles just kept becoming more expensive while efficient countermeasures just became cheaper. Who has been in a plane shot by missiles?"

Aisha raised her hand, remembering what had happened to her three and a half years ago.

"Where was it?" Major O'Malley asked.

"Bishkek, in Kirghizstan," Aisha replied. "Our Russian transport aircraft was shot at when we were landing for a peacekeeping mission."

"Were you hit?"

"No, but we had to abort our landing."

There was some laughter.

"Of course you had to," the major replied. "But you proved my point. If a cheap Russian transport aircraft can escape missiles, what missile can shoot down a fighter aircraft? There is nothing better than gunning down a bandit in a dogfight."

After a few flying hours of combat simulation, Aisha stood out as the best pilot in the group, to the dismay of both Nicolas de Villiers and François Wauquiez. The major himself was intrigued, and decided to test Aisha in a combat exercise, with himself playing the interceptor. He was not able to align Aisha in his sights as she was swinging and turning so forcefully. How strong was the damned girl to stand so much G-force? After a series of hide-and-seeks and intermittent dogfights he completely lost Aisha from sight; then he heard her voice in the wireless:

"B*oom, boom, boom: you're dead.*"

The major concluded that Aisha could stand G-forces much better than the average pilot, most likely because she had lost her legs and the blood could not flow into them.

"At last an advantage of being a cripple," she smiled to the major.

Later that night in the barrack, both Nicolas de Villiers and François Wauquiez called it unfair.

"This is rigged competition," François grumbled. "An amputee should not be able to compete against us. "

"How strange!" Aisha remarked ironically. "At the beginning, during the evac and parachute training, you called me a liability because I was a cripple. Would being a cripple now be an asset?"

"Fuck you, Aisha," Nicolas said.

"Of course, you'd like to," Aisha replied calmly. "You couldn't even in your dreams, though. Your dicks are too small."

"You have no right to be here!" Nicolas protested. "You are a fucking Moroccan. What will you serve in the EU Air Force? Go back to your camel land, you dirty Muslim crippled whore."

Aisha inhaled and exhaled slowly. She looked at de Villiers, and ordered him slowly:

"Repeat what you said, warrant officer."

"Go back to your camel land, you dirty Muslim crippled whore," Nicolas repeated.

Aisha looked intensely at the lower ranked Cadet and said: "Tell me, Warrant Officer de Villiers. What exactly have you done to be French and European? Your only trouble in life has been to be born from the right person. I, on the contrary, have done much more for the European Union than any of you. I am the most European person in this barrack. So, you do twenty push-ups in front of me now."

"Never, bitch!"

Nicolas suddenly cast his fist toward Aisha, who saw it come. She backed a little and eluded the strike, before grabbing his fist with her right hand and casting her left shoulder under her arm. Nicolas fell immediately to the floor, as she pivoted her body. Aisha saw that François was about to strike her. He was hesitating, though, and she struck him with her right fist. Both cadets got up again to fight, but she was quicker and punched them both again in the face. Some female cadets were encouraging Aisha:

"Come on, punch these male supremacist assholes!"

The fight lasted for another couple of minutes, until they were interrupted. The Academy's wing commander had shown up, intrigued by the excitation in the barrack. "Atten-hut!"

The wing commander was a thin and tall Englishman with grey hair and a white chevron moustache.

"What the bloody hell is going on here?" the old man yelled. "Lieutenant Barjaoui. Who punched these two men?"

"I did, Sir". Aisha answered.

"Why the hell did you do that, lieutenant?" he screamed.

"Teaching them gallantry, sir" Aisha answered. "I fear today's youth is not as properly educated as we used to be, sir."

There was some laughter in the barrack.

"Silence!" The Wing Commander screamed. "Some of you take these two cadets to the infirmary. You, lieutenant, you are under arrest."

Aisha followed the Wing Commander out of the barrack.

The next morning, she was standing on her prostheses in the wing commander's office. Her legs were hurting. Major

O'Malley was also present, standing slightly behind the commander's chair.

"Who do you think you are, Lieutenant Barjaoui?" The Wing Commander asked as she stood at attention.

Aisha did not answer.

The mustached officer went on: "Are you Eugene Bullard? Are you the new Eugene Bullard, punching your way out of racism and bigotry?"

Aisha had no idea whom he was talking about, but the wing commander kept talking:

"After all, you are a former legionnaire, like he was. But remember, Eugene Bullard lost his wings for punching a racist sergeant."

"I don't know Eugene Bullard, sir," Aisha replied calmly.

The wing commander shrugged and said: "You don't know Eugene Bullard... You don't know Eugene Bullard? Google him, stupid!"

"Yes, sir."

"Now, it is my understanding that these two froggies went a bit far." The Colonel admitted. "I shall not take any sanction against you as long as you promise me to behave more like a gentleman."

"Yes, sir. Thank you, sir."

"I've been told you are quite a good pilot. If you join the Fighter Squadrons, we may have a chance to beat the Americans at the next inter-allied exercise. Carry on, Lieutenant."

The training went on. After totaling fifty flying hours on the AF1 Chihuahua, twenty-four cadets only were granted the permission to fly the AF5 Dachshund. The Dachshund had been its nickname because it was long and flat. It was fifteen meters longer than the AF1 Chihuahua, totaling 25 meters (82 ft), but with a wingspan of only 16 meters (53 ft).

Its thin wings and horizontal stabilizer gave it a pleasant look. It was equipped with two CUBIC-R engines and a scramjet. The hybrid air-breathing rocket engines served as reaction jets up to Mach 3, as ramjets up to Mach 6, and as rocket jets in the absence of oxygen. Located beneath the aircraft, the scramjet could be ignited only after the airplane had reached Mach 6, but enabled the Dachshund to reach Mach 17 in atmospheric flight with a ferry range of 10,000 kilometers (6,200 miles).

Using its CUBIC-R engines in rocket mode, the AF5 could do suborbital flights and strike anywhere on Earth within one hour. The AF5 Dachshund was highly performant in high altitude dogfights, but also performed extremely well in close air support missions. It could take off and land vertically if needed. It was the Swiss army knife of the EU Air Force and was able to conduct any kind of mission.

After her very first flight, Aisha adored it. She would gently pull the sidestick while pushing the gas throttle and the sleek beast would soar to the sky, leaving the clouds and rain below. During her second flight, she engaged in all kind of aerobatics until Major O'Malley, who was flying behind her, told her on the radio to take it easy.

Both Dachshunds were flying 12 km (39,000 ft) above the North Sea at Mach 2, and Aisha was now to try the scramjet for the first time. Over the radio, she reviewed the checklist one last time with instructor O'Malley, and she initiated the maneuver.

She pressed a button with her left thumb to push forward the gas throttles in ramjet mode. She felt a thrill of excitement as the CUBIC-R engines, now serving as ramjets, propelled the Dachshund to Mach 6. She pushed another button, and the scramjet was ignited. The Dachshund was now soaring at Mach 17, and they reached reach the Norwegian fjords around Bergen in less than three minutes. Except that they could not see the fjords beneath them: they were over a sea of clouds.

"Crappy Bergen," the major said. "It's always raining here. Next time we will use our scramjet to Spain."

Four minutes later, they were back above Cranwell.

During the fighter module, they were only learning how to fly their planes. They had no firing exercises yet, since that would be the purpose of their third and last year, but Aisha looked forward to it already. She wanted to feel the vibration of the twin Gatling 25-mm guns in her fuselage as she was aiming for air targets.

The module was drawing to an end, and she knew she would be allowed to continue as a fighter pilot rather than a transport or helicopter pilot. It seemed, however, that both de Villiers and Wauquiez would also make it to the fighter squadrons. What the hell! It would only be an extra year with them, and then they would most likely be assigned to different squadrons.

Around the middle of June, Aisha Barjaoui received an unexpected visit. It was Antoine Léger, her former captain from the Foreign Legion. His burnt face scared people away in the base cafeteria.

"*Qu'est ce que tu fais là*? ['What are you doing here?']" she asked as they sat at a table in the mess.

"I'm starting a four-week course with the EU Air Force pararescue school," he answered. "There is a partnership between WARSEC and the EU Air Force, among others. Their staff may train using WARSEC's facilities. In exchange, they provide some courses for the WARSEC astronauts."

"What can a security specialist learn from the air force?" Aisha asked.

"Well," Antoine answered, "I am a trained mountain guide, I have been trained in basic safety concerning nuclear reactors, spaceship evacuation, and I have been in space."

"Lucky you," Aisha said.

"Yes," Antoine replied. "I have even done a few spacewalks already. But I have never jumped with a parachute. I need to train in basic parachute jumping before learning how to jump from the orbital station in an escape suit."

Aisha grimaced and said: "Do you really have to be able to do that?"

"Only if you are a safety specialist, a space medic or a pilot. Engineers, doctors and scientists don't have to. Anyway, that's why I am taking this course organized by the Air Force para-rescue school."

"You are with the pararescue students? Yeah, I see who there are," Aisha replied. "We don't spend much time with them. I just heard they spend some hard time in the pools at the beginning of their training."

Antoine looked at Aisha and said: "You know you could earn a few extra euros working for them?"

"How?"

Antoine explained: "They organize disaster simulation, where their para-rescuers have to take care of a maximum of casualties. To make it more realistic, they hire cripple soldiers who have really lived through traumatic situations."

"Are you suggesting I play a victim in a rescue simulation?"

"Why not? Could be a change of air." Antoine replied. "How is your training going?"

"Fine. I have very good grades. I will be admitted to the fighter squadrons."

Aisha's ex-captain looked surprised.

"Fighter squadrons?" he asked "Why do you want to join the fighter squadrons?"

"Because I'm good at it. I'm one of the best. I dream of

shooting down drones."

Antoine looked long at Aisha and finally said: "I see what you mean. The thrill of shooting with a twin 25-mm Gatling gun. Who hasn't dreamt of it? But what happens next? What will you do in ten years, when you are too old to be a fighter pilot?"

"I have my Commercial Pilot License," Aisha replied. "I could convert to an airline."

"And what would an airline prefer?" Antoine asked. "A fighter pilot with 2,000 flying hours on a Dachshund, or a transport pilot with 10,000 hours on an Airbus 590C. Make no mistake, Aisha. Fighter pilots rarely fly, they cost too much. The fighter module you just took... 100 flying hours in two months... it's the time when a fighter pilot flies most. Fighter pilots are grounded most of the time."

"What? Are you telling me I should join the heavy transport squadrons?"

Antoine leaned forward over the table and said: "Listen, Aisha, I'm gonna tell you what I know. WARSEC will hire a lot of pilots in the next five years. I know the Space Coordination Center director. He's an American. He is from the submarines in the US Navy. He despises fighter pilots. They are cowboys to him. What he wants is bus drivers, people who put the safety of their passengers ahead of their ego."

Aisha chuckled, but objected: "Come on, captain. Even if I joined a transport squadron, I would never qualify to become a space pilot."

"You never read the press, do you, Aisha?" the former legionnaire captain replied. "The EU Air Force has purchased about fifty Space Hounds and two hundred Space Bears from the WARSEC lunar factory."

"Why would they do that?" Aisha wondered.

"The Space Bear is any general's dream," Antoine replied. "With its suborbital flight and VTOL capability, a single Space Bear can transport two infantry companies or one armored infantry platoon anywhere in the world within two hours. Besides, politicians can use it to pay a visit to the orbital station. Our new president, Guido Niedling, wants to use Space Bears instead of the Albaspace as his EU Flight One. A way for him to show he is not a friend of the Vahlroos Corporation."

"As long as taxpayers stand the bill, why not?" Aisha said sarcastically

"As such, some of the heavy transport squadrons will become space transport squadrons as soon as January next year. With your grades, you could easily make it to the space transport squadrons."

There was a long silence.

"I had never thought about it," Aisha finally admitted.

On Friday 25 June 2100, in the ranking ceremony, Lieutenant Aisha Barjaoui was called first of all the cadets to decide her assignment. She surprised everybody by choosing the transportation branch with a major in heavy transport.

At the end of the ceremony, François Wauquiez and Nicolas de Villiers, who had both chosen to become fighter pilots, went to see her.

"Well, lieutenant," Nicolas said. "At last, you have become sensible".

"Well, my dear warrant officers," she replied, "You have no idea how sensible I have become. The thrill of manning a 25-mm twin Gatling gun is, after all, best for childish male supremacists. As for me, I don't want to reach for the sky. I want to reach for the stars."

23: A CARELESS ALPINIST
(JUNE - JULY 2100)

Samir Benyamina graduated from the community college in June 2100. He now had a Bachelor of Science in robotic engineering. Emily was quite happy as he would hopefully get a better-paid job than his current part-time cook position, and they would be able to move out of their student flat.

However, corporations were not hiring over the summer, and both Samir and Emily wanted to enjoy a summer mountaineering in the Alps. They traveled to Paris by train on Friday 25 June, and they spent the night in Samir's father's flat, located in the Parisian suburb of Beaudottes. They did it more for social reasons than anything else, as both would have preferred to fly directly to Genève and reach the Chamonix valley from there, as they could now afford it.

They forced themselves to see Samir's father once in a while, especially for Abdelkader's sake. Samir's youngest brother was the only sibling left in the parental apartment. He would turn eighteen the following year and go somewhere to do his European Service. Samir wondered if any of the siblings would visit their father after Abdelkader had left the paternal home. He doubted it.

After spending a horrible Saturday in Beaudottes, they left the next day for Chamonix. Sunday evening, they pitched their tent in their usual camping site in Montroc, at the end of the valley. It was as international as it had always been. There were a lot of English, Scottish, Germans, and Italians, not to mention the usual careless Russians.

Russians in the Alps were hard to miss. They would listen to loud music, quarrel with most of the people around them and, when it came to climbing, they obviously had a different understanding of what the word 'safety' meant. They would walk on glaciers without crampons and secure themselves on badly built belay stations, when they were belaying themselves at all. Samir and Emily had always wondered how they could have so few casualties. Beginner's luck, perhaps.

Beside Samir's and Emily's tent was a camping car with a Finnish number plate reading 'SPACE BITCH'. The owner seemed to be Russian, and most of the other Russian Alpinists seemed to know him. He had a hairy, brown sausage-looking dog tagging along with him.

While Emily and Samir were eating bread and *saucisson* in front of their tent, the dog went to them and sat down in front of them.

"What does he want?" Samir wondered.

"Food, I guess," Emily replied.

She cut a slice of saucisson with her Swiss Army knife and threw it to the dog.

"And… you are doomed," a voice said. "She will keep begging for food if you give her some just once. She is a real bitch. Both literally and figuratively."

It was the owner of the camping car.

"Sorry," Emily apologized.

"Name's Anatoli, by the way," the Russian said. "Astronaut."

Samir couldn't help laughing.

"Name's Samir, unemployed."

"And I am Emily, nurse."

"I looked at your gear," Anatoli said. "You look pro. Have you been doing mountaineering for a long time?"

"A couple of years," Emily answered,

"Any plans for tomorrow?"

"We are warming up," Samir said. "We just arrived. We will do something we know. The Arrête des Cosmiques."

"Where is it?" the Russian asked.

"By the Aiguille du Midi," Emily replied. "You know, where the cable car goes."

"I should do it as well," the Russian said.

Emily looked at Samir. Both laughed.

"You know, Mr. Astronaut," Emily said. "The fact that we will warm up on it does not mean you should attempt it solo, just like that. Have you done some climbing before?"

"I have done some hiking in Lapponia," the Russian replied.

"*Oh, putain.*" Samir commented. "*Encore un Russe qui va crever.*" ('Fuck. Again a Russian who's gonna die.')

"*Celui là a l'air particulièrement con,*" Emily replied with a slight English accent ('This one looks particularly stupid.')

"Sorry, I don't speak French," the Russian said. "I will go back to the Russian Alpinists. Don't spoil my kokoni bitch too much. I don't want her to grow fat."

"What's her name?" Emily asked.

"Calypso," the Russian answered. "You know, Calypso, like that Greek Goddess bitch who raped Ulysses twice."

Samir gave the dog some more saucisson, and she climbed on him, licking his face.

"*Oh, putain!*" he exclaimed. "Her mouth stinks like hell. Go and lick Emily instead. She loves being licked."

They finished packing their gear for the next morning and went to bed early. The next morning, they took the 6:10 train to Chamonix and the 7:30 cable car to the Aiguille du Midi. In the cable car, there were only climbers and mountaineers. That was the advantage of getting up early, they were skipping the tourists, though some Russians may have earned that title.

At the Aiguilles du Midi, they went past everybody to the exit to the glaciers. They quickly put their crampons on, roped themselves, and went down on the narrow snow arête to the

Vallée Blanche. Samir went first, and Emily was behind, the rope tight between them.

"*On s'échauffe avec la traversée des Pointes Lachenal,*" Samir said as they were taking more slack for the rope to cross the glacier ('We warm up with the traverse of the Pointes Lachenal'). He led the Emily to the eastern side of the Pointes. As they started climbing it was pretty icy.

"OK, will put in a couple of ice screws."

Ice technique was not like biking, Samir felt. One could easily forget the tricks while not practicing it. He had trouble setting the ice screws ("*Putain de glace! Putain de glace!*"). When he was finally certain the first screw was holding, he clipped a quick draw and put the rope through it. He progressed laterally, before setting a new ice screw, and so on. They eventually made it to the ridge.

"*Bon, bah cette glace, elle m'a fait chier,*" he said to Emily ('That ice pissed me off.').

"Ice wise, we kind of suck today," Emily admitted. "We make it to the pointe, and then we go back down to the start of the Arrête des Cosmiques, OK?"

"That's OK for me, Emily."

They reached the start of the Arrête des Cosmiques, located below the cable car station, at around 11:30. There were now a great many less-experienced Alpinists wandering about the Vallée Blanche, one of the few glaciers left in Europe.

"OK, I lead," Emily announced.

They took off their crampons, as the ridge was completely dry. They attacked with tight rope, and it would have been a very enjoyable climb if it had not been for all the Alpinists and climbers queuing on the ridge.

They finally arrived at an abseil ring, where Alpinists where queueing to rappel down. They decided to take advantage of the forced halt to eat some energy bars. They were under a fantastic blue sky with little wind. Above them, Alpine choughs were circling, waiting for food to scavenge.

"Damn," Emily suddenly said. "I forgot to put some more sun cream on."

"Ok, I can get it out of your rucksack."

"You see the cloud above the Mont Blanc?" Emily wondered.

"Yes," Samir answered. "Strong winds in altitudes. It will not be that nice this evening."

"Hey," Emily said. "A solo climber is coming behind us."

Samir turned his head to have a look, further down on the ridge.

"He looks not very confident," Samir said. "A lot of rocks falling. Definitely not climbing like a cat."

"Jesus Christ!" Emily exclaimed.

"I don't think that's Jesus", Samir replied.

"No, but I mean…" Emily started. "I think that's the Russian from the camping site. He does not even have a harness, though at least a helmet."

Two minutes later, the Russian climber was at their anchor

point, completely out of breath.

"Greetings," he said. "Well, it seems I will beat you to the top, after all."

"Take it easy," Emily told the Russian. "There is an abseil here, and you don't even have a harness."

"Damn it," the Russian said, "But I saw people bypass it by going down there further on the right. I just have to go down, back a bit."

The Russian climber turned around, and it was finally Samir and Emily's turn to abseil down. They were quick with the rope and managed to go past two rope teams. They arrived at an icy section and were too lazy to put their crampons back on. They took their ice axes and carved a few steps in the ice. It was a short section, and they were soon progressing on the rocky ridge again.

They finally came to the breach with the slightly difficult climbing step, which both thought was really easy. The only issue was the queue.

"Thanks for carving the steps on the ice; that was helpful."

It was the Russian astronaut again.

"Are you still alive?" Samir asked.

"From here, it's only easy climbing to the cable car," the Russian replied. "You make a lot of fuss with your climbing equipment, but I just do it like this, and I don't find it very hard."

It was now Emily's turn to climb the step. She led, and was

soon on a ledge to belay Samir up. They moved up on the ridge. In front of them was a rope team of older Spaniards, while the Russian was right behind them.

"Why are they so slow?" the Russian ranted.

"Take it easy, just let them take their time," Samir replied, irritated.

"It's not like that the great Anatoli Boukreev climbed the Everest," the Russian ranted, and he moved forward to go past Samir and Emily.

Doing so, he lost balance and fell.

"Fuck!" Emily yelled, "He just fell. I did not push him! Can you see him?"

"Hold me," Samir said as he went to the side of the ledge to look. Emily was holding him tight with the rope around a spike.

"Emily!" Samir called. "The lucky bastard has fallen on a snow cornice. I don't know how long it will hold."

"How far?" Emily asked.

"Ten meters down."

"Hold on a second. I'll remove all my rope rings. I will belay you down."

Samir set a camming device in a crack and anchored himself to it. While Emily was preparing the rope, he took three of his longer slings to be ready to grab the Russian when he reached him.

"Ready," Emily shouted. "Down when you want."

Samir removed his anchor and let himself be lowered to the Russian's level. He could not see if he was alive, but he passed a sling around his chest and locked it with a carabiner to his harness. Then he passed a sling around his left leg and right shoulder as well as another sling around his right leg and left shoulder. He held the whole together with a set of knots and locker carabiners. It was a workable harness, he thought. As he was standing on the snow cornice, it suddenly collapsed under both their weight, and they were both hanging by the rope.

"I have him," Samir screamed. "But we lost contact."

"Samir," Emily yelled back. "Crevasse pulley system. Be patient."

Samir suddenly understood that Emily was planning to build a crevasse rescue system with her gear. But still, with two people hanging, it would be difficult for her.

"Damn it. It's like I am sucking your dick," a voice said.

It was the Russian climber. He was hanging on Samir's harness, and his head was indeed between Samir's legs. Samir wanted to punch him, but he refrained as he noted that Emily was pulling them up.

A moment later, they were all three up to an anchor station Emily had built.

"Have you called 112?" Samir wondered.

"The Spaniards have," Emily replied

It did not take long before they heard the sound of a

helicopter. It wore the white and blue colors of the mountain gendarmerie.

A minute later, the helicopter was autorotating above their head. It was absolutely horrible. Samir and Emily had never experienced being in such a noisy environment. The wind turbulence caused by the rotors had the snow and gravel hitting them in the face and exposed area. None of them had had any idea that a helicopter rescue could be so painful for passersby located at the wrong place.

A mountain rescuer was lowered to their level. He set himself loose from the cable and anchored himself to their belay station, while the helicopter flew away.

"*La victime,* ze victim, *c'est qui*?" He asked ('Who is the victim?').

"*Ce mec là.* Samir replied, indicating the Russian. "No harness, fell about fifteen meters off the ridge onto a snow cornice."

"OK. I will pass him on a better harness."

"Wait," the Russian said to Emily and Samir. "You guys, you can drive?"

"Yes," Emily answered.

"I give you the key to my camping car. You know the plate. A Finnish plate number. "Space Bitch" is written on it. You take it to the camping and take care my dog."

"You left your dog in the camping car?" Emily asked, horrified.

"No. The bitch is at the camping. With the wife of some Russian Alpinist. Here is my business card with my phone number. Call me when you have the dog."

A moment later, the helicopter was back in geostationary position above their head, and the wind turbulence was worse than ever. The cable was lowered, and both the careless Alpinist and the rescuer were airlifted before the helicopter flew down toward the valley.

"*Putain, quelle histoire*," Samir concluded.

"Look on the bright side," Emily said. "We have just won a camping car."

"And a smelly dog," Samir added.

Later that afternoon, they drove the camping car back to the camping in Montroc and took the dog back from a Russian lady. They checked the business card the Russian had given them. It read "Anatoli Govorov, PhD, Warp propulsion specialist, World Agency for the Regulation of Space Exploration and Colonization".

"Anatoli Govorov? WARSEC?" Emily wondered. "Wasn't he the Russian who did the first warping of the *Alcubierre*?"

"And rescued Sanne from Mars?" Samir added. "That must be him. And Calypso must be the first dog to have tested warp technology. Let's call the guy."

Anatoli had been transferred to a hospital in Sallanches, further down the valley. He told them that he had broken a leg and dislocated a shoulder. He would have to be evacuated to Finland on a medical flight. He had asked two friends of his to come and get the camping car and the dog. He asked them if they would be kind enough to take care of the dog for another week before a Tintin Mutombo and Thierry Diakité came and pick her up.

They accepted. They did not mind having a vehicle, however impracticable it was, at their disposal.

Samir and Emily were back in Cambridge at the end of July 2100. While Samir was starting to look for a job as a robot engineer, he was surprised to see that a video had become a viral hit on the Internet. It was entitled '*Careless when committed – the story of a Russian astronaut*', and had been filmed and edited by a rope team a bit below on the ridge.

With the help of comments and arrows, the video was explaining to the layman in the field how careless the Russian Alpinist had been. He was shown falling, and later being rescued by Samir and Emily.

Samir was not thinking about it anymore when he received an email from a certain Glover Johnson, who was the global safety director and Space Coordination Centre director at WARSEC (always windy titles, Samir thought). The latter had heard about him from Anatoli, Tintin and Thierry. He had heard that Samir had just graduated in robotics from a community college. WARSEC was looking for robot engineers with a dedicated focus on safety. The next recruiting sessions was scheduled for October. Why didn't he apply?

Samir mentioned the email to Emily. She was against it. Why would he move to Finland? Sanne and Amina, on the contrary, thought it was a good idea.

They had both somehow managed to solve their supervisor issues. Amina had eventually persuaded Dr. Cooper that her research could lead to the first Nobel Prize in Physics for geologists ever. Did he want to get it? Meanwhile, Sanne had had to get some help from Ralf Åhman, who had threatened her supervisor that he would sue the University and claim back the WARSEC funding, if Sanne was not allowed to pursue her PhD normally.

They were now confident they would both take their PhD in the spring 2101 and had both been given some hints about job opportunities at WARSEC.

They tried to convince Emily to apply to WARSEC as a medic. Emily was soon to be 25, Samir soon 23, they had their lives before them.

Emily, however, was very resistant to that idea. She might have considered it if the WARSEC headquarters had been located somewhere else, but Finland?

Samir found a compromise. He would look actively for any job in Cambridge and in the UK, but would also apply for a position at WARSEC in case he did not find anything else. He was not even certain he would be accepted. Emily hoped he wouldn't.

24: NEXT PLANS
(AUG 2100)

The second week of August 2100 had been calmer than usual at the UN, and the secretary-general decided to spend a few days in Vaasa, to visit the WARSEC headquarters. It was definitely cooler in Northern Finland than in New York City and Hira Dorjee-Sherpa decided that she might even enjoy her stay.

"I have not seen many people at the office," Hira told Ralf, as they were meeting in the latter's office.

Ralf led her to his sofa corner and explained: "It's too early. Most of the people in the administration here are watching the Summer Olympics in Quito at night. Half of the office currently lives on Ecuadorian time."

"Oh, I see."

"It's not an issue," Ralf added. "It's quite calm at the moment."

"Same in New York," The secretary-general replied. "The new European President, Mr. Niedling, is more reasonable than former President Bonavita. It makes all our lives easier."

"Yes, but US President Fang's office ends in January next year. The current Republican candidate seems to be likely to win the elections, and he is going to be tough on the UN."

"Silverbane?" Hira asked. "Let's hope he becomes more reasonable if he becomes president."

"I won't hope for it," Ralf replied. "However, as long as not all the heads of state of the major powers of this world are lunatic at the same time, the UN can handle it."

"You almost make me regret accepting a second term at the head of the UN."

"But I thank you for renewing me another for five years at the head of WARSEC," Ralf said. "I finally feel we are going somewhere."

"In September," the secretary-general said, "the General Assembly will ask us to explore more stellar systems and look more actively for potential planets to colonize."

"I'm aware of it, madame," Ralf replied. "We are working on some bigger warpedo probes to automatically explore more stellar systems. However, to configure them, we need to first launch more human-led missions. As you know, robots can't take initiatives. If we start launching warpedoes on automatic exploratory missions, there is a high risk that they either disappear or come back with no relevant information at all."

"I understand," Hira said. "What are our next plans for human exploratory missions?"

"We plan to send four starships of the Forward class to the

closest stars," Ralf answered.

He wanted to show her on a stellar map which was hanging on his wall, but then he realized that Hira did not have her earGlasses and could not see it.

Instead, he said: "The closest of these stars will be Sirius, which is 8.6 light years away. It's the brightest star in the sky seen from the northern hemisphere. It's actually a binary star system."

Ralf went on: "The second star system we want to go to is Epsilon Eridani. It is 10.5 light years away, with a star weaker than our sun. Strong data indicates we may find exoplanets, there, though probably not habitable."

"Sirius and Epsilon Eridani", the secretary-General repeated. "What are the other stars you're targeting?"

"We have 61 Cygni, also a binary star system. It is located 11.4 light years away. Uncertain we will find any exoplanet there. Last but not least, we want to go to Tau Ceti, 11.9 light years away. We know there are exoplanets, though the probability of finding a habitable planet is also very remote."

"In short, all the planets are within a range of 9 to 12 light years," Hira Dorjee-Sherpa summarized. "That means on average some two-and-a-half year- missions."

"You are correct," Ralf replied.

"When can we send these expeditions?" Hira asked.

Ralf looked a short moment at the stellar map hanging on the wall and finally said:

"We would like to wait for January 2102. By April 2101, next year, we will have only four Forward class starships ready. This means no back-up ship for a rescue mission. By December 2101, we will have seven starships, so it will be much safer."

"Thank you for your input, Ralf," the secretary-general said. "I will keep that in mind when asked by the General Assembly. I had another question, regarding our relationship with the Vahlroos Corporation. As you know, because of them, the USA have requested the International Court of Justice to give their opinion on the validity of the Vienna Treaties."

Ralf sighed and said: "This is correct. The ICJ should give their verdict by the end of August, but I do not expect any unfavorable surprise."

"Neither do I," Hira said. "We have both knowledge of International Law, and quite a reasonable idea of what the International Court of Justice will say. I am more puzzled about our overall relationship with the Vahlroos Corporation."

Ralf shrugged and said: "Aren't we all? Their relationship to us is rather ambiguous. Ideologically speaking, Michael Vahlroos clearly despises us, hence his refusal to be part of WARSEC Ventures. On the other hand, their Albaspace sales have been booming since the opening of the orbital station and they have successfully launched their Albaspace Neo. WARSEC will acquire three of them. With them, we will be able to shuttle space workers from here to the lunar base in only eleven hours."

"Perhaps," the secretary-general tried, "I should acquire an

Albaspace Neo for the UN Secretariat."

Ralf smiled but objected: "The UN member states would oppose it and see it as a waste of their taxpayers' money. However, WARSEC could put an Albaspace Neo at your disposal anytime the schedule permits it."

"Perhaps a clever way of making Vahlroos feel more positive to the UN?" Hira commented.

"His general manager, Sophie Couillard, is already more positive," Ralf noted. "In fact, cooperation between us and them has increased somewhat lately. As you know, Vahlroos Travel already operates the space attraction center in the orbital station. As the orbital station will be further extended within the next three years, they will also open a space casino and a space spa, though I wonder what it will be. We have also teamed up with V-Space for the design of easily deployable space stations. The first one will be launched around the Moon in April next year, and be opened to the public a year later. We also let Vahlroos Travel deploy a tourism center on the Moon, close to the lunar base. Last, but not least, within three years, we will lease them Forward class ships and enable them to expand their tourism activities to Mars."

Hira Dorjee-Sherpa was thoughtful a moment.

"In short," she concluded, "they don't want to be part of the standard WARSEC cooperative framework, but they have an extended à la carte cooperation with us. A bit like Switzerland and the European Union."

Ralf could not agree more.

The conversion then drifted on to the quality of life in Vaasa. The main issue was to have proper nights of sleep in summer, though, because of the quasi absence of nightfall. Ralf was about to tell Hira how lucky she was to be blind but realized just in time how misplaced it would have been.

As he led the secretary-general out of his office, Ralf could not help thinking of the next interstellar exploration wave.

He had been renewed for a five-year period at the head of WARSEC. If the next wave were to find, against all odds, a habitable planet, then he may have a chance to be the WARSEC director initiating the first interstellar colonization project.

Published books in the WARSEC series

Available now for paperback and Kindle on Amazon!

ABOUT THE AUTHOR

Ash Gawain is an EU citizen living in Northern Europe. When not working, writing, nor drinking, Ash is being kept in adequate physical shape by an ex-Swedish military, in order not to die of heart failure before the WARSEC series is complete.

About the WARSEC series:

When I went to the cinema and watched Christopher Nolan's INTERSTELLAR, in January 2015, I first thought I had got into the wrong theatre room. The film opened like a kind of documentary about farmers. After overcoming the first moment of surprise, I admitted the concept was brilliant, though I was willing to challenge everything else about the film.

At that time, I was studying political science, while spending a lot of my time with earth and ice scientists. This, added to a good dose of Finnish Vodka, led to the WARSEC interstellar series.

More on: **www.ashgawain.com**

ACKNOWLEDGEMENTS

The first four books of the WARSEC Interstellar Series could not have reached their final stage without the help of Deborah Murrell, whose thorough edits and comments in the margin have been critical. Any error or mistake is my sole responsibility. I am also forever grateful for Lisa Robbins's valuable feedback and advice, and most of all for her patience with a non-native English-speaker.

Of course, the book could never have been without a book cover. I would like to thank Mark Thomas, not only for his wonderful cover design but also the beautiful paperback edition.

Finally, I would like to thank my family and friends for their support and encouragement, especially Eliah, for reading so many of drafts, and Lumi for forcing me to spend less time in front of my screen and more time exercising.